# THE UNREAL ADVENTURES OF JAKE VON HAMMER

## THE BRAT LIFE

### RN SHELLY

*Illustrated by*
RN SHELLY

GOOEYE DESIGN & PUBLISHING

# THE BRAT LIFE

Dedicated to all Military Brats and Karateka worldwide.

This book is a work of fiction.

# PROLOGUE

Back in the 1970s, there was a goofy kid from a dysfunctional family named Jake. He avoided any type of commitment by idling until the Air Force transferred his family to the next duty station. By 1975, their transfer was well overdue, and Jake's backpack began to fill up with unfinished work and progress reports. Finally, one day coming home from school, Jake and his brother, Ryan, found a note left by their mother:

Dinner is on the stove. Make your own spaghetti noodles. Your father will be home next month. Start packing——we're moving to Hawaii. Aloha, Mom.

Jake and Ryan danced around the kitchen high fiving.

Over the next few weeks, Jake, Ryan, and their older sister, Lyndsey, blew off school and threw away everything that didn't fit into their footlockers. They carefully packed their parent's brass treasures and beer steins, spackled the walls with toothpaste, and spit-shined the floors.

Mustering in the driveway alongside their mother, they waited for the blue staff car to arrive. They hadn't seen their father in two years. Sergeant Von Hammer climbed out of the car, slung a duffle over his shoulder, and marched toward them.

Jake's lip curled. "Who's that?"

Ryan said, "No idea."

"Imposter," Lyndsey replied.

"Shush!" their mother admonished.

Sergeant Von Hammer dropped his bag and hugged his wife while the kids looked on, wondering how to react.

During the ensuing month, they shuffled the kids to Ellington Air Force Base for a barrage of injections, dental work, and medical exams.

On one such trip, Jake sat in the backseat massaging his arm and asked his mother, "Why do we need so many shots to go to Hawaii?"

His mother replied, "Change of plans. We're going to the Philippines."

"Huh? What?" Jake said, "Where's that?"

# 1

Mashing his face against the window, Jake pinned his eyes downward to catch sight of his new island home. As the airliner descended, he grabbed a copy of Sky Magazine and stuffed it into his carry-on. The stewardess looked at Jake and smiled—after sixteen-hours—she was ready to get rid of the irksome brat. She fastened Jake's seatbelt and pulled it snug and said, "Where are you from?"

*I hate when people ask that,* Jake thought.

He shrugged at the stewardess. "I'm not from anywhere."

The Von Hammers landed only a few minutes before deboarding on the tarmac at Clark Air Base. As they exited the plane, they were immediately mugged by suffocating heat and humidity. Heatwaves rising from the sun-scorched runway made the whole landscape look like it was melting. Walking toward a massive air hangar, Jake turned to see Mount Arayat, a dormant volcano dominating the eastern landscape, for the first time. Following his family into the building, Jake slumped into a metal chair waiting to clear customs. An industrial fan eked out a dissonant buzz, broken every few minutes by the rip of fighter jets taking off from a nearby airstrip. Rivers of sweat carried make-up down Jake's mother's face as she sat clutching her enormous vinyl purse. In a soft drawl, she said, "I've nevva been more miserable than this."

An equally tortuous taxi ride took them to their new home located a few miles off-base. Leaving the main gate was total chaos with jeepneys, street peddlers, and beggars packing the street. On the front steps of the Von Hammer's new home stood a tubby Filipino woman wearing a light-colored moo-moo dress and house slippers. She smiled and waved at the family.

"Hello, hello. Welcome! Let me help you with your bags," she said, extending her hand. Jake gave her a bag, and then another.

She said, "My name is Trini, and you are?"

Cracking a half-smile at the housekeeper, he said, "I'm Jake."

"Come in, come in!" Trini exclaimed while ushering the family into the house.

Jake climbed the stairs and called dibs on the first room by throwing his suitcase onto the bed. The taxi's engine revved as it drove away, and Jake leaned out the window to take in the view of his new neighborhood.

Sometimes, Trini cooked traditional Filipino dinners but spared the family bizarre dishes like Balut, an egg with a dead duck inside. She'd make spring rolls stuffed with pork called Lumpia—Jake always ate more than his share of those. Milk and ice-cream were reconstituted from powder and everyone gagged at the taste. Jake opted for eggs or French toast every morning with a glass of juice made from the oranges that grew beside the house. Trini's husband, Steve, came every Friday to tend the roses and various fruit trees. He showed Jake how to climb the coconut tree, but twelve-year-old Jake never got halfway up that fifty-footer before he'd shimmy back down. The mango tree was easier to climb, but the fruit wept sticky juice, and the branches were always covered with ants.

Jake's father, Senior Master Sergeant Von Hammer,

returning from the Vietnam War, was stationed at the nearby airbase but never talked about his job. He'd leave for days, sometimes weeks, on what the Air Force called TDY (Temporary Duty Yonder), and not even Jake's mother knew where he went. During those times, Jake's older brother and sister tortured him mercilessly. His older brother, Ryan, a whole head taller and twice as strong, would often pulverize Jake during their weekly fist-fights. Lyndsey, the oldest, was more interested in boys and sneaking out with her friends than anything else. In those days, Lyndsey and Ryan were close and considered Jake a pest. They liked to tease him by thumping his ear or knuckling his thigh as they passed by.

Kind of a loner, Jake explored the village on his own. A ghetto by any account. The road, only sparsely paved for a few hundred feet, was cratered like the Moon. The Von Hammer home, situated in the middle of a small enclave of houses, was constructed mainly of cinder blocks and plaster. Most of the village lived in ramshackle houses made of plywood, tin roofs, and dirt floors. They'd share electricity by running extension cords from house to house. The home at the end of the street barely had enough power to light a single bulb.

Even though Trini and Steve did all the household chores, the Von Hammer parents gave the kids small allowances to keep them quiet. The exchange rate of thirteen to one substantially increased the family's buying power. One afternoon, Ryan and Jake walked across the street to buy sodas from a sari-sari store, which is really a house with a small convenience store in the front room. Most of the things they sell are super sugary knock-offs of popular American candy, sodas, and gum. Jake grabbed an orange drink from a cooler and swirled it around to stir up the sediment resting on the bottom. He held it up to illuminate the floating particles and grimaced; *Yikes! What the blazes is that?* Then he put the drink back and grabbed one less questionable.

One of two women tending the counter sat breastfeeding a baby while she sifted through a large bowl of dead June beetles.

Jake motioned toward the bowl. "What're y'all doing with those?"

"We eat dem," she replied.

His eyes widened. "Nah... Really?"

Then she plucked one from the bowl and bit the insect in half with her rotten teeth.

Jake cringed, "Ewwh!"

The woman held up another and said, "You like?"

Ryan laughed and turned to Jake using his nickname, "Go ahead, Goobs, don't be shy."

Jake gave Ryan a wry eye and tossed a quarter onto the counter to pay for the drinks. The women laughed as they left the store.

Further up the road, the village was more rural. Houses called Nipa Huts, made of bamboo and thatched straw, hovered several feet above the ground on piers. Those people were farmers who grew crops and raised pigs, goats, and chickens. If they were lucky, they owned a carabao, a type of water buffalo used to pull plows and carts. There were few automobiles except for the brightly painted jeeps left over from the war used as taxis. You'd often see as many as a dozen Filipinos hanging off the sides of those jeepneys.

One of the local Filipino boys saw Jake on the street one day and said, "Kumusta ka."

Jake looked at him and replied, "Huh?"

"Kumusta... Hello!"

"Oh, Hi... I don't speak Tagalog," Jake replied.

"I'm Benji. What your name?"

"Jake."

"You from New York?"

"Nah, Texas."

Benji nodded with a clownish smile. "Cowboys!"

*Wow,* Jake thought, *even in small villages halfway around the World, they've heard of the Dallas Cowboys.*

Benji lived on a small farm with his parents, three brothers, and two sisters in a large Nipa Hut. His uncle, Tam, lost a leg when a krait snake bit him. Those snakes are so poisonous the locals call them two-steppers because you die before you're able to take a third step. Many mornings, you'd see Filipinos walking large hogs up and down the road, guiding them around potholes with bamboo switches. At times, smoke from cooking and trash burning wafted through open windows, stinking-up Jake's whole house.

Monsoon season in the Philippines is rain, rain, and more rain. For three months, rainfall varies from drizzle to washout conditions. Swollen rivers spill into streets carrying all sorts of trees, animals, and trash. When the rain subsides, the Sun comes out, and the temperature soars, making the air thick and sticky. Sitting on Benji's steps one afternoon, Benji noticed Jake's puffy red face.

Benji leaned against the railing and said, "You go swim?"

Jake wiped his brow and replied, "I'm swimming in sweat."

"No, no, you want go swim?" Benji said.

"Heck ya, but where?"

Benji led Jake to the rear of the village and down a jungle path partially blocked by overgrowth. Fighting their way through thick foliage, Jake walked face-on into a spider web and jumped about doing the jungle dance, swatting and swiping as he whirled around.

Benji said, "It's on your leg, on your back, your back, on your head, your hair, in your hair!"

Jake whipped his hair into a frazzle and looked at Benji.

"Where is it? Where is it?"

Benji said, "Your face, on your face,"

Jake slapped himself in the face several times, and Benji started laughing.

Realizing Benji was spoofing him, he leered at Benji, "Man, that's not funny."

Benji replied, "Haha... You a bad dancer."

After hiking a half-mile, they climbed a large grassy hill covered on one-side by a patch of jungle. Benji led Jake down a trail to an old well. Leaning over the edge, Jake saw a sparkling pool of crystal clear water under a rusty metal roof.

"Wow, this is so cool," Jake said. "It must be fifteen feet wide and thirty feet deep."

"The water come from underground," Benji said.

Using his walking stick, Benji banged the edges of the well and said, "Animals come here to drink. I scare them away."

They shucked their shirts and shoes and jumped in.

Jake screamed, "Yahoo!"

Benji said, "Bet you can't reach de bottom."

Jake took a deep breath and dove, passing through levels of cooler water every few meters. He decompressed his ears and still hadn't reached the bottom. Forced to return to the surface, his teeth chattering.

He said, "I couldn't reach it."

Benji smirked. "Ah ha, you not sweating now. No-one can swim to the bottom
anyway."

When they were tired of swimming, Benji took Jake to a deep pit not far away. Shimming down a tangle of thick vines, they reached the bottom and found a large cave opening.

Benji said, "During the war, they store ammo here."

Jake ran his hand along the wall and discovered niches carved into the dirt.

"Cool," he said. "This must be where they put lanterns."

The cave narrowed to a wormhole where a hint of light

guided them toward the exit. Following Benji, Jake crawled, then belly squirmed, inching toward the light. Jake saw Benji squeeze out, but the tunnel was too tight for him. Unable to move forward or back, Jake struggled to free himself.

He felt the cave crashing down and screamed, "Help. Help me!"

Benji tried to pull him through but couldn't. Benji said, "Go back. "

"I can't, my chest is stuck."

Benji said, "Okay, I come back tomorrow when you lose some weight."

"No! Don't leave me!" Jake pleaded. "Get me out of here!"

Using a stick, Benji picked-out some dirt and said, "Try now."

Jake wriggled side to side to no avail.

Benji grabbed his hands. "You blow real hard, and I pull you out. Ready... one, two, threeeee!"

Jake exhaled, and Benji dug his heels in and pulled him free.

Jake said, "Whew! Salamat (thank you)! That was scary. I never wanna do that again."

Benji patted him on the belly. "You too fat for that one."

They emerged near three old defensive bunkers for which Bunker Hill is named. Etched in the top of each one, was the date and names of the Army battalions who built them. Large caliber ammunition peppered the bunkers on both sides. Jake held his hand against the bunker, comparing his finger's size to one of the slugs.

Benji said, "That's a big one."

Jake pushed his thumb into the hole. ".50 caliber."

Looking downrange, Jake imagined himself a soldier trying to hold the hill and thought, *man o' man, it must've been pure hell out here.*

The boys jumped on a bunker, and Benji pointed toward the rice terraces on a distant hillside. Two fighter jets dusting the eastern range flipped on the afterburners and rocketed straight up. The deafening roar of the engines shook the ground as the boys watched them disappear into the clouds.

Jake said, "Wow, I never get tired of that!"

Benji replied, "We having chicken tonight."

"Huh? What're you talking about?"

Benji bumped his chest. "Heart attack."

Jake grinned and shook his head, thinking, *Benji says the craziest stuff.*

When they returned to the village, Jake told Benji goodbye and continued on home. As he walked down the street toward his house, he passed several villagers carrying dead chickens.

A few weeks later, Jake and others were goofing around before math class. A girl named Fritz, with tightly wound blonde curls, was showing another student how to get out of a choke-hold. Jake watched, thinking, *that's lame.*

"Bet you can't escape my choke-hold," Jake said.

Fritz replied, "Wanna try?"

Jake stood beside her and reached out to capture her neck in his formidable grasp. As soon as Jake's fingers touched her shoulder, Fritz turned and kneed him hard in the groin. Jake crumbled to the floor. The teacher came into the room, and everyone quickly took their seats, but Jake lay there clenched in a tight ball.

The teacher asked, "What's wrong with Jake?"

Several students blurted out, "Fritz."

The teacher gave Jake a minute to recover, and he crawled into his seat. Everyone was watching the teacher when Fritz peered over her shoulder and smiled at Jake. He thought, *I don't like her.*

The last period of the day was one of the unique electives offered by Wagner Middle School called Jungle Survival. The small class of eight boys and one girl learned about the plants and animals of the Philippines. It was Jake's favorite class because it involved a lot of goofing-off except on Fridays when a special forces commando came to teach survival techniques. In a swath of wild jungle behind the school, the students constructed a campsite where the commando taught them to build campfires and produce drinkable water from large banana trees. They also learned how to identify edible plants and insects—eating them earned extra credit—Jake never got extra credit.

Jake liked to sit in the backyard jackfruit tree at sunset to watch animals come out of their hiding places. One evening, as Jake watched bats dart around feasting on insects, he saw something out of the corner of his eye. A giant cloud rat climbed down from the treetop and stopped on an adjacent branch just a few feet away. Jake froze. The large rodent raised-up on his hind legs and lifted its nose into the air. Jake slowly exhaled. The rat looked at him, whiskers twitching. Then it jumped onto the concrete fence and scampered toward the empty house behind them. Suddenly, a silhouette of a male figure emerged and moved suspiciously around the yard. Jake watched, thinking, *Oooh, he's gonna rob that house.* The burglar rounded a corner, and Jake waited to hear a window crack. But, he saw no sign of him, or the rat again.

The following Saturday morning, Jake was goofing around in the backyard and heard voices coming from the empty house. He climbed the jackfruit tree, glimpsed over the fence, and saw two Airmen attacking each other with a large knife. Jake watched them take turns practicing self-defense techniques. A few minutes later, Jake choked on his own spit when he saw Sergeant Fujioka walk into the backyard. The special ops commando who taught Jungle Survival at school was teaching the airmen combat skills.

When the airmen left, Sergeant Fujioka picked up a bamboo pole and swung it like he was fighting invisible men. He turned in Jake's direction, and Jake ducked, hoping Sergeant Fujioka didn't see him. Jake waited until all was quiet before rising to peek over the fence again. When Jake's eyes cleared the top of the wall, he saw Sergeant Fujioka standing right there looking back at him, *oops, busted.*

Sergeant Fujioka said, "Hello there!"

Jake stood up slowly and replied, "Uh... Hi, Sergeant Fujioka."

He smiled and said, "Hey Jake, how are you? Do you live here?"

"Um, ya," Jake replied, "a few months,"

"I moved in a week ago. Looks like we're neighbors."

"Ya, that's cool."

"Are you busy?" Sergeant Fujioka said. "Would you help me with something?"

"Uh, sure."

Jake climbed over the fence, and Sergeant Fujioka handed him a bamboo stick like the one he used. The commando placed Jake's hands in the correct position and taught him to strike. They played stick fighting for a while before they went into the garage. Jake saw animal cages stacked against the back wall and asked, "What are those cages for?"

Sergeant Fujioka replied, "That's why I need your help. I'm going TDY for a few days and wondered if you could help us?"

Sergeant Fujioka picked up a small bell and rang it. They waited a short minute, and then Jake saw the giant cloud rat enter the garage and climb onto a cage.

Jake said, "Wow, that's a giant rat. I've seen him in the yard!"

"His name is Griffiss," Sergeant Fujioka said, just before a small black rat came and climbed onto the other cage, then a brown one a moment later. Sergeant Fujioka said, "The black one is Elm. The brown one is Travis." Sergeant Fujioka reached out his arm, and Elm climbed onto his shoulder. "Elm and Griffiss are tame, but don't touch Travis; he's a biter!"

Jake replied, "You named them after Air Force bases?"

"You know your bases. Elm is short for Elmendorf."

"Well, ya, I've been to all of those," Jake said.

"Oh, yes, I'm sure you have. I was hoping you could fill the water and food dishes each morning? They can open and close the cages themselves."

"Okay, I can do that."

"Great! I'll show you where I hide the key.

The morning after Sergeant Fujioka left, Jake climbed the fence to feed the rats. Only Elm was waiting as he filled the bowls and rang the bell. Travis and Griffiss arrived a few minutes later and ate while Jake snooped around the garage. In the corner was a collection of weapons like he'd never seen. He picked up a sickle-like thing and ran his finger across the blade to test the sharpness.

"Owch!"

A drop of blood hit the floor, and Jake went inside to find a napkin to wrap around his finger. Sergeant Fujioka's house had little furniture or decorations. Just a few pictures of older people Jake assumed were his parents. Back in the garage, Elm and Travis had locked themselves in their cages. Jake held Griffiss, scratching him around the neck while Griffiss's massive body draped over his arm. He placed Griffiss back in his pen and climbed back over the fence to get ready for school.

A few days later, Jake climbed the jackfruit tree and saw Sergeant Fujioka had returned home, and went to see him.

"I played with Elm and Griffiss, but Travis won't come out of his cage. He just runs on his exercise wheel. I think it's broken."

Sergeant Fujioka replied, "It's not broken. It only turns one direction. He's being trained."

"Trained for what?" Jake said.

"Sometimes, they help me at work."

"You mean they're rat commandos?"

"Something like that," Sergeant Fujioka said.

"What are the weapons in the corner?"

"Those are traditional combat weapons."

"Commando weapons?"

"Sort of... martial arts weapons."

"You know kung fu?" Jake asked.

"Karate. My father was a Karate instructor."

Jake said, "That's cool. How long does it take to learn Karate?"

"It depends."

"Oh, hmm... Could you teach me?" Jake asked.

Sergeant Fujioka grabbed two bamboo poles from the corner handing one to Jake. They reviewed the strikes Sergeant Fujioka taught Jake before and added a few more. Jake was having so much fun; he lost track of time. Jake heard his mother calling—time to go. Sergeant Fujioka let Jake take the staff home. He hardly slept, staying up all night to practice the movements in his room.

Jake trained with Sergeant Fujioka two nights a week. He'd always have Jake sit and meditate for a minute before warm-up exercises. They'd do leg kicks, more leg kicks, and more leg kicks. When Jake couldn't lift his legs anymore, he'd tell Jakle to get into a horse stance and do blocks for ten minutes. Then he'd let Jake rest and do it all over again.

Jake thought *I have cramps in my legs, and my arms are gonna fall off.*

Sergeant Fujioka taped two lines on the floor and had Jake straddle them using front stances and cockamamie back stances. At the end of practice, Jake worked up a good sweat with jumping jacks and push-ups, then he'd hang on a wall of horizontal wooden bars called the Rack. He'd grab the highest bar and hang there, letting gravity stretch out his tired muscles.

Like Jake's father, Sergeant Fujioka would often go TDY and allow Jake to practice in his garage. In exchange, Jake fed the rats and watered plants. Sometimes, Sergeant Fujioka took one or two rats with him, but usually, Jake cared for all three and nicnamed them Ratcom—short for rat commandos.

While eating breakfast one morning, Jake told Ryan, "Griffiss is huge. Big as a cat."

"Dang," Ryan replied, "I wondered where all the dogs went."

"I know, right! I hear they're delicious."

"Cats too!"

"Ewh!" Jake shook his head. "Nah, Griff mostly eats nuts and fruit. But, don't touch Travis—he's a biter. He has a gnarly tooth sticking out the side of his mouth. I'm sure it's not supposed to grow there. Fujioka said he's tough—if there's trouble—he's gonna start it."

Ryan said, "Well, there's your Jarhead."

Jake practiced stances and movements on the tape lines for over a month, until one day, Sergeant Fujioka removed the tape and said, "Don't look down, look straight ahead."

Standing where the lines used to be, he focused on the wall in front of him. As he stepped forward, his feet knew just where to go.

Sergeant Fujioka smiled and said, "Well done, Jake-san," then taught him a kata called Taikyoku. Sergeant Fujioka said, "Kata is the method ancient masters developed to practice fighting techniques in secret."

In only a few days, Jake learned the kata but was made to practice it over and over, for weeks.

One day, Jake turned to Sergeant Fujioka and said, "I'm getting bored, can't I learn something new?"

Sergeant Fujioka replied, "It's best to master one form before moving to the next."

"What more can I do?"

"The purpose of practice is to strip away the unnecessary. Talk less—practice more.

A month later, Sergeant Fujioka introduced Jake to a wooden post wrapped with rope, called a makiwara. To strengthen his hands, Jake would strike the post with his knuckles. It was painful.

*I hate makiwara days,* Jake thought, *and kata isn't much use either—my brother still wins all the fights.*

Staff forms were his favorite. Sergeant Fujioka broke complex movements into small bits so Jake could understand the techniques.

One afternoon, Sergeant Fujioka told Jake he was going to test him. He sat in a chair and instructed Jake to demonstrate what he'd learned. Even though Jake knew everything Sergeant Fujioka asked, being evaluated made him nervous, and he messed up a few things.

"I failed," Jake said.

Sergeant Fujioka replied, "I'm not testing you for perfection. I'm testing what you know. To know you made mistakes means you learned."

## 2

Sometimes, Benji practiced with Jake and Master Fuji, but karate wasn't his thing. He was more of an artist type, carving animals out of wood and selling them to foreigners. One day, Sergeant Fujioka expanded on a concept he called Economy of Movement. He said, "Take the shortest path. Eliminate unnecessary movement. It's quicker and uses less energy."

After a long hard practice, Jake sat near a fan to cool down and thought about the lesson.

"Why does Benji call you Master Fuji?"

Sergeant Fujioka replied, "He's a funny kid. He shortens Fujioka to Fuji, like Mount Fuji. Master is a high ranking black belt."

"So, in the economy of syllables, can I call you Master Fuji too?"

Laughing, he replied, "Yes, Jake-san, you can call me Master Fuji."

The Philippines doesn't have seasons other than monsoon and hot, but around that time when school is out, called summer, Master Fuji told Jake he would take his next rank test at a school on base with other students. He started teaching Jake to spar. As Master Fuji's kicks snapped around him, Jake thought, *Master Fuji is so fast I can hardly see him move.* Every time he dropped his hands, Master Fuji tagged him in the chest, but never too hard.

*Hitting Master Fuji is like hitting the makiwara,* Jake thought. *He's hard as stone.*

Saturday, Jake's birthday, he bolted downstairs, ready to tear into his gifts. He hit the landing and spun around and scanned the room—nothing. Jake plopped onto the couch, arms folded and pouty faced. *Where is everybody?* A few seconds of silence, then a rooster crowed. He glanced at the clock.

*Awe, 0530, too early.*

He slogged back to bed and lay there remembering past birthdays; *Houston, Alpena, Rome, Anchorage, Homestead—*

Sunlight beamed through Jake's window, and an unknown sound jolted his mind to the present.

*Oh, wow, I fell asleep.*

He opened his eyes and spotted a white pillow hovering over his head. *What the—?*

Ryan crammed the pillow into his face and held him down. "Happy birthday, Goobs... You're finally a teenager. Name ten candy bars."

Ryan and Lindsey punched Jake over and over while Jake spat off names.

"Snickers, Butterfinger, Milkyway... uhh, Three Musketeers... Ow, Um, Marathon,n,n... ooch, Baby Ruth, Ah,h,h, Al—mond Joy... Ouch... Oh Henry... Ahh, ow... I can't breathe, owch, oh, I can't think of any more."

The hazing continued until Jake curled up into a ball and cried, "Stop, stop..."

Showing some mercy, they halted the attack and escorted Jake downstairs by twisting his ear. A frosted chocolate cake sat on the table next to a stack of cards. He bounded toward the table, grinning wide, "Oh my gosh, y'all didn't forget this year!"

"Hey, give us a break," Lynsey replied. "We were moving last year."

Jake picked up a card. "Who's Elsie and Gino?"

Lyndsey said, "That's Grandma and Grandpa. You've never met them."

"They gave me ten bucks."

He picked up another card. "Pam and Gabby, who are they?"

"Our cousins. You never met them either."

Ryan handed him a present. "Open the box."

Jake ripped the wrapping paper away. "Woah, a radio! Just what I wanted, thank you, thank you, thank you!"

He unpacked the radio and turned it on, searching for a station. "How come I only get static?"

"It doesn't work here," Lyndsey said, "we've already tried."

"Huh?"

"We're too far away," Ryan said. "No stations here except AFARTS (Armed Forces Radio and Television Service) and a few Filipino stations."

Jake's shoulders dropped. "Awe, man."

Ryan said, "Let's eat cake."

Shaking a spatula, their mother said, "After breakfast."

Sergeant Von Hammer emerged from the bedroom and handed Jake a case. "Happy birthday, Son."

Jake opened the case and found a military field compass. "Wow, this is cool. Thanks!"

"Take care of it. I used it in Vietnam."

Jake turned it over. "Why does it have a radiation symbol?"

Sergeant Von Hammer said, "It has tritium in it to make the dial glow. Don't open it."

"It'll make your teeth turn green," Ryan said.

"Ya," Lindsey said. "You'll grow another arm."

Later that afternoon, Benji saw Jake in the street with his compass and shouted, "Malygayang Kaarawan (Happy Birthday)!"

Jake waved, and Benji ran toward him, holding out a package.

"I make this for you."

"Salamat," Jake said and took the package.

Jake pulled back the paper and found a wood carving of an F-4 Phantom fighter jet. Admiring Benji's artistic skill, he ran his fingertips over the wingtips.

Benji smiled. "You like chicken?"

"Haha, may we never run out of drumsticks. Thanks so much, Benji! This is the best gift ever."

"Put it away, let's go swim."

On the way to Bunker Hill, Jake said, "Master Fuji is making me take my belt test on base."

"That not good?"

"No. I don't like people watching me."

"My brother, Arnel, like girl, sing in nightclubs."

"Your brother likes a girl who sings in clubs?"

"No, he dress like a girl and sing in nightclub."

"Haha... Why does he do that?"

"He no care. They give him money. He wears a white wig and pretends he Marylin Monroe."

"Oh my gosh, that's funny. Haha."

"Ya, Baklâ Boy laugh all the way to the bank."

They arrived at the well and rapped the sides with a stick.

Jake said, "Watch this."

He filled his lungs with air and dove in. Diving deeper, colder, deeper, colder, he pressed on. When he couldn't get any farther, he blew out half a lung of air and kicked furiously. Inching deeper, he extended his hand and snatched the stone with his fingertips. He exhaled his remaining air to sink to the bottom, and like a torpedo aiming for the surface, he pushed off with all his might. Halfway to the surface, his momentum slowed. Lungs bucking for air, he flapped his arms, pushing upward.

*Uh, oh, not there.* Kick, flap, kick... Jake broke the surface gasping for air, and held up the stone.

"Yay, you did it, you did it!" Benji said.

Jake inhaled some water and started coughing. The stone slipped from his fingertips.

"Oh, shoot!"

They watched as it sank on to the bottom.

Shaking his head, Benji looked at Jake and smiled. "Oops, no-one gonna believe you."

They splashed around until a group of monkeys attacked them by throwing tree nuts. Benji said, "They thirsty."

"Let them have the well," Jake said. "I'm done swimming anyway."

The boys grabbed their shoes and climbed the bunkers. Jake stood and looked around. He could see Mt. Arayat in the east and the Blue Ridge Mountains in the west.

Jake spread out his arms and said, "This is the best view in all Pampanga."

Benji said, "It's late. I'm hungry."

On the way back to the village, they heard the church bell ringing continuously. Benji turned to Jake. "Emergency!"

They ran and quickly arrived at the village to see many people gathered in a field near Benji's house. His brothers were unhooking a plow from the carabao while others attended an injured person. Benji's mother kneeled nearby sobbing. The boys pushed closer but were held back, then Benji's older sister took him away. Jake heard someone say Benji's father was tilling the field when a root stuck on the plow. He stopped to remove the root from the blade, and something spooked the carabao; It lunged forward, trapping Benji's father under the plow. Jake watched as they loaded Benji's Dad into the ambulance and took him to the hospital. The following morning, news spread through the village that Benji's father had passed away from the injuries.

Two days later, mourners spread flower petals up and down the streets, and the whole village came out to take part in the funeral. Friends and relatives poured in from other communities overwhelming the small church. Loudspeakers broadcast the service to the crowd gathered outside. After the ceremony, a walking procession carried the casket to a small cemetery at the village's far end.

The next day, Trini said, "Jake, I made supper for Benji's family. Will you help me carry it?"

"Yeah, I want to."

Trini handed a basket to Jake and carried another down the street. Benji's sister, Melinda, invited them in. The little room didn't have much space, so Jake and Benji went outside and sat on the steps.

Jake said, "This is the worst thing ever. I don't know what to say."

"It bad," Benji said, "but, Tatay in heaven now."

"Yes, he is. I'm sure of that. Is there something I can do? Do y'all need anything?"

"Nah, we good. Just need time to adjust."

"I understand." Jake said, "If you need anything, please ask."

"Salamat, my friend."

When Jake got home, he found Ryan on the couch wearing headphones listening to albums.

Jake sat across from him and asked, "What if Dad died?"

Ryan lifted one of the white mickey-muff earphones. "What?"

Jake spoke louder. "What if Dad got killed?"

Ryan sat up, leaned toward Jake, motioned at the front window. "If two dudes dressed in ballroom blues park out front, just shut the door. Don't answer it."

Ryan snapped the earmuff back over his ear and leaned back into the couch.

*Whoa!* Jake thought, *He doesn't wanna talk about it. Nobody ever does, even though Clark has the biggest cemetery ever.*

The test was a few weeks later, and Jake was nervous that morning. After breakfast, he met Master Fuji and drove to the dojo, where Master Fuji gave him a black uniform and a yellow belt. Jake went to the locker room to change and realized he didn't know how to wear a gi. Studying the picture on the package, he did the best he could. When he emerged from the locker room, Ryan was sitting in the family area, and Jake walked over to talk to him.

Ryan said, "You look like a bumblebee."

"Oh gosh, I feel like a dork."

"Are you sure you have it on right?"

"Why?"

"You look homeless. Try rolling the waistband over to take up slack in the legs."

Jake took off the belt and opened the top. Ryan showed him how to roll the waistband to shorten the legs, but Jake couldn't figure out how to retie the laces.

Ryan pointed to a string and said, "That goes there."

"This one?"

Ryan said, "Ya, like that."

By the time he'd finished, other students had started arriving, all wearing white uniforms. *Why am I the only one wearing a black gi?*

A moment later, the girl with happy knees walked in wearing a red belt. Jake turned away, hoping Fritz wouldn't notice him. She dropped her bag and went to the other side of the dojo to talk to other students. Unable to hide in his black uniform, he faked a smile and tried to act nonchalant. Ryan, the best athlete in all sports, leaned over and gave Jake a fist pump. "Sting like a bee!"

Jake's face drooped, *I'm gonna pass out.*

Master Fuji sat with other high ranking black belts at a long table in the front of the floor. The head of the school, Master Kim, lined everyone up and led the class through warm-up exercises. Then he instructed all the students to sit around the edge of the floor until called by their rank.

When Master Kim called Jake's group, he lined up with five other yellow belts and hid conspicuously in the back row with his black gi. Master Kim instructed them to perform the Heian Shodan kata. Everything proceeded well until the other students executed a high block where Jake's form used a middle block. Jake became confused, lost his place, and stopped. As he waited for the others to finish, he realized he'd just become the focus of everyone's attention.

*Oh, my god! I can't believe this is happening!*

A hot flash swept up the back of his neck, leaving his face flush. The other students finished and stood at attention.

Master Kim looked at Jake, "Would you like to start over?"

"Um... yes, s—sir."

Master Kim instructed Jake to move to the front while the rest of the group sat down. He made his way to the front with the weight of every eyeball sticking to his bumblebee uniform. His heart pounded—air too thick to breathe. *Jeesh, I feel sick.* Clenching his sweaty fists, he assumed the ready position.

Master Kim said, "You may begin."

He stood there trembling—unable to move. Then he heard a whisper.

"Weebles wobble, but they don't fall down."

A few students snickered, and Jake exhaled.

Master Kim said, "Do you need more time?"

Jake sent a telepathic *thanks* to Ryan and snapped, "No sir, I'm ready."

He swallowed hard and tried to focus. Turning left, he executed a low block followed by a punch. *Stop shaking,* He told himself. Then turned to make another block and stumbled. Finally, he completed the short kata, but it was ugly, and he knew it.

Master Kim excused Jake. *Thank god, I can't wait to get off the floor.*

As Jake sat and watched the other students, the pink drained from his face. The higher ranks' ability to execute katas without losing their concentration impressed Jake. When everyone finished, Master Kim allowed a short break to stretch and get a drink of water.

Jake ambled over to Ryan, "Man, I'm so embarrassed."

Ryan replied, "Ya, no-one likes to suck."

"What do I do? I gotta do a staff form next."

"People only remember the last thing you did. Have a short memory and go big!"

The only yellow belt with weapon form was Jake, so Master Kim asked him to grab his staff and move to the middle of the floor. He remembered Benji telling him his brother dresses like Marilyn Monroe and thought, *That'll be big.*

He bowed and came to a ready stance. Master Kim signaled Jake to begin. Envisioning himself as the comic book superhero Drax the Destroyer, he lifted the staff and imagined the supervillain "Thanos!" Jake attacked with a sidestrike, "Bam!" Then a sweep and downstrike, "Wap!" He jabbed backward, knocking Thanos in the forehead, "Dot," and finished him with a downstrike, "Pow!" He dropped to a knee and performed a sequence of side strikes vanquishing Thanos to the Underworld, "Boom,

Pop, Kiai!" Jake popped up and snapped his staff to his side and bowed.

No-one moved or said a thing. Master Fuji sat with a blank expression and Master Kim stood motionless with his head tilted to the side. Master Kim shook his head and quietly dismissed him. Jake trudged off the floor and sat wondering, *Did I blow it?*

Ryan leaned forward catching Jake's attention and gave him double thumbs up.

Jake mouthed, "Thanks."

The other students completed the test, and a short belt ceremony followed. When they called Jake, he stepped forward and received his orange belt.

Afterward, Fritz said, "That was different. Great recovery."

"I was super nervous," Jake said.

"I can tell," She pointed. "Your uniform is tied wrong."

Jake looked down and pretended to know, "Oh ya, haha, it is."

"No worries," Fritz replied. "During my first test, I fell into the judge's table."

They laughed. Jake pointed to her brown belt and said, "Congratulations on your brown belt. How long did that take?"

"Longer than it should've, but thanks. See you at school. Bye for now."

Jake waited until Master Fuji finished talking to Master Kim and said, "Master Fuji, sorry I messed up. I don't deserve the belt."

Master Fuji replied, "That was the test Jake-san."

"What d'you mean?"

"The test IS the test. Overcoming fear is the hardest thing for a young karate-ka."

Puzzled, Jake thought for a second, "What d'you think about my staff form?"

Master Fuji replied, "What is Thanos? ... and what is dot?"

"Oh ya, Thanos is a bad guy in comics. When you jab someone in the forehead, it leaves a dot."

"I see... Keep the sound effects to yourself. Otherwise, you did well. Keep the belt."

Jake's father returned from his TDY trip late that evening. He'd been away for ten days and was still sleeping when breakfast was ready the following morning. Jake wanted to show him his new orange belt. His father slept facing the far wall, and Jake leaned over the bed and shook his shoulder to wake him.

"Dad, Dad, wake up. It's breakfast time."

Sergeant Von Hammer wheeled over and punched Jake in the face, knocking him to the floor, then jumped out of bed and stood over him screaming, "Don't touch me! Never touch me! Don't ever do that again! Never!"

Jake lay on the floor with his arms covering his face. His mother ran into the room and jumped between Jake and his father, yelling, "Stop-it. Wake-up! Wake-up! It's Jake. Leave him alone. Stop it!"

Jake seized the opportunity to crawl behind his mother's legs and squeeze out the door. She found him sitting on the back steps massaging his cheek and sat next to him.

"Sorry that happened," she said. "I should've warned you not to wake your father."

"What the heck is wrong with him?" Jake asked.

"He has nightmares. He didn't mean to hurt you."

"He's psycho!"

"He needs help. Are you all right?"

Jake looked up. "Mom, they stuck me with twelve needles to move here. I can take a punch."

She put her arm around him and rested her chin on his head. "I know."

A few days later, Jake was still excited about getting his orange belt and went to Master Fuji's, ready to learn new stuff.

Master Fuji said, "Jake-san, what happened to your eye."

"I got punched."

"I see. Are you okay?"

Jake replied, "Ya, looks worse than it is."

Master Fuji showed him the next form and taught him a new jumping spin-kick. The kick was hard for Jake to do, and he fell during the first few attempts.

Two weeks passed and Jake knew the kata, but could barely stay upright after the kick. Then Master Fuji dropped a bomb, "Jake-san, I've been transferred to Hickam. I'll be leaving next month. You can continue your training on-base with Master Kim. I've already spoken to him, and you are welcome to join his dojo. I'll be checking on your progress."

Jake didn't know what to say. It felt like a spear had pierced his chest, but as a military brat, Jake knew this day would come. It's just something you get used to. Everyone promises to keep in touch, but that's just what you say to make it feel better.

The new school year was starting soon, and Jake's father was away on TDY. Jake's mother took Lyndsey shopping, and Ryan was at football tryouts. After lunch, Jake wanted to go swimming.

He walked to Benji's. "Hey, wanna go to the well?"

"Sorry. I help my brother today."

"Drats, I'll go by myself."

He started up the trail towards Bunker Hill, humming a song stuck in his head. Jake worked up a good sweat knocking down spider webs and fighting back overgrown foliage.

*Wish I'd brought a canteen, it's a scorcher out here.*

When he finally arrived at the well, he was so relieved, he ripped off his shirt and jumped in cannonball style, creating a giant splash.

As he floated on his back, points of light shined through pinholes in the rusted metal roof. *What a fantastic day,* he thought and closed his eyes, imagining he was an astronaut drifting through space watching stars of every color getting swallowed up by churning black holes. His head bumped into a wall snapping him back to reality. He rolled upright, lifting his head and shook the water out of his ears. The familiar sound of leaves rustling, and birds chirping, was upset by an odd growling noise. *What's that?* He swiveled his head around, locking onto a blurry silhouette. He blinked, bringing the image into focus. A large cobra hissed and reared up with its neck flared.

*Oh, crud! I forgot to bang the side before jumping in.*

Jake back-peddled into the opposite wall and froze. The cobra swayed side to side, tongue flickering, it slipped into the water and swam toward Jake. Holding his breath, he sunk and braced himself against the wall. Not releasing even a bubble, He watched the snake slink through the water overhead, circling above. Lungs begging for air, he was unable to stay submerged. The serpent turned toward him, and Jake splashed at it, trying to ward it away, but that just agitated it more.

Diving deep, Jake kicked off the wall to launch himself to the other side. He surfaced and grabbed the sidewall to pull himself up. His hand slipped, and he fell back into the water. Jake surged upward again, reaching for the edge. As he caught hold of the rim, intense pain shot through his torso and stunned him.

"Arghhhh!"

He pulled his stomach onto the side with the cobra dangling from his back. Jake kicked at the snake, knocking it back into the water. A fang caught his leg as it fell, making a long scratch. He rolled over the side of the well and ran to a clearing with blood trickling down his leg.

Jake felt a cramping sensation in his back and dropped to a

knee. Vision spinning 'round and 'round, his blood percolated like hot coffee under red hot skin.

*I gotta get home...* He squeezed his thigh. *Can't feel my leg.* Heart pounding, he struggled to breathe and laid down gazing toward the sky. *Oh man, This is bad, I need Mom. Help... ...so...moo... oh—*

# 3

___

Jake's mother and sister picked up Ryan on the way home from shopping. When they arrived home, they didn't see Jake in or around the house. Mrs. Von Hammer looked toward Ryan and said, "Find Jake and bring him home."

Ryan walked to Master Fuji's house, "Is Jake over here? Mom wants him to come home."

Master Fuji said, "I just got home myself. Jump in the jeep. I'll give you a ride to Benji's."

Ryan hopped into the jeep admiring its rugged appearance. "Slick ride."

They drove to the end of the street, where they found Benji putting away tools.

Benji pointed to the jungle and said, "Jake go swimming."

Benji jumped into the back, and Master Fuji drove to the jungle trail where they continued on foot. When they got near the well, they found Jake lying on the trail. Master Fuji knelt beside him and slapped his cheek.

"Jake-san, wake up."

He didn't respond. Ryan pointed to the scratch on his leg, "Look at that!"

Master Fuji put his fingers on Jake's neck and barely detected a pulse. He rolled Jake over and saw a large bruise surrounding two distinct puncture holes.

Reaching into his pocket, Master Fuji said, "Ryan, take my keys and get to a phone, call the base—request a Medevac for snakebite."

Ryan beat the wind back to the jeep, turned the key, slapped it in drive, and floored it to the village, weaving around people and animals. He slammed on the brakes and skidded to a stop in front of his house. Ryan crashed through the door—knocking it off the hinges—grabbed the phone and dialed the base.

When the operator answered, he said, "Sergeant Fujioka, send Medevac, Bunker Hill, snake bite, Jake Von Hammer —Pronto!"

His mother and Lindsey overheard the conversation and crowded around, flooding Ryan with questions.

Ryan shook his hands at them. "I don't know, get in the car, let's go!"

Master Fujioka went to the well and pulled a plant from the ground. A growling noise caught his attention. He looked around the corner and spotted an eight-foot King Cobra lying on a nest beside the well. He eased away and reached inside his boot to retrieve a small knife. Placing the blade on the root, he cut away the leathery cover to expose the soft yellow flesh.

Rolling Jake back over, Master Fuji tilted his head and driz-zled the syrup into Jake's nostrils. He placed his mouth over Jake's nose and blew several short sharp breaths, forcing the juice into Jake's sinuses. When Master Fuji heard the helicopter, he motioned to Benji. "Go flag them down."

Benji ran to the clearing waving his shirt overhead. The chopper pilot spotted him and landed in a nearby clearing.

Master Fuji cut two small shoots of bamboo and inserted them into the puncture wounds. Then he hoisted Jake over his shoulder and ran to the chopper where a crewman helped him strap Jake down. The helicopter took off, aiming for the base hospital. While en route, they ran an IV into Jake's arm and administered cobra anti-venom. The chopper landed on the hospital pad, and a crash team took Jake directly into the Intensive Care Unit. The medical team put him on a ventilator and worked a solid hour to stabilize him.

Jake's family arrived and saw Jake lying there unconscious, attached to machines by hoses and tubes. His mother stood shaking while Master Fuji tried to explain what happened. Two hours later, she gave the car keys to Lyndsey to drive herself and Ryan home. Jake's mother retreated to a chair in the corner of the room and stayed the night. The next morning, Master Sergeant Von Hammer landed at Clark and raced to the hospital to join his wife.

The doctor came in an hour later. The nurse updated him on Jake's condition and rolled Jake onto his side. She lifted the bandage over the snakebite, "Doctor, look at this?"

The doctor looked at the wound. "Boonie medicine. Saw a lot of that in Nam."

He removed the bamboo shoots Master Fuji inserted and replaced them with surgical tubes to allow infection fluid to drain.

The doctor said to the nurse, "Good work. Keep administering anti-venom keep me updated of any changes."

The doctor approached Jake's parents, "Hello, I'm Dr. Carver, the primary physician treating your son. Sergeant Fujioka told us the snake was a large king cobra. Cobra venom is a neurotoxin that affects the central nervous system causing paralysis. The venom also destroys tissue in and around the bite location. A snake that size can deliver a large volume of venom. The bite was in the lateral posterior torso close to the kidney. We're trying to protect as many tissues as possible. There is a wound on the leg, but we're not concerned with it. He got bitten about forty minutes before the first anti-venom injection. He's hanging on, and we are doing everything we can. We just don't know right now. I'm sorry."

Master Fuji stopped by and told Jake's parents, "Go to lunch. I'll stay with Jake and call the NCO club if anything changes."

"Thank you, Teuro," Master Sergeant Von Hammer replied. "We need a break."

They left, and Master Fuji pulled the chair beside the bed and sat. He opened a book and read aloud.

"The Warrior Spirit. A warrior fights with body, mind, and spirit, never gives up, never surrenders. A warrior will fight with every muscle. Until the last breath. A warrior fights with an indomitable spirit." Master Fuji closed the book. "Jake-san, you can hear me. You're a warrior, stronger than ten-thousand cobras. Fight the snake, Jake-san."

Master Fuji rubbed Jake's hands and squeezed his feet. Then he placed his hands on Jake's head and chest and meditated. Warmth flowed from Master Fuji's hands into Jake's body. His heartbeat grew more robust, and a rosy color returned to his cheeks.

For the rest of the day, the family took turns standing watch. Jake's mother refused to leave and sat in the corner, praying. Jake's father ferried the family back and forth between home and the hospital. Ryan and Lyndsey brought bags of treats for Jake to eat when he woke, but they ate most of it. Benji came by and spoke entirely in Tagalog—no-one understood a word he said.

The next morning Dr. Carver came and read Jake's chart. He peeled back Jake's eyelids and shined a light into each one. The doctor rolled Jake onto his side and inspected the bite area.

Baffled to see the bruise gone, he eased him back down and noticed his toes flinching. He left the room and returned with a syringe and inserted it into the IV bag. He then attached a squeeze pump to his breathing tube and manually regulated his breathing. He paused to see if Jake would breathe on his own. Jake gagged. The doctor removed the breathing tube and sat him up to cough.

"Jake, you're okay," Dr. Carver said, "You're in the hospital. Family is here."

Clutching the bed rail, Jake's cracked his eyelids open, and his jaw lay slack—like he'd just looked death in the eye.

## 4

The medical staff, amazed, if not confused, by Jake's quick recovery and lack of tissue damage, released him two days later. He stayed in his room and slept.

Benji visited. "I made you a new walking stick. I carve a cobra in the handle to remind you to watch out for snakes."

"Oh, Benji. Thanks! It's my new favorite stick. I'm gonna be real careful from now on."

"You all good now, right?"

"Ya, but tired all the time. I can't remember anything. Tell me what happened."

Benji said, "Master Fuji take juice from a plant root, put it in your nose, and blow with his mouth."

"Ewwh, in my nose?"

"Ya, you baklâ boy."

Jake covered his face, "Noooo!" Benji and Jake laughed.

Benji started waving his hands and speaking fast, mixing Tagalog and English, "Turn sobra—back—stick, tumakbo..."

Jake only caught half of what he said. Then Benji rattled on and on about the cute nurses at the hospital.

School started while Jake was recovering. He'd only missed a few days, but the news of his accident spread quickly through the small school. Many kids asked to see Jake's snake bite. He lifted his shirt to show the others who measured the distance between the fang marks at over one and a half inches. The kids gave him a new nickname—Von Viper.

Jake continued to recover, but the ordeal haunted him when he was alone. He couldn't stop replaying the incident in his mind and became sick to his stomach. One evening, Jake fidgeted with his dinner, unable to eat. Jake's mother sensing his uneasy mood, asked, "Are you all right?"

"I'm not feeling well. Going to lay down."

Jake crawled into bed, rolled-up in a blanket, and drifted to sleep. He dreamed he was climbing Bunker Hill and saw krait snakes in the grass, vipers in the trees, and pythons all around him. Jake ran, but snakes were everywhere. In his house, hanging from windows—he couldn't escape. He stayed still, snakes slithering all around. He woke-up and snapped upright —then realized it was a dream. He laid back, pulling the covers close to his chest, and laid there, staring at the ceiling.

The following day, Jake visited Master Fuji. While Griffiss lay in his lap, Jake stroked his fur and said, "I had a nightmare about snakes... I can't stop thinking about them."

Master Fuji replied, "You experienced a traumatic event. Your subconscious mind is helping you cope." Master Fuji gave Jake a cup of hot tea. "Drink this. It has healing herbs that will restore your energy. You should meditate and concentrate on the healing power of your body. You'll feel better tomorrow."

The next morning Jake's energy returned, and his appetite increased, gaining four pounds in one week. Jake started practicing with Master Fuji, and within a month, he was moving faster and jumping higher than ever before.

Concerned by the speed of Jake's improvement, Master Fuji held up a striking pad and asked Jake to try the jumping-spin kick he learned before the accident. Jake positioned himself in front of the bag and twisted off a semi-decent jumping spin kick. Master Fiji then held the bag higher and asked him to try again. Jake spun up another twist kick, striking the bag squarely, and landed in proper balance. Master Fuji seemed pleased but secretly wondered how much the Wado juice was affecting Jake's physical ability.

Master Fuji said, "Keep practicing but don't overexert yourself."

The following Saturday, Master Fuji was packing to prepare for his move to Hawaii when Jake dropped by to talk to him.

"Master Fuji, the karate school does things differently. Can't I just practice by myself like you?"

Master Fuji replied, "You aren't advanced enough to practice alone. You need a teacher. Master Kim is an excellent instructor. No need to worry, just work hard. I'll talk to Master Kim to see how you are doing."

Master Fuji took a katana from the wall and handed it to Jake and said, "Jake-san, take this sword. It's a good sword, made by many craftsmen working toward the same goal, each adding their expertise to create a work of art. Just as each teacher adds their knowledge to mold a student into an exceptional person. Be careful—it's sharp. When you are ready, I'll teach you how to use it."

"I understand," Jake said. "I'll keep it and work hard."

Master Fuji bowed, "Till we meet again, Jake-san."

Jake said goodbye to Griffiss, Elm, and Travis and walked the long way home talking to no-one. He placed the sword on his dresser and sat on his bed, staring out the window. Memories of the people who've come and gone in the brat life floated through his mind. He felt like crying but couldn't—crying isn't allowed in the Von Hammer family. His father was always quick to bark, Maintain your military bearing!

The following day, Ryan took Jake to the Base Recreation Center. The center was a large gymnasium with an outdoor swimming pool. Jake and Ryan competed to see who could make the biggest splash from the high dive. While Jake clung to the side of the pool, someone yelled, "Snake!"

Jake sprung out of the water and whirled around. There stood Fritz, with her golden curls and tangerine bikini, laughing.

Jake exhaled. "Wow... that wasn't cool. What're you doing here?"

"I come here every weekend—it's my favorite pool. Don't you prefer slimy snake-infested wells?"

"Ugh, don't wanna think about it."

Fritz said, "Guess I'll be seeing you around here more?"

"Ya, maybe. Master Fuji transferred to Hawaii. Said I should train with Master Kim."

"Great, fresh meat!"

"Um... not cool either."

"Just kidding," Fritz said, "We practice Tuesday and Thursday and spar on Fridays. That'll give you all weekend to heal. Haha. See ya!"

Jake took notice of Fritz's toned body as she walked away. Jake thought, *she's gonna kill me.*

Bored with swimming, Jake dried off and found Ryan sunbathing on a pool lounger.

Jake said, "I'm starving, but I don't have any money."

"I don't either," Ryan said, "but Lyndsey taught me a trick. Get dressed."

Ryan and Jake walked a block to the NCO Club's Flame Room Restaurant and ordered steak dinners with dessert. When the waiter brought the check,

Ryan said, "Charge it to Senior Master Sergeant Von Hammer's tab, please."

The waiter said, "Do you have an I.D.?"

Ryan pulled a dependent military I.D. from his wallet and handed it to the waiter. The waiter took it and disappeared into the back.

Under his breath, Jake said, "This isn't gonna work."

"Ye of little faith," Ryan replied.

A moment later, the waiter returned and handed the I.D. back to Ryan.

"Thank you. Come again."

Jake gave Ryan that, did we just get away with that, look.

Ryan replied, "Lindsey and I did this a few weeks ago. Dad never reads the bill."

"Wow, who doesn't notice steak dinners?" Jake asked.

"The room is so dark, and the bill is so long, he never bothers. Mag beer muna tayo."

"Haha, ya, he likes his San Miguel. I don't know how he can stand that stuff. It smells horrible."

"Have you noticed the stare?"

"What stare?"

"He's got war sickness."

"What's that?"

"That's when the war is over, but you're still fighting."

"Why doesn't the Air Force do something?"

"They'll section eight him. He's trying to hang on till he gets full retirement."

"Man, that sucks."

"It does."

That evening, a dead calm blanketed Master Fuji's house. Jake climbed the jackfruit tree with his binoculars and scanned the upper branches—Griffiss wasn't there. He sunk into the tree. *What am I supposed to do now?*

A few days passed, and Sergeant Von Hammer called Ryan and Jake into the living room. "Take a seat, boys."

Jake gave Ryan that; busted look.

Sitting upright, they braced for their punishment. Sergeant Von Hammer said, "I received a call from the base commander."

The boy's eyes grew wide, and the Sarge continued, "They offered us base housing."

The boys exhaled and slumped back into the cushions.

Ryan said, "Does it have air conditioning?"

"Yes."

"When can we move?" Jake asked.

Sergeant Von Hammer said, "How long will it take you to pack?"

Ryan shot back, "An hour!"

Sergeant Von Hammer lifted a brow. "An hour?"

"We're experienced."

Two weeks later, the Von Hammers were settling into their new house near the perimeter fence. Lyndsey spent most of the time at her friend Debbie's house, and Ryan went to football practice everyday. One afternoon, Jake became so bored, he walked fifteen minutes to Master Kim's dojo.

Master Kim said, "Good to see you, Jake. Please, come in."

Jake followed Master Kim into the office and sat in a chair beside the desk. "Master Fujioka said I should train here."

Master Kim said, "He's already called to check on you."

"I'm sorry," Jake replied, "We just moved on base and got unpacked... Do you think I'll fit in?"

Master Kim answered, "Everyone here is a military dependent. Class starts in an hour. Why don't you stay?"

"I don't have a uniform. Master Fuji and I practice in shorts."

Master Kim smiled. "He's old school. I'll give you a uniform. White or black?"

"White, definitely white."

Jake changed into the gi and started warming up. As other students arrived, each of them introduced themselves and welcomed Jake to the school. Feeling out of place, he struggled with the order of things.

"Don't be discouraged," Master Kim said. "You'll get used to it soon."

One of the green belts lived across the street from his new house. Bebout was his last name, and everyone called him Bebout because that's what kids do. Bebout liked skateboards and taught Jake to ride. They raced up and down the streets with other kids and practiced tricks on any smooth surface they could find.

After a few weeks, Jake was blending into the class at Master Kim's dojo and sparring on Fridays. Most of the time, Jake only fought kids similar to his age and rank. Jake and Bebout were favorite sparring partners, but one evening, they paired Jake with Fritz. Fritz bopped around like popcorn, and whatever confidence Jake had ran away.

*Oh gosh, here we go.*

The timekeeper dropped his arm, and she attacked. He dodged, weaved, and backpedaled to avoid contact.

Fritz said, "What's the matter? Are you afraid of a girl?"

Playing it cool, Jake said, "Boys aren't supposed to hit girls."

"Oh, ya! Worry about yourself, Von Viper."

Fritz leaped forward and hook-kicked Jake in the stomach. Jake clutched his chest and fell to the floor, gasping for air.

Fritz knelt beside him. "Thanks! That didn't hurt at all. See you in school, fool."

Jake lay there thinking, *Man, I really don't like her.*

The following week at school, Fritz saw Jake eating lunch at one of the picnic benches. She sat on the other side and said, "Hey, Jake, I see you didn't die."

He grinned, "Ha, ya, I sucked."

Fritz replied, "You should practice more."

"Ya, guess so."

"Jake, I've been taking Karate since I was five years old. I'd be a black belt by now, but we move all the time, and I have to keep starting over. This is my fourth school. My mother said we're moving again after Christmas."

"Where are y'all going?"

"We haven't gotten final orders yet. Maybe Honolulu or Phoenix."

Jake responded, "We were supposed to move to Hawaii, but my father talked my mother into the P.I. (Philippine Islands)"

"Wow! How'd that happen? He oughta sell cars."

"No kidding. Haha. He said the Philippines is just like Hawaii —but cheaper. We thought we were getting Waikiki but got Tijuana instead. I haven't seen a beach since we've been here. Can't wait to get back stateside."

"I know, right," Fritz replied. "I'd love to live near a beach. I'd go every day."

"Me too."

"See you at practice, Ciao!"

"Bye, Fritz."

A few days later, Jake and Bebout were doing jumping kicks against the heavy bag before practice. Several other students joined them and started a high kick competition. Bebout's kick landed on the upper section of the bag. Determined to win, Jake kicked too high and hit the chains. He fell to the floor, clutching his foot and moaning in agony. His cries caught Master Kim's attention, who came over, grabbed Jake's foot, and reset the dislocated toe. The pain went away, and Jake sat massaging his foot.

"This is why we don't horseplay in the dojo." Master Kim pointed at the floor. "Everyone give me fifty."

At the end of class, the students sat in rows according to their ranks, and Master Kim gave them a summary of the day's lesson. Afterward, Master Kim said, "Any questions?"

A student asked Master Kim, "How high is the top of the bag?"

"About six feet, why?"

"Jake's kicked the chain," the boy said.

"Hmm? That would be over seven feet," Master Kim said. "Perhaps when Jake's foot is better, he can try again?"

Jake raised his hand and replied, "Sir, I can do it now."

Master Kim said, "Isn't your toe sore?"

"No sir, look. "Jake raised his foot and wiggled his toes. "It's okay."

"All right, anyone who wants to kick, line up near the bag. We'll start low and work our way up."

Bebout hit the bag with such force; it caused it to swing violently. Several other students went before Fritz. She executed the kick better than most, which surprised no one. She was one of the more skilled students. Then Jake lined up and kicked the bag almost as viciously as Bebout.

Master Kim raised the bag and told the students to try their best and highest kick. Some students declined to try with the bag so high. Bebout ran and jumped, striking the bag above the logo printed on the bag, measuring 5'4". Then Fritz took her turn. She skipped and hit the bag just below Bebout's mark.

On Jake's turn, he ran, jumped, spun, and kicked the bag. A loud pop rang out. Jake landed and caught the bag as it swung back toward him. Everyone gasped. Master Kim measured the height of Jake's impact.

"Almost seven feet. That was unexpected," Master Kim said. "Jake is our winner!"

"Wow, I didn't expect that either," Jake said. "I was only trying to beat Bebout's kick."

Bebout said, "I think Jake's ready to test for his next belt."

"Maybe he should skip green and go straight to blue?" Fritz replied.

# 5

A fter math class one afternoon, Fritz trapped Jake in a corner before he could leave the room.

"Hey Jake, are you going to the Teen Dance at the Recreation Center?"

Jake and Bebout weren't planning to go because they thought it was stupid and didn't know how to dance, anyway. Jake hemmed and hawed around, acting like he knew nothing about the dance. He was about to make up an excuse when Fritz said, "I want to go, but I can't unless my sister finds a date."

Jake replied, "Oh, that's a bummer. Isn't your sister in high school?"

"Ya, she's on the basketball team, and most guys are shorter than her. I was wondering if your brother had a date because he's tall?"

Jake said, "I don't think he's going. I'm sure he has football or something."

"Great, because the football teams don't have games that weekend. Tell Ryan that Marie really wants to go with him. You and Ryan can pick us up at 7:00. I'll let you know what to wear as soon as I figure out what I'm wearing. Thanks, Jake!"

Fritz turned and walked away, leaving Jake speechless and wondering, *did I just get hoodwinked?*

That evening at dinner, Jake told Ryan that Fritz's sister wanted to go to the dance with him. Jake was sure his brother would say 'no way' because he thought dances were stupid too. Ryan dropped his fork and swallowed hard.

Ryan said, "What? Marie wants to go to the dance with Me?"

Laughing, Jake said, "Ya, Fritz can't go unless Marie does, so if you have football practice or something, I won't have to take Fritz."

Ryan replied, "Football practice?... I'd miss the Super Bowl to go out with Marie. I'll talk to her tomorrow."

Jake's mouth fell open. "Huh?"

Their mother asked, "Who is Fritz?"

"She's that cute girl with big green eyes in Jake's karate school." Lyndsey said, "How cute! Jake has a girlfriend."

While getting ready for the dance, Jake felt the willies—like a real date. Ryan and Marie had gone out several times in the weeks leading up to the dance, but Jake and Fritz barely talked about it.

Ryan said, "Marie loves to dance.'

Jake replied, "Gosh, dancing makes me feel like a dork. Can you teach me?"

"I really don't know myself. Just don't dance like a girl. If all else fails, do the Funky Chicken, you'll get a good laugh."

Jake and Ryan took a taxi to the commissary to pick up corsages, then rode to the Pattersen house. They walked up the sidewalk carrying the flowers and rang the bell. Mr. Pattersen opened the door and said, "Come on in, boys," opening the door wider. The boys stepped inside and Mr. Pattersen said, "You guys make yourself comfortable and I'll tell the girls you're here."

When Mr. Pattersen left the room, Ryan whispered to Jake, "Don't look so surprised."

Jake said, "I didn't know Sgt. Pattersen was black."

"Ya, well, he probably expected you to be taller."

Jake tapped the plastic container holding the corsage and gazed around the room. He noticed a piano in the corner of the room. Marie came out wearing a black dress matching her long black hair.

"Hello, Ryan, and Jake," She said. "Jake, you look handsome. Fritz is almost ready; she'll be out in a minute."

Jake replied, "Thanks, you look great too. Is that your piano?"

Marie said, "Oh no, I quit playing long ago. Fritz is the talented one. Maybe she'll play something for you!"

Jake's stomach churned, realizing Fritz was the musical one. She came out wearing a red dress with her curls artfully tied back with a white ribbon. Her warm brown skin glowed against her blonde hair, pearl earrings, and matching necklace.

"Wow, Fritz, you look amazing!" Jake said.

She smiled. "Thank you; you look great too."

Jake tried to pin the corsage onto Fritz's dress. Blushing, he fumbled with the pin and accidentally stuck her.

"Ow!"

Ryan said, "Good thing she's wearing red."

Marie laughed and stepped in to help the flustered Jake, who looked at Fritz and whispered, "Sorry."

Fritz smiled and winked, "Thanks for the corsage, Jake. Irises are my favorite."

As they walked out the door, Mr. Pattersen leaned toward Jake and said, "Watch out, she has a mean kick."

Jake covered his stomach and replied, "Yes sir, I know!"

When they got to the dance, Ryan and Marie ditched them and went to hang out with their friends. Jake and Fritz walked around the Rec Center, looking at decorations, and found the snack table. Jake covertly scanned the floor to pick up dance moves from older guys. He grabbed two glasses of punch and handed one to Fritz, and said, "Wow, there's a lot of people here."

She sipped some punch, "This is so much fun!"

The song "You Should Be Dancing" blasted through the speakers and Fritz got bouncy. She put down her cup and pulled Jake onto the dance floor, swiveling around and taunting Jake to dance with her. A flash of perspiration drained the color from his cheeks; dang, *this is gonna suck.*

Then a brilliant idea popped into his head; *I'll just copy what Fritz does!*

Mirroring her movements, he waved his arms overhead, swung his hips, and twirled. He thought, *I must be doing all right —she's smiling.*

Then Ryan worked his way into his sightline and mouthed the words, "You're dancing like a girl."

Jake started choking and excused himself to the restroom. He leaned over the sink and splashed cold water on his face.

Staring into the mirror, *Can I fake sick and get out of this?*

The bathroom attendant, an old retired Navy Chief volunteering as a dance chaperone, noticed Jake in a fluster and handed him a towel, "Looks like you lost your dinghy?"

Jake took the towel, dried his face, looked at the Chief, and said, "I can't dance."

"Hmm?" said the Chief. "That's odd; you walked in here,"

"Huh... What does that mean?"

"If you can walk, you can dance."

"Ya, well," Jake said, "I can't dance."

The gruff old bosun scratched his cheek, "Come over here. I'll show you." The Chief opened the door and said, "Hear that noise you kids call music?" Jake nodded, and the Chief continued, "Okay, the beat goes one, two, one, two. Now, all you have to do is sidestep, one, two, then step to the other side, one, two, and so on. Now, that gets rather boring, so step back, one, two, and forward, one, two. Mix it up, and don't swing your arms too much—you'll look like a girl."

The Chief led Jake through a few steps and said, "Remember, ladies will give you a lot of credit just for trying. Understand?"

"I think so," Jake replied.

The Chief gave him a dab of cologne and said, "Go get 'em, sailor."

"Thanks, Chief!"

Jake found Fritz waiting by the punch bowl. She said, "I thought you ghosted me."

"Ah, no," Jake replied. "I was talking to someone."

"Was she cute?"

"Um, not really."

"What'd y'all talk about?"

"Uh... I was teaching her how to dance."

Fritz laughed out loud.

Jake continued, "Haha, I know—I'm bad. Can you help me?"

She grabbed Jake by the wrist and led him to the dance floor. Placing her hands on his shoulders, she tapped the beat on his shoulders and guided him around the floor. A few minutes later, Jake got the hang of it and started dancing. When a slow song played, she pulled him close. Firm but soft, her hair smelled like rain. As they swayed to the music, her warmth surrounded him. He fell into a trance.

"Ouch, that's my foot," she said.

He snapped to and winced, "I'm sorry."

"Were you falling asleep?"

"Oh no, I just lost my place," Jake said, "Sorry, I'll clean 'em."

"Ha, don't worry about it. They're too small, anyway."

A while later, Ryan and Marie found Jake and Fritz. Ryan said, "Y'all hungry?"

Jake looked at Ryan, "We're always hungry!"

They walked to the nearby Flame Room Restaurant and charged dinner and dessert on Sergeant Von Hammer's tab—again. When they arrived home, Fritz hugged Jake and said, "Thank you, I had a great time. Wish we could do it again."

Jake replied, "Same to you. I had a blast. Goodnight."

"Ciao"

Over the next month, Jake and Fritz went to the movies with Ryan and Marie. Other times, they'd meet Bebout and other friends at the bowling alley or swimming pool. Jake was developing a crush on Fritz but was too afraid to tell her. During Christmas break, Jake invited her to go horseback riding and took a taxi to the stables. Jake rode his favorite black gelding named Angus, and Fritz rode a mare named Buttercup. After riding across the pasture, they rested under a large monkeypod tree.

Fritz placed her hand on Buttercup's neck, "The horses are sweating badly."

Jake replied, "It's too hot. Let's take the trail through the forest so they can cool off."

The path led to a small creek crossing. Jake guided Angus across the shallow stream without difficulty, but Buttercup stopped in the middle. Fritz gave Buttercup a nudge to encourage her to move forward, but Buttercup reared up, trying to throw her. Buttercup dropped and rolled, knocking Fritz off, then popped up and galloped away. Fritz laid in the creek, startled and soaking wet. Jake jumped down and ran to Fritz as Angus took off in the same direction as Buttercup. He helped Fritz onto the bank to assess her injuries, but the only damage she suffered was a sore bottom and wet perm.

As they walked down the trail toward the stables, they joked about the incident, vowing never to ride Buttercup again.

The conversation lulled, and in a more somber tone, Fritz

said, "We got our orders. We're moving to Phoenix in two weeks."

Jake didn't respond; he just looked down. Fritz sensed Jake's mood and tried to brighten him up.

"What's the matter, cat got your tongue?"

"No," he said, "I don't want you to go."

"I'll send a postcard."

His voice cracked, "That's what we always say."

"I know," she replied.

She grabbed his hand, and they walked back to the stable where Angus and Buttercup were holed up behind the barn. They told the stable-hand what happened and where to find the horses.

## 6

Sitting in one of the large Papasan chairs in his living room, Jake thought about Fritz. Her family left for Phoenix a few days earlier. He fell asleep and dreamed he was in math class, looking at Fritz's empty chair. He looked around the room, and all the chairs were empty. Jake wandered around the school and couldn't find anyone. Ryan told him, "Everyone is gone. We're the only ones left." Jake woke up and realized he was dreaming, but the empty feeling stayed with him.

Jake grabbed his skateboard and rode aimlessly through the winding streets. He found himself in front of the dojo, where Master Kim was updating the outdoor sign.

Master Kim said, "How're you doing?"

"I'm bored," Jake said.

Master Kim replied, "I spoke to Master Fujioka and told him about your flying spin kick. He is very much delighted and coming to visit next month. I scheduled a belt test, and you and Bebout are testing with a few other students."

The news about Master Fuji thrilled Jake. The following morning, he and Bebout worked their new staff forms, and Jake spun his staff aggressively—whistling as it whipped through the air. Jake wasn't paying attention and accidentally hit a concrete carport pillar. The staff shattered, flinging pieces all over the driveway.

Bebout said, "Man, you're really missing that girl, ay?"

With his jaw hanging open, Jake stared at the scattered remnants of his staff.

"Breaking your staff is a real bummer," Bebout said, "but do you realize how fast you were moving? That's crazy!"

Heartbroken, Jake picked up the pieces of the staff given to him by Master Fuji. He and Bebout worked on kata instead. Again, Jake was moving too fast, and they needed to restart several times.

"What's going on with you?" Bebout said.

"I don't know," Jake replied. "Maybe, I'm just not into it today? Let's quit for now. I need to go home anyway."

Jake threw himself onto his bed, and the bed shook, and shook, and shook. Jake realizing it was an earthquake, ran outside. Standing in his front yard, he saw Bebout across the street looking back at him. Together they watched shock waves roll down the concrete street like waves on water. Houses moved up and down like boats in large swells. Then, as quick as it started, it ended. Inside, Jake found pictures smashed on the floor, rearranged furniture, and the china cabinet face down. The sight of his mother's cherished china broken all over the floor made him forget about his staff.

By the time the parents arrived home, Jake and Ryan had already picked up the cabinet and cleaned most of the broken glass. The television news broadcasted images of the damage in mountain villages from the massive earthquake. Sergeant Von Hammer used a metal plumbing strap to attach the cabinet to the wall and warned the family of aftershocks.

Over the next few days, several tremors shook the base. Jake was in science class when an aftershock caused them to evacuate the building. Someone spotted a snake, and several guys, including Jake, chased it and cornered it against a building. The neon green snake became agitated and bit a tree trunk, leaving gooey saliva.

Transfixed by the snake's movements, Jake watched the scales contract and expand with the muscles beneath its skin. He saw the snake move as though it was in slow motion. Long, bright white fangs and glowing red eyes peered fearlessly right at Jake. One teacher pushed the boys back, telling them to clear the area. When Animal Control arrived, the crowd quickly lost interest and dispersed as officers captured the snake and put it into a barrel in the back of their truck.

Jake said, "What kind of snake is that?"

The officer took off a glove and replied, "Don't know. We've never seen one like it. It's a mean green dangerous animal."

"What will you do with it?"

"We'll take some venom and release it where it won't harm anyone."

The following Friday, Jake and Bebout were sparring with other students. Jake was fighting well, so Master Kim paired him with Chuck, an older black belt student. Powerful and fast, they considered Chuck the best fighter in the dojo. Jake used his speed and agility to avoid Chuck's attacks, but Chuck pulled no punches and tagged Jake a few times. Master Kim called, "Time." and Jake quit fighting and dropped his guard. Chuck stuck him with a side thrust kick to the ribcage. Stunned by the impact, Jake covered his rib and backed away.

Chuck said, "Sorry, I didn't hear the call."

Initially, adrenaline masked the pain, but by the end of class, Jake felt the stabbing pain of broken ribs. Later that evening, he lay down to sleep but couldn't find a comfortable position, so he propped-up pillows and slept upright. The following morning, Jake's whole side was sore, and it hurt just to put on a shirt.

Jake went to see Master Kim, "My rib is real sore. I won't be able to practice for a while."

Master Kim replied, "You may not be able to train your body, but you can train your mind. On Tuesday, you will train with my brother, Master Lanh."

Master Lanh, a Buddhist Monk and a 4th-degree black belt, was younger than Master Kim, but taller, bald, and spoke softly. He and Jake talked about his injury and different methods of training his mind through meditation. Jake found meditation exercises difficult because, as usual, thoughts and images flooded his mind making it difficult to concentrate. Master Lanh invited Jake to the Buddhist Temple for a better meditation environment, and Jake went the following Saturday. When Jake arrived, he checked the address twice because he thought he was at the wrong place—the Temple looked like an ordinary house.

Master Lanh opened the door and invited Jake inside. White sheets hung over walls and windows, making the whole interior look sterile. Master Lanh introduced Jake to a small Chinese woman named Ms. Han. She took Jake to a room and sat him down on a small pillow. Then handed Jake an illustration of a person lying down with their arms and fingers spread to each side.

Ms. Han pointed to the paper and said, "You do like picture."

Jake laid down, and Ms. Han sat beside him, "The purpose of meditation is to clear your mind. Random thoughts will break your concentration. You try to concentrate only on your belly button. It go up as you inhale and down as you exhale. Use your mind's eye to watch your belly rise and fall. This will occupy your mind and help stop outside thoughts from entering."

Ms. Han set a timer for five minutes and placed it near Jake, and said, "Do your best."

Jake closed his eyes and focused on his breathing, imagining he could see his belly and watched it fill and deflate. Within a short time, thoughts of everything from car horns to school work poured into his mind. It became increasingly difficult to concentrate on his breathing. After what seemed like forever, the five-minute timer buzzed.

Ms. Han entered the room and said, "Now, you take a short break and try again."

The second meditation session was better than the first, but he still couldn't stop his mind from drifting away on random thoughts.

Ms. Han gave him a pamphlet to take home, "Your focus will get better with practice. Know you are always welcome here. When you can meditate five minutes, you then meditate for ten, fifteen, and twenty. You train your mind like you train your body. Your ability to focus will get better with practice."

Jake read the pamphlet and meditated in this manner twice a day and with Ms. Han on Saturdays. Within a month, his attention span increased, he could focus better, and his grades improved.

One of his teachers said, "I thought you were cheating, so I gave you a different test, and you still scored higher than your classmates. Whatever you're doing, keep it up."

Imitating Ms. Han, Jake said, "Meditation, it good for you."

Jake's rib healed, and he returned to full practice at the dojo. Master Kim allowed Jake to choose a staff to replace the one he broke. The new staff was smooth, light, and slightly longer than the old one. Jake asked Benji to carve a viper around the midsection, "Paint it green—give it red eyes."

He called it the Viper and vowed to be fearless like the neon green snake dubbed Mean Green. Every day he practiced until he knew his hand positions by the feel and balance of the weapon. He became so fluid and fast, Master Kim taught him an advanced form he could use in competition. The form was long and complicated, but Jake practiced it obsessively and added extra rotations just for show. By the time of the belt test, he could run the complete form at almost tournament level.

Sergeant Von Hammer invited Master Fuji to dinner the night before the belt test. While sitting at the table, Jake said, "Benji told me you made medicine from a plant growing near the well."

Sergeant Von Hammer asked, "What kind of plant was that?"

Master Fuji replied, "It's a rare plant related to ginseng. You know, we study botanicals in jungle training."

Sergeant Von Hammer replied, "Hmm? That's interesting. I don't recall that one."

Mrs. Von Hammer, "How lucky are we that it was growing just where it was!"

Master Fuji replied, "Probably planted by soldiers during the war. Who knows?"

Quickly changing the subject, Master Fuji looked at Jake. "Are you prepared for your test?"

"Yes, sir! I've been working hard. I'm ready!"

"That's very affirmative, Jake-san. Has Master Kim helped you with your concentration?"

"Yes, sir! I've been working with Ms. Han at the Temple."

"I see," Master Fuji said, "I can tell it's working. How is school?"

"It's still boring, but I'm making better grades."

"Sounds like things are going well?"

Jake thought for a moment and responded, "I guess they are."

Jake excused himself from the table and walked to his room.

He sat on the bed and thought, *Huh, things really are getting better.*

Jake and Bebout rode their skateboards to the belt test arriving an hour early so they could practice. Parents and friends entered and filled the spectator section. Master Fuji wore a heavy black gi and sat at the judge's table with Master Kim and several senior black belts. The students lined-up by rank. Master Lanh, speaking in his soft manner, told the students, "Relax, have fun, and you will do well today."

Master Lanh asked them to sit—mook jong—meditate. "Imagine yourselves performing perfect forms."

After a few minutes, they warmed-up and demonstrated static blocking techniques. Master Kim ran the students through a lengthy exercise program of kicking and punching handbags, after which many students were walking around wincing and panting.

Master Kim said, "Maintain a warrior mindset and posture."

Master Kim asked Jake to sit down while the other two students completed the first Heian kata. Then Master Kim told Jake to perform the Heian Shodan kata in the manner taught to him by Master Fujioka. Jake came to attention and bowed once to Master Kim and then to Master Fuji. Jake took to heart what Master Lanh said—relax and be yourself. Before he started, he cleared his mind, thinking of nothing but the form. Jake took a deep breath and slowly exhaled. Exploding into the first movement, he moved crisply, using good technique, and Kiai'd powerfully.

Lyndsey whispered to their mother, "I think his voice just changed."

When the kata was complete, he returned to a ready stance, knowing he'd done his best, and it was the best he'd ever done.

The other orange belts joined him to perform the Heian Nidan kata. Jake executed the kata with the other students, but something was different about Jake. They returned to the ready position, and the judges scored their kata. Master Kim instructed them to get their weapons.

Jake grabbed the Viper and moved to the center of the floor between the other two students. Trying to stay in sync with the others, Jake's staff snapped from strike to strike. *Everyone is moving so slow,* he thought. He made adjustments, and the group completed the simple form. While the other ranks completed their forms, Jake noted the time and started meditating. Ignoring the surrounding noise, he went into a trance, clearing his mind of thought and emotion. After a while, Jake opened his eyes and looked at the clock. He'd been meditating for twelve minutes.

After individual belt testing was complete, the senior belts performed a weapon demonstration. Master Kim asked Jake, "Would you like to present your competition form?"

*Oh wow! Way to put me on the spot.* "Um... okay, sure."

He grabbed his staff and took it to the center of the floor. Master Kim addressing the dojo and family members, said, "Jake has only recently learned this form." Then turned to Jake and said, "No pressure. Just do your best," and winked.

Jake thought, *Oh, no pressure. ...ya right, just fifty people... Breathe, be calm like Master Lanh. Om mani padme hum...*

Jake exhaled and spun the staff around, bowed, and came to the ready position. Master Kim gave him a nod, and Jake snapped to attention. His head turned left, the staff spun as he kneeled for a low strike—popping as it struck his side. Jake quickly moved through several attacking positions and paused. Turning his head right, as if something caught his attention, he jumped to his feet and burst into a side strike, then another, and another. As Jake stepped across the floor, he whirled the Viper through a flare sequence that caused the wooden staff to appear to bend. The form ended with Jake jumping and turning 180 degrees landing on one knee in a low strike. He stood, spun the staff, and bowed to Master Kim. As Jake returned to his seat, he thought, *that wasn't so bad.*

The belt ceremony followed, and Jake and Bebout received their new belts.

Ryan said, "Good job! That stick thing is cool."

"Thanks. I was nervous."

"Couldn't tell. You looked like the Fuge out there."

Ryan walked away to talk to the new girl, and Master Fuji approached. "Congratulations, Jake-san! I'm happy to see you improve so much. You've been working hard?"

"Yes, sir, Thanks for coming."

"Glad to be here, Jake."

No living person had ever seen a Hābu-Té develop, and Master Fuji wondered if Jake's budding abilities would soon draw the wrong kind of attention.

## 7

B efore Master Fuji left, he gave Jake a gift with a note that read; I'm proud of you. Enjoy the Okinawan tea. Master Fuji departed for Hawaii the following morning after sending a message to the Grandmaster asking for a meeting to discuss Jake's situation.

The following Tuesday was another ordinary boring school day. Jake, feeling blase, took a shortcut home. A postcard in the mailbox lifted his spirits.

Hi Jake,

Here's the postcard I promised you. I hope you're doing great and missing me a lot. The school here is a year ahead of Wagner. Marie and I have to catch up. I found a great dojo near our new home. I get to learn everything all over again. Oh, joy! Okay, your turn.

Ciao, Fritz

Happy to hear from Fritz, Jake pulled a letter from his desk drawer he'd written a month earlier. After reading it, he crumpled it up and tossed it in the trash. He grabbed a Philippine postcard and wrote a less doting note, ending with the phrase: Having a great time. Wish you were here!

A couple weeks later, Jake, Bebout, and another friend, known as Bone Jaw, planned to sneak into the restricted area near Mars Hill for a jungle hike. Benjamin was Bone Jaw's real name, but a large head and protruding jaw gave the kid no chance. The older kids dubbed him Bone Jaw, and it stuck, so he went with it and became a sort of a cult celebrity. Jake and Bebout generally referred to him as BJ.

The three of them raided their kitchens filling backpacks with soup cans, beans, crackers, Zippo lighters, and anything else they could steal.

In the early morning darkness, donned in their father's Vietnam era gear, they snuck past two guard towers and crossed a bridge spanning the Dolores River. During the rainy season, torrents of water rush through the pass, chiseling a swath of destruction through the forest. During the dry season, water barely trickles through the spillway, allowing Jake and his friends to navigate the jungle by following the stream.

After crossing the bridge, the boys quickly ran to the cover of tree limbs, masking a concrete embankment. When they looked down, they saw a monster python coiled up in the very spot they needed to jump.

"Whoa!" BJ said. "It's as thick as a watermelon. Gotta be a fifteen-footer."

Jake replied, "Is anyone missing?"

Beabout and Jake were debating whether to abort the hike when BJ threw a stick and hit the snake. It didn't move, and ants started crawling over the body.

BJ said, "Hey, look, it's dead!"

"Alright then," Jake replied, "we're right behind you."

Bebout pushed BJ aside, "I'll go," and jumped down the five-foot embankment, landing just inches from the beast. Bebout nudged the snake with his boot, "Yup, it's toast."

"I'm sure it starved to death," Jake replied.

The spillway opened to a vast ravine covered by a thick canopy where inky ankle-deep water flowed around large stones. The musty odor of a gazillion mold spores filled their mouths with the taste of jungle.

Bebout's nostrils flared. "I love that smell."

Stepping gingerly, Jake eyed the riverbed for slithering monsters.

"These stones are slippery," he said.

"Be careful," Bebout replied. "Twist an ankle out here, and you stay here."

Having made their way to a ledge at the base of a steep volcanic wall, Jake paused to sip from his canteen. His gaze wandered around the primeval world laced with monkey vines and tropical fauna. "What lurks here, snakes, leeches, giant lizards?"

"More like typhoid, typhus, and cholera," BJ replied.

Bebout sang, "These are a few of my favorite things."

They continued along the ledge until reaching a narrow filled with giant boulders that blocked their path. Bebout tied a line to a grappling hook and tossed it over the blockade catching a chink in the rock. Using the line for leverage, he scaled the large stones and helped Jake and BJ do the same. From the top of the boulders, they could reach shallow divots to use as handholds. The vertical wall spanned thirty feet across. Bebout led the way, hand to hand, boot to boot, handhold to handhold. As Jake made his way across the wall, he saw a small shed snakeskin in one of the divots that made him pause. Being twenty feet above the stream, he had no choice but to whisk it away and keep going.

They reached another ledge and walked along the side of a deep chasm. Over eons, the river wicked its way through the pass, eroding porous rock and created an underground labyrinth of caves. One slip on the moss-covered path and they'd fall into the river and be trapped forever in the maze of tunnels. As Bebout pressed on, Jake and BJ stopped to view a spectacular web sequined with glimmering dewdrops hanging overhead.

BJ pointed. "Look at the size of that."

"Yeah, ...but where's the spider?"

"Dunno—must be huge."

Jake nudged BJ. "Let's get outta here."

The trail ended where the crevasse narrowed to a gap only five feet wide. They removed their backpacks and prepared to jump to the other side. Bebout, the confident one, leaped, making the jump look easy. Jake tossed the gear to Bebout, who stacked it out of the way. Jake stepped to the edge and focussed on the landing. He jumped, overshot the mark, and fell into the bushes.

Bebout quipped, "You should be on the track team."

The smallest of the group, BJ, worried about the jump. Jake stood on the landing, waiting to catch him. BJ ran and vaulted, leaping as far as he could. Landing on the edge of the rift, he wobbled. His eyes grew big, arms whirled 'round and 'round. BJ started falling backward. Jake stretched out and grabbed his hand and held him there. Slowly, Jake leaned back, trying to help BJ regain his balance, but his boot slipped, and BJ's weight pulled them both toward the abyss. Bebout latched onto Jake's belt and dragged both of them safely onto the ledge.

BJ said, "Wow, I thought I was a goner."

"Thought I was going with you," Jake said.

"No way," Bebout replied. "I'm not carrying all this stuff by myself." He picked up his backpack and continued along the way.

Another half-mile later, the ledge ended beside a waterfall. The hikers stripped down to their swim trunks and carefully descended the slippery rocks to a large pool at the bottom of the falls. After a quick scan for critters, they hoisted their bags overhead and waded into the water, making way to a sandy beach on the other side. In a fire pit, they burned a plant Master Fuji called sepium to keep insects away. In another hole, a fire heated cans of soup and beans.

After lunch, they played under the waterfall and explored the jungle where spaghetti-like vines made it difficult to penetrate. They all kept a watchful ear for any signs of a dangerous flash flood caused by rainfall in the mountains upstream. If caught off guard, a flash flood could sweep them downstream if they couldn't climb the river bank fast enough.

When the fire died down, Jake searched for more firewood. He found dead bamboo hanging over the edge of the water and reached up to break off a piece.

"Ay-ouch!"

Jake pulled his hand back sharply and squeezed it tightly with his other hand—afraid to look.

Bebout said, "What's wrong?"

Jake stood there white as chalk with his mouth hanging open. Blood streamed down his arm as Bebout rifled through bags searching for the first-aid kit. After the initial shock subsided and Jake realized he wasn't going to die, he mustered the courage to look at his hand. The bamboo split longways, cutting the web of his hand to the bone. Bebout gave Jake a fistful of gauze and cotton and said, "Here, apply pressure!"

Minutes later, the bleeding slowed, and the boys rested. Jake wrapped a t-shirt around the blood-soaked bandages, then wrapped tape around that. Bebout glanced at his watch and decided it was time to move on, so they cleaned up the campsite and snuffed out the fires.

They walked barefoot along the sandy river bottom in half-calf-deep water. An hour later, the stream widened into a shallow marsh covered by elephant grass taller than themselves.

They put on their boots and hacked through the swampy maze using machetes.

Jake said, "There's no better way to find a cobra than this."

Bebout replied, "You'd be the one to know Von Viper."

The trio trudged through a mile of meandering marsh until they came to a clearing. The water had eroded away half of a large hill, exposing a forty-foot wall of sand. Bebout and BJ threw rocks at the sand wall to see who could knock off the biggest chunk. The debris fell into the river forming a narrow stream at the base of the hill. They followed that stream for another mile, cutting through thick foliage, emerging on the golf course, muddy, tattered, and exhausted. A group of golfers stopped to watch as the paramilitary clad boys casually strode across the fairway carrying large machetes and bolo knives.

Jake dragged himself home, took a shower, and fell asleep. He woke up a few hours later when he heard his brother. His hand throbbed uncomfortably, and Jake went to the bathroom to replace the dressing. When he peeled back the jungle bandage, he saw bone and thought, *dang, I need stitches.*

But, he knew he'd get in trouble, so using tape, he made butterfly stitches like Master Fuji taught them in survival class and closed the wound.

Ryan asked. "What happened to you?"

Jake said, "I cut my hand on some bamboo in the Mars Hill jungle."

Ryan said, "Boy, you better not tell Dad. He'll go ballistic. That area is dangerous and off-limits."

Jake said, "I know, but you gotta see that place. It looks like a Tarzan movie. It's the wildest thing you ever saw."

The following week, Jake and his friends were heading up to the school to ride skateboards. Jake's covered his hand with a thick bandage and a duct-tape cover.

Bebout said, "Jake, how's your hand?"

"Getting better," Jake replied.

At karate practice a few days later, Jake wasn't wearing a bandage at all.

Bebout asked Jake, "Did you get stitches?"

Jake replied, "No, I didn't want to tell my parents. I held it together with tape and told them I cut it in the garage."

"Wow, it seems impossible for a cut like that to heal so quickly. You must be some kind of alien!"

---

## 8

Master Fuji traveled to the old city in Okinawa to speak to Grandmaster Matsumura, leader of the secret Order of Tē. Initially created to protect Shuri's capital city from invaders, the group expanded their focus after WWII to stabilize World governments and prevent war. Some OTé members used the Wado plant to enhance their strength, speed, and endurance while on spy missions. The Wado also had the power to heal life-threatening injuries in the same manner Master Fuji saved Jake. Children and teens often died because of the Wado's toxic properties, but a child would survive and develop sustained abilities in rare cases. They referred to these children as Hābu-Té, meaning reborn in the way. Because Jake was a Wado survivor, he'd be asked to join the OTé. If he refused, he'd be culled to protect the secrecy of the group.

They met in Grandmaster's dojo before the morning class. Sitting down with a cup of tea, Master Fuji said, "Thank you for this meeting, Grandmaster. I need to consult with you about Jake-san's situation. I believe he is exhibiting signs of Hābu-Té."

Grandmaster Matsumura replied, "This is a concern. If Jake is Hābu-Té, he must be guided carefully."

"He has an adventurous spirit. Someday, he'll be a valuable asset. For now, though, I believe it's best to let him experience a normal childhood."

Grandmaster nodded. "If that's possible... I'm sure you will handle it well." The Grandmaster took a sip of tea and continued, "Teruo, go to the mountain."

The following evening, Master Fuji ascended the mountain using a full moon's glow as his only light source. He climbed the cliff using no safety line or anything else that might leave a trace. Master Fuji rested on a ledge and looked out over the open sea, recalling the first time he climbed the mountain. He was a young man and gave Grandmaster an onyx stone to signify his unbreakable commitment to the OTé.

Master Fuji continued climbing, and when he reached the top of the mountain, he climbed down another cliff face to enter the cave where the Wado grew. Deep in the cave, an opening in the ceiling allowed sunlight and rain to reach a small area. Master Fuji cleared away dead leaves accumulating around the plant's base, took root cutting, and wrapped it in a damp cloth. Then he removed a dead fish from his gear bag and buried it under the plant. When Master Fuji returned to Hawaii, he planted the cutting on a hill in a protected location. The Wado grows slowly and would take many seasons to grow to a good size.

Meanwhile, Jake travelled with his parents along suicide road to Baguio City. The road winds up and down through steep mountain passes. Jake's mother buried her head as the Rabbit bus they were riding skirted around hairpin turns. When they finally arrived, Jake's parents went to a pub to calm their nerves while Jake visited the Negrito village. Aeta pygmies are the indigenous people of the Philippine Islands who migrated across land bridges 25,000 years ago. Although they have their own language, many are multilingual and speak Tagalog and English. They are small in stature. A mature man is no larger than a young American teenager.

Jake watched a Negrito warrior shoot papayas using a bow and arrow. The warrior never missed, even though the fruit swayed from long vines tied to a high branch. Jake asked if he could try and missed several shots before grazing the side of a papaya with the warrior's help. Jake bought a bow and a quiver of arrows from the man and spent months shooting banana trees in the backyard, but no-one cared; monkey bananas aren't good eating, anyway. Steve cut down the damaged trees and built Jake a target using a cardboard box stuffed with yard clippings. By the time the banana trees grew back, Jake's accuracy improved, and he could hit a papaya from across the yard.

Jake was in Bebout's garage playing pool one Saturday when Bebout mimicked his mother's British accent. "Aye mate, we're moving to bloody ol' England this summer."

Jake replied, "Your Mum must be happy, Aye?."

"Mighty pleased, ol' chap."

"We just found out we're getting transferred to Edwards," Jake said. "We're moving in August!"

"Roy toe!"

It was the first weekend of summer break, and Jake and Bebout were exploring the countryside. They would often discover unknown caves by prodding hillsides with walking sticks. Sometimes, they'd find rusted ammo clips, handguns, helmets, and other things in the caves left behind by soldiers. Bomb techs always reminded everyone on the base not to touch the old ammo found in the area because it was unstable and could explode.

While hiking the undeveloped area of the base, they found an undiscovered cave in a hillside. Jake and Bebout were careful to check for snakes and giant tarantulas before squeezing through the tight entrance, which expanded to a large cavern. Using a Zippo lighter as a torch, they found an old grenade embedded into the soil on the cave's floor.

Jake said, "That's an American MK2."

"What's it doing in a Japanese cave?" Bebout asked.

"Don't know. It could blow if we dig it up."

"Let's put a firecracker beside it. I've got a few triangles."

"Okay, gimme one," Jake said.

Bebout dug through his pocket and pulled out a triangle firecracker, and handed it to Jake. "Here, I'll find a punt."

Jake placed the powerful triangle firecracker next to the grenade then squeezed out the opening. Bebout lit the end of a long stick and let it burn until it was red hot, then blew out the flame. With half his body hanging out of the opening, he held the lighter in one hand and the makeshift punt in the other. Bebout placed the ember's tip on the fuse until it fizzled and backed out of the cave. He and Jake took cover and waited. A few seconds later, pop and a whisper of smoke wafted from the hole. After the smoke cleared, they found the grenade unphased.

Bebout said, "Maybe, two triangles will do the trick?" and twisted the fuses together. He wedged the triangles under the old bomb and lit the fuses. He and Jake retook cover. A loud salvo rang out, and a grey cloud billowed from the cave. They used a leafy branch to whisk away the smoke and found the grenade dislodged, but it didn't detonate.

"I'm out of firecrackers. What now?" Bebout said.

Jake replied, "Gimme a shoelace. I've got an idea."

Jake tied a slipknot in the shoelace and attached it to the end of a stick. He snared the grenade and lifted the old explosive from its resting place. With the grenade dangling, he walked it to a clearing and placed it on the ground. Hovering over the old bomb, Jake pointed and said, "The pin is intact."

Without hesitation, Bebout reached down and picked it up, "Think it'll blow?"

"It's thirty years old," Jake said. "Probably a dud."

Bebout replied, "Let's try."

Jake said, "Hold the hammer down and pull the pin. Be sure to throw it far."

The boys took cover behind a small berm, and Bebout pulled the pin.

"Ready?" he asked.

"Throw it far," Jake said.

When Bebout reared back to heave the old relic, they spotted a patrol jeep racing toward them. The boys ducked.

"Shoot, put the pin back in," Jake said.

"It won't go in."

He tried again, and the rusty pin broke, "What now?"

The jeep carrying two Military Police skidded to a stop, "What are you boys doing here?"

Jake hopped up, raising his arms to distract the MPs while Bebout tucked the grenade behind his back.

"Just messin' around," Jake said.

"You guys popping firecrackers?"

"No sir, just throwing rocks."

"We heard several pops."

Bebout brows lifted, "We didn't hear anything."

Jake shook his head, "Nope, not a thing."

"You kids get out of here. This area is off-limits. It hasn't been cleared by EOD (Explosive Ordnance Division)."

"Yes sir," Jake said, "On our way."

"If we catch you out here again, we'll arrest you. Got it?"

Bebout salutes. "Yes sir, got it."

As the MPs drove away, Bebout sat up holding the grenade, "Now what?"

"Don't drop it. Wait till the MPs get down the road."

When the jeep was out of sight, Bebout tossed the grenade into the cave. Seven, six, five, four, three, two, one, and... nothing.

"See, told ya," Jake said. "It's a dud."

"Oh well, let's go before the Keystone Kops come back."

Jake and Bebout climbed to the top of the hill and walked the ridgeline toward the housing area. They'd made it about a hundred yards when—KaBOOM! An explosion staggered them. Dirt and shrapnel hurled from the cave shooting a cloud of smoke into the air.

"Woe! did you see that?" Bebout said.

"Oh, my gosh," Jake replied, "that was killer!"

A jeep kicking up a dust cloud came racing toward them.

"Crap!" Bebout said, "The MPs are coming."

They legged it to the other side of the hill and hid in a gully. The patrolmen canvassed the area while Jake and Bebout snuck along the ravine.

Jake grabbed Bebout's arm and put his finger over his mouth, "Shhh... I hear 'em talking. They're bringing out the dogs."

Bebout said, "Shoot, we gotta scram."

The boys hoofed it down the gulch and ducked behind a mound of dirt. Bebout gestured, "We have to cross that flat to get to the wire."

"We'll be out in the open."

Then a dog bark echoed across the hill, and Jake looked at Bebout.

"Run for it!" Bebout said. "See you on the other side," and took off.

They made it halfway across the field before a voice screamed, "Hey, stop!"

They hoofed it to the fence separating the restricted area from the rest of the base. The two slipped under a wire fence, bolted down a dirt road, and ducked between two houses. While Bebout caught his breath, Jake peeked around the corner.

"I think we lost 'em."

"Ya," Bebout replied. "them suckers ain't got nothin' on us."

The boys strutted down a hill and crossed the road to Bebout's house. A grey car speeding down the road screeched to a halt. Two security policemen jumped out and charged toward them, shouting, "Stop!"

Jake and Bebout froze.

"Put your hands on your heads and turn around."

Jake whispered, "Busted."

Bebout placed his hands on his head and said, "I want a lawyer."

They handcuffed the boys, took them to the police station, and locked them in a cell. A staff sergeant looked at their dependent IDs and gasped.

"So, Timothy, your father is head of 3rd Security Police, and Jacob, your father is the EOD First Shirt? What in the Sam Hill were you two thinking?"

"Um," Jake said, "we're just goofing off."

Bebout perked up, "I want a lawyer."

"Slow down," said the Sergeant, "tell me what happened. Did you guys make an explosive?"

"No," Jake said. "We found a MK 2 in a cave... It kinda blew up."

The staff sergeant looked confused, "The patrol sergeant said they heard several explosions?"

Jake said, "We had a few triangles."

The sergeant shook his head, "You two are lucky you didn't blow yourselves up. Make yourselves comfortable while we sort this out."

When the staff sergeant left, Bebout said, "You shouldn't say anything without a lawyer."

Jake said, "Be more afraid of my father."

The Sergeant entered an adjacent room where Colonel Stoddard sat on a desk with arms crossed, staring at the floor.

"Did you hear that, Colonel?"

The Colonel turned to the Sergeant, "I did... What in tarnation was an MK2 doing in a Japanese cave?"

"That's a mystery, Sir."

The Colonel smirked, "Leave it to a bomb tech's kid to find it... Where'd you grow up, Sergeant?"

"New York, upstate, Sir."

The Colonel cracked a smile and looked at the wall, "I grew up on a little farm in Iowa... When we got bored, we'd grab some rope and make crop circles in cornfields. The alien invasion was the talk of the town."

"Haha, we had nothing so exciting. When the ice came, we'd grab bus bumpers and skitch down roads. Our parents swore we'd kill ourselves."

The Colonel stood up, walked across the room, placed his hands on his hips, and looked out the window.

"We drag these brats from post to post. Stand tall, toe the line! We forget, they're just kids, curious, adventurous, and daring as hell." He threw up his hands. "What did we expect? Given half a chance, I'd be right out there with them."

The Colonel sat in the chair and leaned back, "You know, ...I commanded the team that extracted Sergeant Von Hammer from Nhat Lan... That was a sight you never want to see..."

Colonel Stoddard stood and slammed his hand on the desk, "I don't want this to be a stain on a long and distinguished career. Read those boys the riot act and send 'em home."

The Sergeant snapped to, "Yes, Sir!"

A week later, Jake celebrated his fourteenth birthday. It was also the first anniversary of Benji's father's death. A taxi took Jake to the village to see Benji. When Benji saw Jake's taxi arrive, he ran to the car waving, "Maligayang kaarawan, maligayang kaarawan... (Happy Birthday)"

Jake stepped out, "Salamat, Benji, How are you?" and they embraced in a bro hug.

"I'm good, good. How is your family?"

"We're all fine. How 'bout yours?"

"Good, good. I'm glad you came today. We take flowers to tatay. You come?"

"Yes, I want to."

Benji's family gathered in front of the house. As they walked down the main street, a neighbor stepped out and handed Benji a flower. They walked a little further, and another villager stepped forward with a flower and gave it to his sister, then another neighbor handed one to his brother, and another, and another. By the time they reached the cemetery, they were carrying dozens of colorful flowers.

Jake said, "Wow, you've got great neighbors."

"Yes, we know them all our life. They family."

Awestruck by the generosity and the deep connections Benji had with his family and other villagers, Jake's eyes filled with tears. He'd never known anyone for more than a year or two. They put the flowers into small vases filled with water and placed them around the tombstone. Benji pulled out a yellow flower and handed it to Jake.

"For your birthday."

Jake took the flower and said, "Thank you, I'll never forget your father."

Benji smiled. "I'll never forget your birthday."

When they left the cemetery, Benj's family told Jake good-bye, and he and Benji walked around the village talking.

Jake said, "Have you been to the well?"

Benji replied, "A few times, with my brothers on hot days."

"Will you take me there?"

"Sige (okay)."

They grabbed sticks and hiked up the trail toward Bunker Hill. As they reached the top of the hill, Benji reenacted Master Fuji's run to the helicopter. When they got to the well, Benji pulled a weed from the ground and showed Jake how Master Fuji made the medicine, put it in his nose, and blew. Jake stared into the pool, trying to remember, but only bits of his memory came to him.

They walked to the other side of the hill and climbed a bunker.

Jake said, "How's your family doing?"

"We good, Arnel does most of the work... My sisters take care of ina (mom). I'm saving money to go to Industrial School in Manila."

Jake said, "We're moving stateside in August. Going to Los Angeles. I'm ready to leave, but I'll miss everyone. You've been a good friend. Salamat."

Benji smiled. "I miss you too, Hollywood."

Jake laughed. "Hollywood, haha..."

A week before Bebout left, he and Jake rode their skateboards to FM Hill. The blacktop road to the top was steep, and nobody had ever successfully ridden down it on a skateboard. Jake and Bebout climbed the hill to the first bend. Standing with their boards in hand, looking at the route, Jake said, "Looks challenging."

"Challenge accepted," Bebout replied.

They jumped on their boards and accelerated rapidly on the steep grade. Felt like they were going 60 mph when the boards started vibrating.

Trying to maintain control, Jake yelled, "Ayee yah!"

Bebout screamed, "Whoa ah oh a!"

Then they lost control and wiped out. Jake crashed into a bunch of banana trees and laid there, taking inventory of his limbs. He heard Bebout moan and stammered to his feet, holding his shoulder. Grimacing, he ran to where Bebout was lying. Bebout rolled over, exposing a forearm sticking up at thirty-degrees. Jake staggered down to the road and flagged a car. The driver, an Airman on his way to work, helped Jake walk Bebout down the hill and put him in the car. Bebout cursed all the way to the hospital. The boys were taken to an emergency room and treated. A nurse putting Jake's arm into a sling over-heard Bebout screaming obscenities as a doctor reset his arm.

She smiled and said, "I haven't heard that one before."

"He's British," Jake replied.

Jake and Bebout sat in the recovery room, admiring Bebout's cast and laughing about the whole mess. Jake borrowed a pen and said, "Let me be the first to sign your cast." Bebout lifted his arm, and Jake drew a skateboard and wrote, FM Hill Challenge, JVH. As Jake put the final touches on his artwork, he said, "FM Challenge—haha—that was stupid."

"Ya," Bebout replied. "The best times usually are."

Jake said, "My mom says I'm hanging around the wrong kind of people."

"Haha, Mine says the same thing."

The hospital contacted their parents, who came to pick-up their daredevil children. Bebout's mother gave Bebout a good tongue lashing in her thick British accent and took him home.

Mrs. Von Hammer looked at Jake and said, "What is wrong with you?"

Jake replied, "We were just having fun."

She whispered, "I don't care what you say. That Bebout kid is trouble."

Jake last saw Bebout the night before his family moved. They hung out in the garage dining on frozen pizza while listening to Zeppelin.

"Man," Jake said, "it's gonna suck around here without you."

"Aye, it's been a wild one. Let's keep in touch."

Jake smiled, "Yup, let's do that."

The following morning, Jake woke up feeling apathetic. He couldn't find interest in anything. He drank a cup of Fuji tea and went to the Temple to meditate. Outside, Master Lanh led a morning stretching class, and Jake sat under a tree to watch. Master Lanh, who always spoke softly, led the group through the Temple Exercises.

Master Kim noticed Jake sitting under the tree and said, "Good morning Jake. What brings you here this morning?"

Jake replied, "I'm bored... My shoulder is stiff, I broke my board, and Bebout is gone. I'm sick of military life. I want to live like a normal person."

Master Kim said, "I see Jake. Let's get something cold to drink."

They walked across the street to Master Kim's office, where Jake sat in a chair while Master Kim filled two glasses with iced tea and gave one to Jake. He sat down and took a sip of tea.

"You know, Jake, when I was a young boy, we lived on a small farm near a village in my home country of Korea. Our neighbors were farmers, and all the children helped their parents work the farms. The days were long, and we often had little to eat. In 1950, the Northern Korean Army invaded our village. My older sister snuck Lanh and me out of the village just before the attack. The soldiers who killed my parents burned the village to the ground. Friendly forces found took us to an orphanage. We got separated, and Lanh was taken to China. I never saw my sister again. They sent me to Japan, where I worked in a labor camp with other orphaned refugees. When I was ten, a Korean family living in Tokyo adopted me. Since I was Korean, the other students shunned me. I didn't have many friends, and that gave me a lot of time to practice karate. When I graduated, I worked in a dojo as a Junior Instructor until I was twenty-four years of age.

One day, the Chinese Kung-Fu Demonstration Team came to Tokyo. I was chosen to help the team get around the city. A member of the group told me my resemblance to a Korean monk named Lanh surprised him. A year later, I traveled to China. I knew Lanh was my brother as soon as I saw him. He looked the same, only much taller and less hair, but he had that smile like my mother. It took a long time for Lanh to remember the family because he was young when it happened. Lanh trans- ferred to Clark just three years ago. We are still getting to know each other. You see, there is no normal life, Jake, only moments. Be happy for the life you have."

Lost for words, Jake said nothing. Master Kim asked, "What's wrong?"

"I'm embarrassed for being so selfish."

"One person's suffering doesn't cancel another's pain," Master Kim said.

Jake's face wrinkled, "That sounds like something Master Lanh would say."

Master Kim smiled. "You caught me."

Jake laughed.

A few weeks later, Jake went to the dojo and started limbering up before class. Master Kim stood next to Chuck and said, "Everyone listen up... Today, we're very proud to announce; Chuck has enlisted in the Navy."

All heads turned to Chuck, hooping and hollering. Many students approached him and shook his hand. After Chuck led the class through an exhaustive work-out, Master Kim instructed everyone to the dojo's rear.

"Jake-san," Master Kim said, "Perform Heian Godan (the fifth Pinan kata)."

"Yes sir," Jake replied.

Jake stepped smartly to the center of the floor and bowed. Moving crisply, he completed the form and waited.

Master Kim said, "Well done. Get your staff."

Jake returned with his staff.

Master Kim said, "Do the intermediate form."

Jake bowed and spun the staff around to the ready position.

Master Kim nodded.

Jake lifted the Viper overhead and executed a downward strike. The staff whirled around him as he spun into another downstrike. Moving with precision, Jake completed each movement and ended with a flurry of strikes. He popped to attention and bowed.

Master Lanh was his demonstration opponent for the Self-Defense portion of the test. One technique used a hair grab technique. Jake improvised by grabbing Master Lanh's ear. Everyone started laughing.

Master Kim said, "Jake get your sparring gear." Then motioned over to Chuck to pad-up as well.

Chuck showed no mercy, punching and kicking hard. Jake took a stout punch in the chest that knocked him back a few feet. He regained his balance and tapped his chest. "Good shot."

They touched gloves and restarted. Jake adjusted his technique and mounted a counter strike. When Chuck threw a reverse punch, Jake executed a roundhouse kick that caught him in the lower ribcage. Chuck winced and paused to shake it off. After resetting, Chuck attacked and hit Jake in the head with a spinning back-fist, knocking him to the floor. Jake popped back up, ready to fight, but Master Kim stopped the match.

Chuck grabbed Jake's shoulder. "Good job! You're the best green belt I've seen."

"Thanks!" Jake replied. "I'm glad you're on our side."

Master Kim, Master Lanh, and Chuck stood at the front of

the class and called Jake forward. Master Kim read his blue belt certificate and awarded him his new belt.

The following Saturday, Jake walked to the dojo to see Master Kim and Master Lanh.

"Thanks for everything. I'll never forget you guys."

"Thank you, Jake-san," said Master Kim. "We shall miss you too. Keep training. We shall meet again."

Master Lanh said, "Work hard and don't forget to meditate." He put his hands together and bowed.

Jake bowed in return and smiled, feeling genuine gratitude toward his teachers.

The next day, a moving company picked up all the Von Hammer's belongings and took them away. Mr. and Mrs. Von Hammer gifted the family car to Trini and gave Benji money to go to school in Manila. The family moved into the Clark Hotel for a few days until their flight to Los Angeles.

# 9

It was nighttime when the Von Hammers landed in California. A courtesy van from Edwards Air Force Base picked up the family and drove them to temporary housing. The jet-lagged Von Hammers woke up late and caught their first glimpse of Southern California. The rolling jungles of the Philippines were replaced by paltry shrubs scattered across a flat desert plain. Crisp air and mild temperatures made the drive to a small cafe in the nearby town of Rosamond refreshing.

Sitting at a table sipping glasses of ice water, Jake and Ryan salivated over the abundance of selections on the breakfast menu. When the waitress came to take their order, Jake asked, "Can we still get breakfast?"

The waitress replied, "You name it; we got it."

Jake said, "Great, I'll have scrambled eggs."

"Fresh out," the waitress fired back.

The Von Hammers chuckled. Jake said, "Okay, I'll take pancakes instead."

"Sorry, out of pancakes."

Ryan said, "Can I get a glass of orange juice?"

"Just ran out."

Dismayed by the waitress's responses, Jake asked, "Do you have cereal?"

"Any kind you want."

Jake smiled and slapped his hand on the table. "I'll have Lucky Charms!"

She pointed her pen at Ryan. "You want Flakes too?"

Jake and Ryan ate Corn Flakes with real cow's milk for the first time since moving to the Philippines. The rest of the family ate donuts—Lindsey swore they were stale.

Two weeks passed before they settled into a rental home in Lancaster, a small town southwest of Edwards Air Force Base. Jake and Ryan were forced to share a room in the tiny three-bedroom house. Gone were the days of maids, yard boys, and ten-cent taxis. Their small weekly allowance barely covered the price of a movie in Southern California. Luckily, the yard didn't have a blade of grass. Neither Jake nor Ryan liked yard work.

After missing a few weeks, they enrolled in the local public high school where Jake started ninth grade. The school was six months ahead of Wagner, and Jake was swamped with make-up assignments. He'd met neighborhood kids at the bus stop, but not all of them were friendly. Most were cliquish and snubbed Jake with his outdated clothes and awkward slang. The Philippines had been a time capsule, and Jake didn't know the movies, music, or television shows other kids watched. He'd only seen Armed Forces Radio and Television Network for the past eighteen months, and they only broadcast old reruns. Theater movies were six months old when they made it to the Philippines, and Jake was the only kid in California who hadn't seen Star Wars.

Since it would be a month before their furniture and household items arrived, Jake borrowed a bicycle from the base to get around. He searched for dojos near his house he could peddle to and found one only a few blocks from his home. The new dojo placed more emphasis on physical conditioning—spending half the class on grueling exercises. A large sign on the wall read, "Karate is Conditioning." Whenever someone whimpered about the exercises, Master Yamada pointed to the sign.

Things were bad at school. Jake struggled to catch up and had few friends. Football season started, and Jake's PE class was playing flag football when someone asked, "Hey Hammer, are you gonna try-out for the football team?"

Jake replied, "Nah, I have karate practice after school."

Several kids sneered, and one boy mocked Jake by making exaggerated karate motions and goofy Kiai sounds. For the first time, Jake realized karate wasn't cool and didn't mention it again.

One day, Jake waited with a group of kids for the afternoon bus to take them home. Some kids were talking about going to the beach the upcoming weekend.

Jake asked, "When are y'all going?"

The kids stopped talking and looked coldly toward Jake.

One guy said, "It's a private party—you're not invited."

Then the whole group turned and moved away from Jake. Taken aback by the rude response, Jake stood there flush with embarrassment. Two girls overheard the conversation and approached Jake.

The red-haired Janis Joplin looking one said, "Hey Jake, I'm Tammy, and this is Carla. We're going to the beach—come with us."

Jake said, "Uh..." *They seem friendly enough.* "Okay, thanks."

The following Saturday, a blue Chevelle Malibu Classic, sporting mags, and loud pipes, arrived at Jake's house and honked the horn. Tammy opened the passenger door and tilted the seat forward, inviting Jake to sit in the back with Carla. As Jake climbed into the car, the driver, Tammy's older brother John, leaned over the seat and said, "Hey, are you Ryan's brother?"

"Ya, you know him?" Jake replied.

"Sure do. He's a great defensive player; we're glad to have him on the team."

They drove to Ventura, where hundreds of school kids from all over gathered. People were everywhere playing frisbee, football, and volleyball, while others skated up and down the boardwalk. The waves were rolling, and John said to Jake, "C'mon, let's go body-surfing."

Jake said, "I don't know how."

"I'll teach you, c'mon."

Jake swallowed a lot of water before he caught a wave that carried him a long way. He and John rode wave after wave until John grew tired. They found Tammy and Carla sunbathing on the beach and sat beside them. Tammy raked Jake's ruddy brown hair with her fingers and parted it in the middle.

She said, "You should part your hair this way because it looks better."

"Thanks for bringing me," Jake said. "I'm having a blast."

Tammy replied, "Glad you came. You're keeping John entertained."

A week later, Jake and his PE class played dodgeball in the gym. A few guys partially deflated the rubber balls and slung them as hard as they could. The balls stung and left large welts on the kids' arms, legs, and faces hit by the balls. They hit Jake with one and knocked him out of the game.

During the next game, Jake grabbed one of the deflated balls and hurled it, striking one of the offending kids, named Miles, on the back of his leg. It left a puffy red imprint that made Miles furious. He told a huge Hawaiian boy named Keiko that Jake called him pilau *(stinky)*. Keiko angrily confronted Jake and pushed him, saying, "You call me pilau?"

Jake replied, "I don't even know what pilau means."

A coach came over and broke it up.

Keiko said, "Bumbai brah! *(Later)*."

Jake asked one guy, "What was that about?"

He replied, "No-one likes you."

Jake kept to himself the rest of the day and caught the bus home. Jake knew he'd have to fight Keiko but feared it wouldn't turn out well. Keiko was twice his size and three times stronger. The next morning at the bus stop, he tried to act normal, but the other kids acted weird.

One of them told Jake, "Keiko is gonna crush you."

By the time he got to school, Jake felt uptight. He wasn't so worried about a bloody nose, he was more concerned that the whole school seemed to hate him, and he didn't understand why. Jake kept his head down and went straight to his first class and opened a book. Each time the bell rang, he was one period closer to gym class. By the third period, Jake found out Keiko wasn't in school. Relieved, he kept to himself the rest of the day, avoiding Keiko's friends.

While at the dojo that evening, Jake told Master Yamada about the situation and asked for advice.

Master Yamada said, "Have you ever played Tic Tac Toe?"

"Ya, it's pointless. You can't win."

"Exactly, you lost the game before it started."

"What do I do?"

Master Yamada said, "Unfortunately, the choice is not yours. Be like the crane."

Jake's brow curled. "Crane?"

Master Yamada continued, "Long ago, a white crane was drinking at the edge of a lake. A hungry tiger spotted the crane and wanted to eat him for dinner. The tiger pounced, but the crane jumped just in time to avoid the attack. Each time the tiger lunged toward the crane, the crane jumped, and the tiger missed. Frustrated, the tiger gave up and walked away. You see, Jake, tigers, and bullies have little will to fight. They want to win quickly and easily. The longer you draw out the contest, the less they want to continue. Trust your training."

The next morning, Jake was nervous and told Ryan about Keiko. Ryan said, "His brother, Aukai, is a guard on the football team. He bowed-up to me at practice, and I decked him. That was a while ago. We're friends now. Just punch him in the nose."

After talking to Ryan, Jake felt more confident, but the kids at the bus stop still shunned him. When he got off the bus, he walked straight to his locker, where he saw Keiko talking to some kids. Jake ignored them, and no-one paid much attention to him. While in his first class, he heard rumors Keiko planned to beat-him-up after school.

At gym class, Jake stayed with a friendly group of kids until they split them into flag football teams. They put Jake on a team with Keiko's buddy, who gave Jake dirty looks but didn't talk to him. Keiko was on a team playing on the opposite field.

The game started, and Jake ran a pass pattern and turned around just in time to see Keiko bearing down on him. He dropped to all fours, and Keiko flew right over him. Jake jumped to his feet. Keiko took a violent swing, and Jake ducked. Each time Keiko lunged forward, Jake backpedaled, and Keiko whiffed.

A crowd surrounded them, creating a pseudo-fighting ring. Jake avoided Keiko's attacks until some kids pushed him in the back, knocking him into Keiko. Immediately, Jake pushed his hands into Keiko's face, and one of his fingers poked Keiko in the eye. Keiko howled and covered his eyes with his hands. Miles snuck up behind Jake and sucker-punched him in the back, knocking him down. Miles quickly slipped back into the crowd before a coach stopped the fight. He took Jake and Keiko to the principal's office, where Jake pleaded self-defense. The principal gave him three days of in-school-suspension (ISS) and suspended Keiko for a week.

Jake hated ISS and spent a lot of time meditating and thinking about his situation. He didn't understand why some kids disliked him so much. At practice one evening, Master Yamada asked, "Jake, why are you so quiet."

Jake replied. "I'm having a hard time at my school. No-one likes me."

Master Yamada patted him on the shoulder. "Have faith. It's darkest just before the sun shines."

Several weeks later, Jake received a letter from Fritz.

Jake,

I'm so jealous! I would kill to live close to the beach. I'd never leave. We're still in Phoenix. It's beautiful, but it's a desert, and the closest thing to a beach is a rocky lakeshore. I'm petitioning the Air Force to transfer my father to Hawaii. I pray we go there for a family vacation soon. Marie is getting her driver's license. Send me pictures. Ciao, Fritz

## 10

J ake often watched the older students in the dojo. One guy, in particular, was fantastic at kata, and Jake asked him for help. Sam agreed and worked with Jake once a week. Sam had Jake do the kata super slow, trying to maintain balance. This exercise increased Jake's muscle memory and strength. When Jake could keep his balance at a low speed, Sam said, "Now, end each movement with a quick snap."

Master Yamada noticed Jake's dedication and taught him a kata. Jake practiced the form for several weeks with Sam's help. One evening, Master Yamada looked on as Jake practiced by himself and walked over to him.

He said, "Very well done, Jake. There is a regional competition in Los Angeles this November. Would you like to compete?"

"I don't know," Jake said. "I've never been in a tournament. Don't think I'd be any good."

"How did you learn to ride a skateboard?"

Jake replied, "My friend Bebou— ...Oh, I get it. Okay, I'll do the tourney."

On tournament day, he packed his gym bag and rode to the

Los Angeles Convention Hall with Sam, who was many times a tournament champion.

Jake said, "I'm nervous. Can you give me some tips?"

Sam replied, "Don't watch the other competitors—it'll mess you up. Many professional athletes use mental imagery to improve their performance. In your mind's eye, see yourself executing perfect form. This will condition your mind to perform at a high level."

"Like meditation."

"More like dreaming."

"Oh, I know how to do that."

After checking-in, Sam and Jake separated and went to their respective competition areas. The crowded convention hall was challenging to navigate, and Jake had difficulty finding his ring. He got to the area just in time and gave his folder to the judges. Before he could sit down, the judges called his name to be the first competitor.

Because Jake didn't have time to think about it, he didn't feel nervous stepping into the ring. He announced his kata and began. Moving through the form, Jake remained focused and snapped like Sam taught him, making only a few minor mistakes. He finished and waited for his score. *Maybe they didn't notice.* The judges flashed his scores.

*Dang, they noticed.*

He sat and watched the other twelve participants perform katas from Kung Fu, Tae Kwon Do, Hapkido, and Tai Chi.

*Now, I know why Sam told me not to watch. These guys are good. I wanna change everything.* When the group finished, the judges compiled the scores, and Jake was in fifth place.

Jake found Sam on the other side of the hall, "I messed up and landed in fifth place."

Sam said, "Did you do the things we talked about?"

"Didn't have time. I was first."

"That's tough," Sam replied. "It's hard to go first."

Jake said, "I don't care; I learned a lot."

Sam smiled. "Attaboy."

Jake meditated while waiting for the weapons competition to start. He imagined himself going through the form flawlessly like Sam taught him. Several competitors went before Jake, but he paid them no mind. By the time they called Jake's name, he was relaxed and unaware of the scores. Master Yamada and Sam looked on as Jake walked to the center of the ring and bowed.

The judge said, "You may begin."

Jake exploded into the form, moving quickly, his staff buzzing as it whipped through the air. Jake executed strike patterns in all directions with near-perfect stances. He jumped high and spun around, landing one knee and jabbed backward, ending with another striking sequence. He popped to the ready position and bowed.

The judge handed him a small third place trophy. With a big toothy grin, his chest grew large as he held it up to show Master Yamada. Master Yamada and Sam posed with Jake for a victory picture.

Sam dropped Jake off in front of his house, where Ryan and Lyndsey were sitting on the car's trunk. Jake slung his gym bag over his shoulder and walked toward them. Holding up his trophy, he said, "Look what I got."

Lyndsey said, "Wow, that's small."

Ryan said, "What's that, a participation trophy?"

"Nah, I won third place." Jake lowered his chin. "It's kinda lame, huh?"

Ryan laughed. "Just kidding, Goops. Good job!"

"Ya, that's pretty," Lyndsey said.

Jake smiled and walked toward the house.

Lyndsey said, "I wouldn't go in there."

"Why?"

"Mom and Dad are fighting. Dad came home drunk and started the Sarge routine—you know—he orders everyone around like a drill sergeant. Mom wasn't having it and threw the salt shaker at him."

"What?"

"Yup," Ryan said. "Hit him square in the noggin. Sounded like a homerun."

Lyndsey said, "I think she's thrown half the kitchen at him by now. You can hear dishes smashing from here."

"Dang," Jake said. "I'm starving."

Lyndsey laughed, "I know, right?"

Ryan sat up, "Hey, there's a Denny's on the boulevard. I've got five."

Jake reached into his bag, "I got three."

"I have enough," Lyndsey said. "Let's go."

They walked to Denny's and sat in a booth at the back of the restaurant. The waitress came over and said, "What'll y'all have to drink?"

Ryan said, "Coke."

"What kind?" She asked.

Ryan laughed, "Are you from Texas."

She looked up, "Ya, from Waco. Where are y'all from?"

Ryan said, "We're from everywhere. We lived in Houston, that's how I recognized your accent."

"Where's your accent?"

"It comes and goes. We move around a lot. Wanna hear my New York accent."

"Haha, are y'all military?"

"Ya, unfortunately," Jake replied.

"Awe, why do you say that? I never left my hometown until my husband joined the Air Force. When he told me we were moving to California, I was so excited. I couldn't wait to go to the beaches and see the mountains."

Lyndsey said, "Oh, how do you like it?"

"Well, we live at Edwards and don't get out very much. We work all the time. You know everything is so expensive out here."

"Ya, we know," Ryan said. "I'll have a Dr. Pepper."

Jake said, "I'll have one too."

"I'll have 7up," Lyndsey said.

"Okay," the waitress replied. "I'll be right back with your cokes."

After they finished eating, they walked home and found Sarge passed-out on the couch, and their mother locked in the bedroom. Ryan dragged the big trash can in from the garage, and Jake started sweeping while Lyndsey wiped down the counters. Within twenty minutes, they had the kitchen inspection ready and went to bed.

A few days later, Master Yamada asked Jake to show the class his tournament kata and staff form. Jake walked to the middle of the floor and performed the forms.

Master Yamada stepped up and said, "Jake, please remove your belt."

Puzzled, Jake removed his belt. Sam stepped out of the office, carrying a purple belt and a certificate. Master Yamada placed the belt around Jake and said, "I'm promoting you to 4th kyu."

"What? Oh, wow!"

The class applauded. Jake bowed, thanking Master Yamada and Sam for all their help.

A month later, Jake received a phone call.

"Hi Jake, how are you?"

Jake perked up. "I'm great, Master Fuji. How are you?"

"I'm doing well. What's new?"

"I went to a tournament with Master Yamada and won third place and got a trophy, and I got promoted to 4th kyu!"

"That's fantastic!" Master Fuji said. "Master Yamada is teaching you well."

Jake replied, "Ya, we do a lot of conditioning. I'm getting strong."

"That's great, Jake-san. Keep working hard. I sent you some tea."

"I got it. Had a cup yesterday—delicious. Thanks!"

## 11

Carla and Tammy were popular among a segment of the teenage skater population and introduced Jake to Tommy and Dustin. Occasionally, Jake would meet them at a neighborhood skate park. They helped Jake select a new board with more upgrades than the old Shark Board he used in the Philippines. The new board had a wider deck with stiffer trucks and urethane wheels. Tommy and Dustin were expert skaters and taught Jake new tricks like the heelflip and nollie over the winter months.

During the Spring, Jake and his friends would ride busses from Lancaster to Ventura's beaches to skate on the boardwalk and body surf whenever the waves were good. One Saturday, he and his buddies were having a lot of fun body surfing in eight-foot barrels. Tommy and Dustin wore themselves out and washed up near the beach.

Tommy yelled to Jake, "Yo! We're going in to score some hotdogs."

Jake waved them on. "Go ahead. I'm gonna catch a few more waves."

Jake swam out to the breakers and caught a few, but as it always happens, the tide changed, and the swells retreated. He swam to an area where some waves were still breaking. He'd race to catch one and ride it as far as he could, but they lacked the energy they had earlier. Seeking larger swells, Jake swam out further, but they seemed to fade away faster than he could swim.

Treading water, Jake turned around to find landmarks on the beach and realized he was much farther from the shore than he thought. He drifted by a large red sea buoy covered with sunbathing seals and realized a rip current had carried him out to sea.

Jake knew great white sharks hunted seals, and scenes from the movie Jaws flickered in his head. Careful not to splash, he swam parallel to the beach until he cleared the rip current and was well away from the buoy.

Far offshore, Jake spotted a fishing boat speeding in his direction. Waving his arms overhead, he yelled, "Help, Help!"

The sport-fisher veered toward him but never slowed down. Jake paddled as fast as he could to avoid getting run over. *Crud, they didn't see me.*

It was late afternoon, and Jake floated on his back to conserve energy. Stinging from saltwater, he closed his eyes, navigating by the warmth of the sunlight on his cheek. As he inched toward shore, he'd crack his lids open now and then to spot landmarks and check his progress. To keep his mind off sharks, Jake thought about his mother, who taught him how to float when he was young. She told him, "One day, it could save your life."

The strong current kept pulling him farther and farther from shore. He lifted his head to scan the horizon but saw nothing but water and distant mountain tops. A plane passing overhead left contrails across the sky. Jake used them as guides until they faded away. He'd back-paddle for a while, rest, and back-paddled some more. Small fish tickled him by nibbling on his leg hair. Two hours later, he started to shiver and realized he could no longer feel his legs. Lifting his feet, he counted, *One little piggy, two little piggies,* and so on until he accounted for all of his toes.

The Sun sank lower, and Jake clenched his teeth so the chatter wouldn't attract bigger fish. Dozing off, he started to dream. His mother and sister talked in another room while Jake lay in bed, cozy and warm. He began to sink, and waves lapped over his face and woke him.

He shook the water from his face and gazed up at a brilliant orange sunset spread across the sky. One little star twinkled overhead. Jake stopped shivering and felt a blanket of warmth surround him. Hallucinating, he heard splashing. He turned to look and saw a school of piranhas darting toward him. He rolled over and swam to escape. The water surface churned as the flesh-eating fish closed-in. To protect himself, Jake created a force field, and the piranhas smashed into it, killing themselves. Jake floated into the sky and woke up on the beach with dozens of people standing over him.

By the time Jake's mother arrived, the doctors had wrapped him in electric blankets to bring his body temperature back to normal. While a heart monitor blipped in the corner, she sat beside the bed weeping. A man came into the room and talked to her.

He said, "Our triathlon team was swimming near Faria Beach and ran into him. He was delirious and tried to fight us." Rubbing his chest, he continued, "Kid has a good punch. We brought him ashore, administered CPR (cardiopulmonary resuscitation), and called an ambulance. They brought him here and treated him for hypothermia."

"Oh, thank God, you were there," she said. "I can't imagine what we'd do if we lost him."

The following month, Jake enrolled in a CPR class at the local Red Cross. An older gentleman said, "I'm surprised to see someone as young as you interested in this."

Jake looked up. "I probably need it more than anyone else. According to my mother, I'm in debt to my guardian angel."

## 12

When school let out, Master Yamada stood in front of the class and said, "There's a national competition in Las Vegas this July. Anyone who wants to compete should see me after class."

Several students stayed behind to sign-up for the tournament, but Jake did not. He picked up his bag and skateboarded home without talking to anyone.

A week later, on a sunny Saturday afternoon, Jake was skateboarding around the neighborhood and became thirsty. He stopped at a convenience store to grab a soda and a Snickers bar. As he walked to the sales counter, Keiko and two of his friends opened the door and walked into the store. One of Keiko's friends noticed Jake and pointed. "Look who it is!"

Jake looked at him and said nothing. Keiko approached Jake and stood in front of him, blocking his way to the counter. Keiko looked down at him and said, "We got no beef with you."

Jake nodded. "Sounds good,"

Keiko stepped aside and walked toward his friends at the drink cooler. Jake paid for the items and left the store. Cruising down the sidewalk, Jake thought how things had changed and remembered when Master Yamada told him, "It's darkest just before the Sun shines." *I really owe my senseis gratitude. Where would I be without them?*

While putting clothes away, Jake's mother found the tournament flyer stuffed into Jake's sock drawer. When Jake came home, he sashayed into the kitchen where his mother was stirring a pot of chili. She pushed the tournament flyer toward him and said, "I found this in your sock drawer. Why didn't you say something?"

Jake replied, "Oh ya, it'll cost a lot. It's in Las Vegas. Besides, I probably won't make it to the finals anyway."

"We could use a vacation," she said. "If you want to go, I'll talk to your father."

"Really!"

"I've never been to Vegas. I feel lucky."

At his next practice, Jake approached Master Yamada and held up the flyer. "I can go to the tournament."

"Fantastic!" Master Yamada said. "Since you placed in the regionals, you get to skip the qualifying round, but still, you must work hard."

"I will."

A few months later, all the Von Hammers, except Lyndsey, packed the Ford LTD for the five-hour trip to Las Vegas. Lyndsey stayed behind to attend a friend's birthday party. They arrived on the strip at lunchtime and stopped at the Tower of Pizza, where Jake and Ryan made pigs of themselves. After lunch, Jake took a nap before heading to the convention center. Standing in the middle of the enormous arena, Jake gazed side to side, imagining crowds of cheering spectators. He raised his arms taking in the glory of his adoring fans, and bowed, and bowed again. A voice called out, "Hey, what're doing?"

"Uh!" Jake popped up, lifting his entry form. "I'm here to check-in."

"That's next door."

"Oops, sorry."

Later that evening, Jake and Ryan went to the hotel swim-ming pool and kicked-back on pool chairs. Jake told Ryan what happened in the store. Ryan said, "Eh, I expected that. Keiko is really a good guy. The real bullies are his friends who are too chicken to fight their own battles."

On Saturday morning, the family ate an early breakfast and headed to the convention center. Master Yamada and others were practicing at the far end of the hall. Jake knew he wasn't the best at kata and asked Sam to give him some pointers. As Sam went through the form explaining where to pause and where to go fast, he said, "Be confident. If you mess up, keep going. Everyone messes up somewhere. The goal is to mess up less than the others."

Jake replied, "I understand. Thanks!"

At 0900 sharp, the opening ceremony began, and the orga-nizers gave ring assignments. Master Yamada walked with Jake to his competition area, "I'm judging another ring. I can't stay."

"Thanks, I'll do my best. See you later."

"Good luck."

Jake handed his folder to the judge and took a seat beside the ring. The judge started the competition, and the first competitor stumbled after completing a jump. The second froze in the middle of his form. Jake thought, *Man, I know exactly how that feels.*

Then the judge called Jake. He raised his hand, requesting permission to enter the ring. The judge waved him through. Jake walked smartly to the center of the square and faced the head judge.

"Judges, my name is Jake Von Hammer. My sensei is Master Yamada. Today I will perform Pinan Nidan. With your permis-sion, I will begin?"

The judge signaled him to begin. Jake bowed and came to a ready stance and announced, "Pinan Nidan!"

He burst through the first three movements and changed direction, attacking the other side with the same ferocity. Jake executed a sidekick. "Kiai!" And, three more knife-hands, ending with a spear hand. "Kiai!"

Turning three quarters, he completed four rapid knife-hands, followed by an arm sweep, punch, and front kick. Repeated the same movement on the other side before finishing with four blocks he copied from Sam's dramatic snapping technique. "Kiai!"

He finished and bowed to the judges. The judges flashed his scores, and he sat beside the ring to watch the others.

After watching a few participants, Jake lost interest and scanned the room. Spotting his parents sitting just a few rows back, he smiled. *They seem happy. I hope it lasts.*

The last competitor finished, and the judges called Jake and two other competitors to the center of the ring. To Jake's surprise, the judge awarded him third place and shook his hand. He held up his trophy to show his parents. His father gave him the old strong-arm flex while his mother cheered.

Anxious to tell Master Yamada the great news, Jake gave his trophy to his mother and set off to find him. While wandering around the convention hall, he remembered seeing a water cooler near the front. Weaving his way through masses of people, Jake spotted the cooler in the corner and aimed that direction. When he got to the cooler, a young lady turned around, looked at Jake, and dropped her cup, splashing water all over him. They stood there speechless before bursting into laughter.

"Oh my God, What are you doing here?" Fritz said.

## 13

J ake wiped the water from his face and said, "I needed a drink, but I'm all good now."

"My goodness, I'm so sorry, you startled me. This is unreal!"

Jake pointed, "Wow, you're a black belt now. Congratulations!"

"Thank you. I tested a few months ago," Fritz replied. "Did you compete yet?"

"Ya, I placed third."

"Wow, that's great! My competition is in an hour."

Jake and Fritz walked, and she showed him where her family was sitting. "I needed to go practice my form," she said. "I don't want you to watch because it'll make me self-conscious."

Jake asked, "When did you become self-conscious?"

"I caught it from you, I guess."

"Haha, good one. I'll see you later."

As Jake walked away, he turned to steal another look. Fritz caught him and smiled while shooing him away.

Jake heard Sam's name called and worked his way to his ring. He noted how confidently Sam projected himself. A large, powerful man, Sam rarely, if ever, made a mistake. His movements were crisp and stances so low, you wondered how he could hold them. When Sam punched, his heavily starched gi popped like a whip. He'd been competing for many years, and his ring savvy was unmatched.

After watching Sam win his competition, Jake made his way back to Fritz's ring and found a spot in the back where she wouldn't see him. His gaze fixated on her as she sat waiting her turn. Her curls, longer and looser than they used to be, were tied back with a black ribbon, and her skin glowed with that golden tan she always had.

When the judge called her name, Fritz entered the ring and announced her kata, "Empi!"

She stepped out, kneeling into a low block. As she moved through the form, Jake forgot to blink, watching her graceful lines. She performed her turning jump, landing solidly in a back stance. Fritz won second place and received a large trophy. When she finished talking to her sensei, Jake handed her a cup of water. "Here, I won't throw it at you."

"Haha, thanks."

She took a drink. "Did you watch?"

"Ya. The jump was perfect. You should've gotten first."

About that time, Ryan and Marie appeared.

Marie said, "Hi, Jake!"

"Oh, wow! Hi, Marie."

Ryan looked at Jake and Fritz. "Proud of you guys for beating everyone!"

Fritz's father approached.

Jake said, "Hi, Mr. Pattersen."

"Hey, Jake, good to see you again."

"Yes sir, what're the chances?"

"Better than the blackjack table, believe me."

Marie said, "Fritz and I are going to lunch with our parents.

You guys make plans to see us later."

Jake and Ryan returned to the hotel room and crashed for a few hours. When they woke up, they found their mother's note:

*We're going to the casinos with the Pattersens. You'll have to fend for yourselves tonight? I left some money on the nightstand. Don't stay out too late. Love, Mom*

The guys showered and met Marie and Fritz in the lobby of their hotel. Walking down the strip, they found a 50s themed diner and sat in a booth in the back of the restaurant. Fritz fed a quarter to the little table jukebox and said, "I love this song."

As the song "Dreams" by Fleetwood Mac played, they ordered burgers and talked about life after the Philippines.

Afterward, they strolled beneath glowing lights and found a carnival-like area where they stopped to play games. Jake tried to win a stuffed animal but choked on the final dart throw.

The game operator said, "For a dollar, I'll let you have a do-over."

Jake agreed and paid the man. He took a dart and straightened the warped plastic flight, and aimed carefully. The dart hit a balloon dead center and bounced off.

Jake cried, "Foul. That's unfair!"

Seeing several people looking on, the game operator said, "Go ahead. Pick a prize. Just be quiet. I don't want to give away the whole farm."

He asked Fritz, "Which one do you want?"

She pursed her lips and looked at the selection. "Um..." Pointing at a yellow pony. "That one."

"Ouch! You don't have good luck with yellow ponies, Buttercup."

"Tee hee, don't roll me, girl."

Jake spotted an undulating chain-saw of rotating cars called The Zipper. "Oh, we gotta ride that one."

Ryan said, "Y'all go on. We're going to play a few more

games."

Jake and Fritz climbed into a car, pulled the seatbelts over their heads, and buckled-up. As the ride filled, their car climbed higher until they reached the top, where they could see the whole strip. Excited, Fritz grabbed Jake's hand. Jake looked into her eyes, glittering with the kaleidoscope of colorful lights. Fritz smiled, and their car flipped over, suspending them upside down. With her curly hair dangling from her head, she turned to Jake and said, "Your face is turning red."

"My heads gonna explode."

The ride started, and the car spun around. They laughed and screamed and said colorful things. Buttercup broke loose and bounced about the cage. Fritz tried to catch it, but it escaped the car and tumbled out of sight.

"Darned, there she goes," Fritz said.

When the ride ended, they searched for the stuffed animal but couldn't find Buttercup.

Jake said, "Ah, well, easy come, easy go."

They couldn't find Ryan and Marie either, so they made their way back to the hotel. On the elevator, Jake pointed to a sign.

"The rooftop lounge closed at 2100 hours."

"If we get off on the 49th floor, we can take the stairs. Marie and I did it last night."

After climbing the stairwell, Jake pushed the door. Sure enough, it was open, just like Fritz said. They leaned over the rampart, looking over the street.

Fritz asked, "What are you doing for your weapons competition?"

Jake replied, "I'm running a new staff form. What are you doing?"

"A sai form I learned for my black belt test."

"Woe, that's cool. Can you show me?"

Fritz left and came back with a pair of sais, a three-pronged weapon resembling a trident fork. "Stand back in case I accidentally throw one."

She began by balancing on one leg with a double overhead block. Jake noted how much taller she was and how her hair seemed longer and softer. He became entranced watching her move, hardly paying attention to the kata. Fritz completed her routine and asked, "What d'ya think?"

He sat there in a daze looking at her. "Beautiful."

Fritz smiled and walked over to Jake and said, "Beautiful?"

She put down the sais, grabbed Jake's hands, and stood in front of him, looking at him with her sparkling green eyes.

Jake said, "You're not gonna make me dance, are you?"

She giggled and pulled him closer. Jake's heart pounded. When her lips touched his, and a flood of sensations swept over him. He tasted strawberry lip gloss and smelled her delicate perfume. She rubbed her nose against his and said, "How was that?"

"Um, better than a kick in the groin."

"Hehe."

Sitting beside each other on a couch, Jake said, "I didn't think I'd ever see you again. It was tough for a few days."

Fritz replied, "A few days? I didn't know you liked me that much. Haha."

Jake said, "I wish we weren't leaving tomorrow."

Fritz replied, "Maybe we can visit LA soon and go to the beach. I'm gonna be a marine biologist so that I can live near a beach."

Jake replied, "I ain't that smart. I don't know what I want to do, but I ain't joining the military."

"Ha, you'll figure something out."

"Gosh, I hope so."

"You have the early time slot," Fritz said. "You should go to sleep."

"I don't wanna go."

"I know. I'll meet you at the hall in the morning."

Jake leaned forward and kissed Fritz one last time before she got up and walked away, saying, "I'll see you tomorrow."

When Jake got to his hotel room, no-one was there, so he got ready for bed. He laid there thinking about Fritz, wondering what things would be like if they never had to move.

He woke early and ate a waffle in the lobby before going to the convention hall where Master Yamada waited.

"Congratulations on the kata victory, Jake."

"Thank you, Master Yamada."

"The weapon contest is more competitive. Be sharp."

"Okay, I'll try."

Fritz arrived at the convention hall a few minutes later and dragged Jake into a corner.

"Are you ready?"

Jake replied. "Don't know. Didn't sleep much last night."

"Something bothering you?"

"A green-eyed vixen haunted my mind."

"You better do something about that."

Fritz grabbed Jake by the lapel, pulled him close, and kissed him.

Jake said, "It's getting warm in here."

Fritz smiled.The competition announcement blasted through the hall speakers, and Fritz walked with Jake to the competition ring.

She said, "Go kill it for me!"

Jake sat on the side of the ring and watched, but his mind was with Fritz standing near the back of the competition square. She smiled, and the taste of her lip gloss flooded his mouth. He closed his eyes and forced himself into a meditation trance, blocking out the room. He imagined himself lying on a tropical beach beneath swaying palms drinking a pineapple slush. A seabird snatched a mackerel from the surf and flew up into the clouds. Then Jake heard his name called. He opened his eyes, stood up, and raised his hand. "Request permission to enter the ring."

The judge granted permission, and he walked to the center of the ring and bowed.

"Judges, my name is Jake Von Hammer. My sensei is Master Yamada. Today I will perform Staff Form Godan. With your permission, I will begin."

The judge said, "You may begin."

Jake took a step back and adopted a crane stance with the staff angled downward in front of him. Jump-kicking, he finished with a downward strike, "Kiai!"

Turning left, he cat-stepped across the floor in a sequence of high and low strikes. Then spun around, dropping to a knee for a low attack with several strikes. Standing-up, he turned and executed a spin kick and head strike. "Kiai!"

Moving rapidly across the floor, from corner to corner, he snapped high and low strikes. Turning toward the middle, Jake executed a downstrike followed by a forward flip, landing on one knee with a flurry of blows. He stood and turned, facing Fritz in the crane position, arms spread wide. Jake pulled the staff down and performed two jumping spin-kicks, and landed on a knee in a side strike.

Slowly, he stood and turned with the staff held in the front guard position. He jumped, completing a forward flip while down striking. Then Jake took a step back and jumped with the staff rotating like a helicopter stabilizer. He landed in a back stance with the staff in the front block position.

Jake lifted his front leg, assuming the crane position again. Then tucked into a forward roll, sticking one end of the staff into the floor, and vaulted over the top, landing in a cat-stance with the staff behind him. As if pulling an arrow from a quiver, he pulled the staff overhead in a downstrike."Kiai!"

Jake rolled into a back somersault that ended on one knee with the staff in the front guard position. Then spun the staff around and bowed to the front judge, stood and bowed again to the rear judges. Onlookers exploded in applause, and Jake received the highest score, earning him first place and a monster size trophy.

Master Yamada leaned toward Sam and said, "Wish I had filmed that one."

"I never expected that," Sam said. "Amazing performance from a 5th kyu."

"That's my son," said Sergeant Von Hammer as he hoisted the trophy into the air.

Dabbing her eyes with a tissue, his mother said, "We're so proud of you."

Ryan looked at his parents and shook his head, then turned to Jake and said, "Are you embarrassed yet?"

Jake laughed.

Ryan said, "For real, that was insane."

Fritz spun him around, "What was that? Are you trying to impress me? It's gonna take more than that Von Viper. Just kidding. I loved it!"

After chugging a Dr Pepper, Jake and Fritz moved to a quiet spot to prepare for her match.

"I don't know how you do all those jumps and flips, but I can't do that."

"I dunno either. They just happen. Do it your way. It'll be great."

Fritz said, "You mean beautiful?"

"Yes—absolutely—beautiful," Jake replied.

Jake took a seat in the spectator stands near Marie and Ryan. Fritz was the second to last competitor called, and she stepped to the middle of the floor. Fritz lifted the sais overhead and began a series of blocks and jabs to one side then the other. She turned and executed a forward kick, maintaining excellent form. Fritz held each position momentarily to emphasize the strength of each stance. Taking a cue from Jake's performance, she jumped and turned, spinning the sai into a straight jab. She completed her form and received a high score.

The last competitor was the reigning champion, and she was running a sword routine. It was easy to see why she was the champion. Her form was precise and fast. During her finishing run, she turned and lost control of the sword. It flew out of her hand, and everyone gasped as it tumbled through the air, landing by a back-judge. She apologized to the judge and finished the form, but they disqualified her because she lost control of the weapon. Fritz won third place, and she received a trophy.

Marie and Ryan took Fritz and Jake to lunch at a nearby restaurant. In the classic brat denial style, they cut up as if it were any other day. Lunch lasted almost two hours because no one wanted it to leave. Finally, they agreed to meet one more time in the morning and said goodbye.

The next morning, Jake moped around, sulking. Ryan said, "Get your act together. They're leaving soon."

Jake asked, "What're you gonna do about Marie?"

"What can I do? She lives five-hundred miles away," Ryan said,

Jake replied, "Bummer. I don't think I'll ever see Fritz again."

Ryan replied, "You know how this goes. By now, you should be good at saying goodbye. Just don't cry because you don't want her to remember you that way. Come on, let's go do this."

Jake and Ryan walked to the girl's hotel and waited in the lobby. Marie and Fritz came down and sat on the fluffy couches next to the boys. They made small talk and tried to crack jokes.

Marie congratulated Jake for his tournament wins and suggested they do more tournaments so they could all get together again. Everyone agreed, but no one really believed it would happen.

Marie stood and said, "Let's go for a walk. "

Ryan and Marie led the way. As they reached the end of the block, Fritz and Jake ducked into the corner of a building.

Fritz said, "I'll miss you Von Viper."

He replied, "I miss you already."

Tears rolled down Fitz's cheeks, and Jake's eyes welled up. Marie came over and hugged him. "Goodbye, Jake."

Then she put her arm around Fritz and led her away. Jake stood motionless as they faded into the background. Ryan grabbed Jake by the shoulder, "Let's go, Goobs. Back to Cali."

After loading the luggage, Ryan slammed the trunk, and the boys slumped into the backseat while Crystal Gayle's hit song, "Don't It Make My Brown Eyes Blue," played on the radio, framing the somber mood.

A month later, in a stack of mail left on the kitchen counter, Jake found a letter that made his heart race. He took it to his room and plopped onto the edge of the bed. With his feet drumming, he tore open the envelope and unfolded the page.

Hi Jake,

I got your postcard. Thank you for a great time in Vegas. I'll never forget that. My father is retiring soon, and we're moving back to Iowa. Please don't spend too much time thinking about me. We may never see each other again, and I don't want you to miss out on anything. I wish things were different. I wish you the best!

Love, Fritz

Jake's head dropped. Tears dripping from his chin splattered onto the paper and mixed with the ink forming purple blotches that resembled irises.

## 14

In early-August, as the family gathered for dinner, Mrs. Von Hammer announced, "Start packing. We're moving."

"Again?" Ryan asked.

"Wha?" Jake said. "I'm not startin' over again!"

Lyndsey replied, "No way! I'm not leaving Randy."

Mrs. Von Hammer replied, "Alright, I'll see if your father can stop the transfer, but I can't make any promises. They need him at Hickam."

The room fell silent. Jake looked at Ryan, Lyndsey looked at Jake. Ryan looked at his mom and said, "Well then, let's get packing. Jake, get the toothpaste."

"Dang," Lyndsey said, "I'm gonna miss Randy."

A month passed, Jake said goodbye to his friends, and the Von Hammers boarded an early morning flight to Honolulu. Upon arrival, they received the full tourist treatment, draped with leis and fruity drinks. The Von Hammers drove a courtesy car to temporary quarters on Hickam Air Force Base, unpacked their luggage, and went for a drive around their new island home. They landed at Kaka'ako Park on the western end of Waikiki and ate box lunches while enjoying cool tropical breezes. Jake's mother's gaze panned across the landscape, scumbled with brown and green hues, to the cerulean blue bay, and she proclaimed, "I could live like this forever."

A week later, the Von Hammers moved into base housing and enrolled in the local high school. Military brats made up most of the student population at Radford. They welcomed the Von Hammer kids and quickly recruited Ryan onto the football team.

Jake met Master Fuji in a warehouse only a short skateboard ride from his house. Master Fuji said, "Aloha Jake-san, you've gotten taller."

"Ya," Jake placed his hand on his head. "I might need a haircut."

Master Fuji smiled, "Yes, that too."

Jake pointed to Master Fuji's arm. "You got a promotion, Sir! Congratulations, Senior Master Sergeant Fujioka!"

"Thank you, Jake san."

Master Fuji lifted his arms wide. "This is the new dojo. How do ya like it?"

"Me like." Point to the corner, "And, Ratcom, yippee! Reminds me of old times."

Lifting his eyes to the ceiling. "but a whole lot bigger."

Jake walked to the cages and picked up Griffiss, "Umph, I think he gained a few pounds." Elm climbed up his arm and ruffled his hair, "She thinks I need a haircut too."

He put Griffiss down and reached out to pet Travis and quickly pulled his hand back.

"Still a testy little devil, aren't you?"

An Aussie named Seth, who lived a few houses away, saw Jake skateboarding in the street one morning and said, "Ay mate, I'm heading to the windy side for some surfing. Wanna go?"

Jake said, "I don't know how."

"It's like skateboarding, but more fun. Come on! You can use one of my boards."

Jake tossed the skateboard into the back of Seth's orange Volkswagen Thing and jumped into the passenger seat. They drove across the island where waves crested just under five feet. Seth, a tall thin guy with longish blonde hair that lay wherever the wind left it, took Jake to the beach for some basic pop-up lessons, teaching him how to push-up into a standing position. Being flexible and in good shape, Jake caught on quickly.

Seth encouraged him. "Dude, you're a natural."

As they paddled into the surf, Jake got pounded by waves and struggled to make headway. Seth showed him how to punch under the waves using a technique called duck-diving. Once they made it past the breakers, they paddled out to calmer water and waited for a set.

Seth said, "Waves come in threes, and the second and third are usually the best." As a mounding swell approached, Seth said, "Let's take this one lying down so you can get a feel for it."

Jake paddled as fast as he could until the wave picked-up his board and propelled him across the surface. *Woe, this is cool. Feels like boogie boarding.*

On the next wave, Jake tried to pop-up, but immediately lost his balance and fell off. They paddled out for another set, and Jake got onto his feet for a millisecond before falling. Again and again, this continued most of the afternoon. Finally, Jake caught a wave and rode it a good while before falling off near the beach.

Jake stood up, pumping his fist. "Wahoo! That was awesome!"

Seth and Jake surfed whenever they could. Jake was relentless, going out wave after wave, even when Seth was too tired to continue.

Seth said, "You're learning fast. You need a better board than that old beater."

In Jake's homeroom class, he sat next to a pretty blue-eyed blonde girl. He noted her name was Sheri, and she rarely spoke to anyone. One day Jake and Seth were hanging out in the cafeteria, waiting for the bell to ring. Seth's friend Bobco approached.

"Yo, Seth, who's the newb?"

Seth replied, "Aye, man, this is Jake. Fresh arrival from Cali."

Jake gave a slight head shake.

"What's wrong?" Seth said. "Haven't you ever seen a red shag?"

"Um, yeah, but I've never seen eyes that color. Are those real?"

"Dais from my paper," Bobco replied. "My grandmere says that's how she knows I'm legit."

"Huh?" Jake said.

"You gotta listen good," Seth said. "He's straight outta the Atchafalaya swamp."

Sheri walked by, and Jake asked, "Hey, do y'all know her?"

Bobco aimed his chin in her direction, "Her? Dat's Sheri Costa, a.k.a. Sheri Costly. Her daddy is beaucoup bucky."

Jake's eyebrow lifted. "Boo-coo bucky?"

Seth said, "That's cajun for, you ain't gotta chance with that one. Outta your league, brat."

A few days later, Jake and friends were hanging out in his bedroom when Bobco asked, "Ah Jake, whatcha wearing to the Halloween party?"

Jake shrugged. "Don't know."

Bobco pointed to his closet. "Wear dat ninja suit."

Jake laughed. "Ninjas don't wear karate gis. Besides, it's an excellent way to get your butt kicked."

"Oh mon, let's trade. You wear my pirate costume, and I'll be da ninja."

"Okay, but don't tell anyone where you got it."

The Halloween party was at a secluded house in the hills on a dead-end road. More than eighty kids showed-up, and Jake sat on the rear patio with several others talking about surfing. To his surprise, Sheri Costa came out and sat next to him on the couch.

Jake said, "Argh, aren't you in my homeroom class?"

"I think so," Sheri replied

"My name is Jake, and you're Sheri, right?"

"Yes, I know who you are. You hang out with Seth."

"Ya, he's teaching me how to surf."

"Are you good?"

Jake replied, "Um... not really, I fall a lot, but I'm getting better. Do you surf?"

"No way," Sheri said. "I don't feed sharks, and saltwater ruins my hair."

About that time, Bobco came out to the lanai and posed in a pseudo ninja stance screaming, "Wai Tai! Beware the red-headed ninja!"

Jake and a few others laughed. Bobco scrambled back inside and continued acting foolishly.

Sheri said, "That's dumb."

"Oh?" Jake asked.

"Fighting is stupid."

Jake replied, "Um, I guess... What do you do? Have any hobbies?

"School, that's what I do. I'm graduating early, then off to med school."

"Wow! You must be smart."

"No, I just work hard. What about you?

"Um, don't know what I wanna do yet."

"You better hurry-up and figure it out?"'

"Oh, ah... Right now, I'm just trying to finish high school."

In wintertime, waves can get huge on the north shore. Jake had fallen in love with surfing and bought a used board from an airman being transferred back to the mainland. One morning, he rode with Seth to Laniakea Beach where strong shore breezes were blowing the tops off of eight-foot breakers. They waxed the boards and paddled out, battling through rough surf, and soupy white foam. When they reached a flat spot, they sat-up and waited for a wave. A pair of dolphins surfaced near them. Jake got excited and Seth said, "That's good luck."

Seth, a talented surfer, eyed the next wave and carved it up before setting-up the shallow. Jake thought, *wow, he made that look easy.*

A few minutes later, Jake spotted a bomb, a monster fifteen-footer just starting to break. He raced to catch it.

Seth sat up on his board, waving his arms, yelling, "BAIL—BAIL—BAIL!"

Over the wind and crashing surf, Jake couldn't hear him and paddled hard as the water piled higher. Jake felt his legs lift as the wave sucked him into the break. The board slipped out from underneath him and he took a deep breath. The wave crested and sent him over the falls. Tumbling uncontrollably, he hit the bottom with such force, it knocked his breath out. The wave crashed down on top, pushing him to the bottom where he bumped into razor-sharp coral slicing his shoulder to ribbons. A powerful surge whipped him around like a rag doll in a washing machine. Jake bobbed to the surface coughing and gagging before being buried by another wave. Choking on mouthfuls of seawater, Jake floated into the shallows where blood oozing from his shoulder turned the wash red. Seth paddled through churning surf, grabbed Jake by the arm, and dragged him to the shore. Others ran to help. They laid him on his side to help flush the seawater from his lungs and wrapped his wound in towels. They loaded Jake into the Thing and Seth raced to an emergency room.

After Jake recovered the doctor said, "Tough day. That's four for coral, zero for surfers. Coral wins. Come back in ten days to get the stitches removed. Are you allergic to penicillin?"

"Don't think so, why?" Jake asked.

"The nurse is going to give you an injection. Right or left?"

"Huh?

"Butt cheek."

"Oh, left, I guess."

Jake put his clothes back on and met Seth in the waiting room.

"Wow, you're still here?" Jake said. Thanks for pulling me out. I didn't mean to ruin the day."

"Ah, no problem, mate. I thought you were going for the Kwan."

"Kwan?"

"The zone. When you hit it, you'll know it. Anyway, everyone started fishing after you chummed the bay."

Jake called Master Fuji to tell him what happened and that he'd miss a few weeks of practice while the wounds healed.

Master Fuji said, "I understand Jake-san. Take your time. I have to leave for a while, anyway. Can you take care of Ratcom? I'll be back about the time you're ready to train again."

Jake replied, "Sure, I can do that. Have a good trip."

A few days later, Jake dried off after taking a shower and turned to look at his stitches in the mirror. They looked strange, and he couldn't see the small cuts anymore. He called the hospital, and they told him to come in because he might have an infection. While examining the lacerations, the doctor noticed Jake's skin healing swiftly, making it difficult to remove the stitches.

The doctor asked, "Is it normal for you to heal this quickly?"

"I don't know... guess so," Jake replied.

The doctor said, "You're definitely a gifted healer."

The wave snapped Jake's board in half, so Seth took Jake to a guy who sells cheap boards near Waimea Bay. On the way home, Seth turned on an uphill road, and the Thing car strained to make the steep climb.

Jake pushed on the dash as if he was helping the car up the hill. He said, "If we go any slower, we'll be moving backward."

"That's 46 horses," Seth replied.

Jake said, "Hope we don't blow the head."

They stopped on a lookout overlooking the bay.

Jake said, "Wow, what a view!"

"Aye," Seth said. "Where are you from, anyway?"

"Ah, man, I hate that question," Jake sighed. "I've been everywhere, but I'm not from anywhere. Like gypsies, we move whenever the wind blows. Rad is my sixth school."

"You're lucky to travel like that."

"Meh. It gets old. No family, no friends, and it's impossible to keep up in school."

"Yeah, I suppose. I've never known one of you military types for long. Saw you talking to Sheri at the Halloween party. How'd that go?"

"Not good. We're on different islands."

Master Fuji returned and met Jake at the warehouse. Jake was putting Elm back onto her cage when Master Fuji asked, "How is your shoulder?"

Jake replied, "The doctor said I'm a gifted healer."

Master Fuji handed Jake one of two wooden swords and said, "These are bokken. We'll use these to practice until you learn to handle the weapon. This way, you won't cut yourself."

"Oh yeah, good idea," Jake replied.

They spent most of the practice learning to sheath and unsheath the sword. Afterward, Jake was cleaning the dojo when his parent's recent argument came to mind. He paused to ask, "Master Fuji, have you ever been married?"

He replied, "No. I was engaged once, but we couldn't work it out. Why do you ask?"

"Just wondering. Everyone your age seems to be married—at least once."

A few days later, Jake practiced with the bokken in his driveway. Seth came by and said, "That's a fancy toy. Teach me some knightly sword."

"Can't. I'm learning myself... but I can teach you the staff."

Jake grabbed a broomstick and handed the Viper to Seth. Admiring the carving, Seth said, "Did you make this?"

"No, my Filippino buddy carved it."

"Ripper."

"Huh?"

"Ripper, awesome."

Jake walked him through the basic form several times, but he had trouble maneuvering the weapon.

Seth said, "I feel like a wanker. Show me the good stuff."

"Like this?" And, Jake whipped through his tournament form.

"That's fully sick, mate! You really are some kinda ninja."

"Ah, it's easier than it looks—just takes practice."

A few days later, Jake took a shortcut through the lunchroom and spotted Sheri sitting by herself. He sat down across from her with his hands cupped on the table. He leaned forward, "Hi Sheri, whatcha reading?"

She tilted the cover toward him, "A book for English. What are you doing—did you lose your friends?"

"Nah... I just wanted to come over and say hello."

"Oh, okay, Hi Jake," and continued reading.

He bit his lip and said, "Do you ever go to the movies or anything?"

After a heavy blink, Sheri lifted her eyes toward Jake. "Why?"

"Ah," he leaned forward. "Dunno, just wondering if you'd like to go to the movies sometime?"

"Haha," Sheri closed the book, "Are you asking me out?"

He leaned back, "Nah... it's just, you know, there are good shows out like The Warriors, Star Trek... Apocalypse Now."

"Oh no, I don't think so," Sheri said. "But... maybe I'd like to see The Rose."

"Um." Jake's brow wrinkled. "The Rose?" "Okay, how about Saturday?"

"Hum?... okay... but, no funny stuff."

"Nah, yeah, just friends... I'll check the movie times and get back to you."

Sheri opened a notebook and scribbled. Tore it out and handed it to Jake.

"Call me."

Jake waited in front of the theater. Sheri arrived in a convertible Mercedes driven by her father.

Dr. Taub said, "Hey, Jake, how is everything?"

Jake stiffened up and smiled. "Everything is great, Sir! Thanks!"

Getting out of the car, Sheri said, "You two know each other?"

"Kinda, he stitched me up after my surfing accident."

Walking into the theater, Jake said, "I didn't know Dr. Taub was your father,"

"Stepfather. My real dad lives in California."

"Wow! Small world," Jake said.

"No, small island."

The Rose was a movie about a female rock star who struggled to deal with career pressure and an overbearing manager. When the movie was over, Sheri went to the restroom, and Jake waited in the hallway reading movie posters. Bobco and his friend Alex were coming out of another movie when they saw Jake and talked to him.

Bobco said, "Ay Jake, didn't know you were coming out to da movies today. You should've called."

Jake said, "Oh, hey, I didn't know you guys were here either. What d'you see?"

Bobco replied, "Awe, we saw Trek. You seen it?"

"Um, no, not yet... I just saw ...um... The Rose."

Bobco and Alex laughed. Bobco said, "Are you wearing panties now?"

Jake's face turned pink, and Sheri walked up behind him.

Bobco said, "Cho, Sha!... You here too? What'd you see?"

"The Rose," Sheri replied. "Good movie. You should see it."

Bobco's mouth hung open, "Ooh, ah... Okay, ya, I getcha now." He smiled. "See y'all 'round. Call me, Jake. Bye, Sheri."

Bobco and Alex walked away, and Jake and Sheri walked to the concession stand to buy sodas. As they left the theater, a group of younger kids ran in. One of them clipped Sheri, knocking the drink out of her hand. Jake reacted by sticking out his foot and caught the cup, balancing it upright on the top of his shoe. He pulled Sheri close and shielded her from the rest of the raucous bunch as they passed by. When it was clear, he lifted his foot, grabbed the drink, and handed it back to Sheri.

"Dang! "She said. "Good reflexes. Thank you!"

Walking through the mall, they found a clothing store. While Sheri skimmed racks of blouses, Jake browsed price tags. *Whoa, must be the Aloha upcharge.*

After Sheri bought two blouses, they went to the food court to grab a bite. Sheri said. "I know you like to surf, but what else do you do?"

"Oh... just skateboarding and hanging out with my friends. What about you?"

"I don't have hobbies because I'm always studying. Sometimes. I hang out by the pool and listen to music, but that's about it."

Jake said, "Do you go to the base pool?"

"Not in a million years. We have a pool," Sheri said.

"Wow, that must be nice. Wish I had a pool."

Sheri said, "Hmm, why don't you come over and swim sometime?"

A few days later, Jake put on a swimsuit and visited Sheri at her house. Sheri greeted him at the door, "Hi, Jake, this way to the backyard."

She led him to the patio. "I'll be right back with something to drink. Do you like lemonade?"

Jake replied, "Sure, anything with ice."

Sheri went back into the house while Jake walked around the backyard, marveling at the garden and the well-manicured landscaping. He heard a car door slam, then a gate. Seconds later, two large reddish-brown dogs running full blast rounded the house and headed straight for him. Panicked, with nowhere to run, Jake jumped onto a brick wall surrounding the garden. The dogs circled below, barking at Jake until Sheri came out screaming for her stepfather. Dr. Taub apologized to Jake and corralled the dogs, locking them in the side-yard.

Sheri said, "Jake, I'm so sorry! My father didn't know you were back here. How did you ever get onto that wall?"

"Uh... I jumped."

"I know, I saw you! That wall is over eight feet tall. I'm sure that's a new Olympic record. Are you sure you're okay?"

"I think so. Is it safe to come down yet?"

Jake jumped off the wall and walked over to the pool area with Sheri. She gave him a glass, and they sat by the pool sipping lemonade.

"What are all the plants and white pipes for behind the wall?"

"That's my stepfather's hydroponic garden. He swears it better for you, but I can't tell the difference."

"Hmm?" Jake said, "Do you want to swim?"

She sat on the steps in the shallow end while Jake plunged into the deep end.

Sheri said, "I don't want to get in because the chlorine turns my hair green."

Jake thought, *that's weird. Fritz has blonde hair and swims all the time.* He swam the length of the pool underwater, surfacing near Sheri.

"How many laps do you think you can swim without coming up for air?"

Jake said. "Don't know. Let's find out."

Sheri looked at the second hand of the pool clock and told him when to start. Jake took a deep breath, kicked off the wall, swam to the other side, and turned around. He made it back to the shallow end and turned for another lap, and another lap, and another lap. Jake completed eleven laps before coming to the surface for air.

"Jake, you were underwater for almost four minutes."

"Really? Thought it was longer than that."

Jake rested on the steps in front of Sheri, "Thanks for inviting me. I haven't been to a pool in a long time. This is nice. ...How do you graduate early?"

"Take lots of extra classes. I should have enough credits by the end of next year."

"That's cool."

Jake felt Sheri touch his shoulder. She said, "Is this where you cut yourself surfing?"

"Ya. your stepdad gave me twenty-three stitches."

"They're healing really well. You can barely see them now."

Then Sheri noticed two dots on Jake's right side that refused to tan. "And, what are these scars from?"

"Um... That's where I got bit by a cobra."

Sheri snickered, "Are you serious?"

"Ya, I almost died."

"Really?" she said.

"Ya, really. I wouldn't have made it if not for my brother, Benji, and Master Fuji."

"Who's Master Fuji?"

"I mean Master Sergeant Fujioka. He kept me alive until I got to the hospital. I don't remember anything except how pissed that snake was when I jumped in and woke her up."

"Oh, how do you know it was a she?"

"Just a guess."

## 15

Radford High students planned a Spring Break party at a local beach park. Jake asked Sheri if she wanted to go, but she declined because she had other plans. But, only a few days before the party, she changed her mind. Upon arrival, Seth and Bobco recruited them for their volleyball team. The team huddled in the grassy area to strategize.

Jake confessed. "I've never played."

Bobco said, "What, you're from Cali?"

"I barely lived there a year."

Bobco said, "Aw , just uppercut da ball. All ninjas know how to do dat, don't ya?"

"I can do that," Jake replied.

"All right," Bobco said. "just hang in the back row and let us professionals handle da net." Motioning with his hands, "Remember, uppercut."

Seth pulled Jake aside and showed them how to use two hands to set the ball. A few minutes later, the game started, and Sheri served the ball to the other side and scored.

Jake said, "Wow! You're pretty good."

"I am a Cali girl."

She continued to serve, scoring four points before Alex knocked the ball out of bounds, losing the serve. They continued to play well, and the game remained close until the end. On the next serve, Seth set the ball for Bobco, but a wind gust blew the ball close to the net. A player on the other team jumped and spiked the ball hard off Bobco's face—winning the game. The sting knocked Bobco to the ground, where he lay stunned for a moment, then he popped up unaware the ball left an imprint on his forehead.

"My face is out of bounds. Dat point no count."

Everyone busted a gut.

Sheri worked up a sweat and rested on a shaded bench while Jake searched for something to drink. When he returned, he reached out to give Sheri a water bottle and said, "That was fun, eh?"

She sat motionless behind her oversized sunglasses as if she didn't notice him at all.

Jake said, "Yo, hot stuff!"

It always annoyed her when Jake spoke that way, but still, Sheri didn't respond. Jake sat close to her and nudged her with his shoulder, and whispered, "Hey Sheri."

She turned to him and grabbed his forearm and said, "Hey Jake, You're back."

"Are you okay?" Jake asked.

She replied, "I'm feeling a little sick. I should go home now."

Seth offered them a ride, dropping Sheri off at her house.

Seth said, "What'd you do, piss her off?"

"Nah, she's sick. I seem to make her sick a lot. I'm surprised she came at all."

Sheri never stayed out for more than a few hours, but Jake didn't mind because he could always find other things to do. He was in his driveway tricking with his skateboard when Seth yelled, "Ay Jake, let's go sailing."

"Sailing?" Jake replied.

Seth said, "C'mon, it'll be fun!"

Jake chucked the skateboard into Seth's Volkswagen and hopped in. They drove to the North Shore, where Seth's mother's boyfriend owned a house and an eighteen-foot catamaran.

"Jake, help me drag it to the beach."

While they hanked on the sails, Seth taught Jake a few sailing terms and how the controls worked. After donning life jackets, they pushed the cat into the surf and jumped on the trampoline.

Seth said, "One hand for the boat, the other for yourself."

The wind freshened, and the boat sped up, crashing head-on into breaking waves. The bow rose abruptly—almost flipping over—Jake lost his hat. They beat through the white water and hit the swells, climbing slowly up the face and racing rapidly down the backside. Seth steered the boat into smoother water farther offshore.

Seth told Jake, "Move over to the windward side and hold on."

He put the boat on a beam reach, and the little cat sped up quickly in the brisk offshore breeze. The windward hull lifted slightly, and Jake hiked-out to balance the boat. The white hulls skated effortlessly across the surface, and the boys soaked up the moment, neither uttering a sound. Jake's thoughts wandered, mesmerized by how powerful, yet graceful, the boat moved, reminding him of Fritz and her sai form. He wondered how she was.

A humpback whale surfaced in front of the boat, jolting them out of their trance. Panicking, Seth over-steered to avoid hitting the whale, causing the catamaran to pitchpole, flipping end over end. Catapulted into the rigging, Jake landed on the sail. He quickly untangled himself as the boat turtled.

"Seth!" Jake called out, "where are you?"

No one replied. Jake swam to the capsized boat and climbed onto the submerged trampoline searching the water. He spotted Seth floating twenty feet away and gathered a line, tying one end to the boat and the other to his jacket. Plunging into the water, Jake swam to Seth and latched onto his collar, pulling him to the vessel.

Jake slapped his cheek. "Ay, wake up, wake up."

Seth groaned and placed his hand over his face. Blood streamed from a cut across the bridge of his nose and ran down his arm.

"What happened?" Seth asked.

"We crashed," Jake said. "The boats upside down."

"Awe," Seth moaned. "That dang whale."

The whale resurfaced close by, and the spray from its blow-hole wafted over the wayward sailors. Seth cursed, blaming it for their current situation. A few seconds later, a much smaller whale surfaced, and they realized the bigger whale was protecting her calf.

Still partially dazed and bleeding, Seth said, "You gotta tie a line to the starboard hull, so we can flip the boat over."

Jake attached a line then put all his weight on the hull but couldn't flip the boat.

Seth said, "We need to untie the mainsheet and let the boom go."

Jake took off his life-jacket and wrapped a line around his waist to prevent him from drifting away. Underwater, everything was a blur. He located the boom and felt his way to the end, but the knot was tight. He swam back to the surface, "I can't get the knot undone."

Seth replied, "Find the traveler and unhook the block."

Jake took a few deep breaths and dove under the boat again. Scanning the horizon for boats, Seth spotted a fin with a white tip. He pulled Jake's tether to signal him to the surface, but Jake was busy fumbling with the traveler. The fin came closer, and Seth jerked the line frantically until Jake popped to the surface.

"What the heck! I almost had it done!"

"Get out of the water," Seth said, "Get out, now!"

"Why?"

Seth pointed. "Shark!"

Jake hopped onto the trampoline and spotted the whitetip.

He turned to Seth and said, "Whoa, Dude, blood is dripping off the end of your nose into the water."

Seth replied, "That's not the worst part, Bud. The starboard hull is taking on water."

"Oh, crud. Maybe that's why we couldn't flip it?"

The boys moved over to the port side to take weight off the sinking hull. Seth removed his shirt and tied it around his face to create a makeshift bandage.

Jake said, "New Aussie fashion? You look like you're gonna rob a 7-11."

Seth said, "Delaying my lunch date with Noah."

"Ha, why do Aussies call sharks Noah?"

"Don't know," Seth replied, "Maybe because shark rhymes with Ark."

"That makes no sense at all."

"Fair dinkum."

A half-hour passed, and the starboard hull was almost underwater.

Seth pointed, "Look, Noah has a chap."

"Chap like Charlie?" Jake replied.

"Nah, Chap, like friend, but I like Charlie."

Jake looked around. "We really messed up this boat. Think they'll be mad?""Only if we survive," Seth replied.

Noah swam close and rubbed his sandpaper skin against the sinking hull. Jake lifted an ear, "I hear a helicopter."

"Yeah, Nah, that's just Noah scratching an itch?"

"Nah, yeah, listen."

A sightseeing chopper rose over the horizon, and the boys lifted their orange life preservers overhead.

"Here, over here!"

The chopper turned toward them and circled while the pilot hailed the Coast Guard on the radio. Unable to land, the helicopter could only watch as the starboard hull sank. Jake and Seth climbed onto the port hull as Noah and Charlie bumped against the hull. The hapless sailors shredded Jake's t-shirt, making makeshift gloves by wrapping strips around their knuckles.

Seth said, "Punch them in the nose if you can. If not, hit 'em the gill."

A few minutes later, they watched as Charlie lost interest and swam off, and Noah disappeared. Jake and Seth pounded their chest and shook their fist.

Seth said, "They scared!"

"Yeah!" Jake said, "We eat shark for breakfast."

Moments later, Noah surged in, chomped down on the end of the hull, and shook it, knocking Seth into the water. He scrambled to get back onto the hull but was unable to climb out. The shark charged, hitting the submerged trampoline.

Jake yelled, "Grab my hand. Hurry, grab my hand!"

Seth stretched out and latched onto his arm. Noah circled back and darted toward Seth. Pulling with all his strength, Jake yanked Seth onto the hull just before Noah reached him. The shark slammed into the hull, chomping down on the pontoon.

Jake said, "We're going down."

A Coast Guard Rescue Helicopter racing toward the sinking catamaran arrived just as the boat sank. The crew dropped yellow dye cans with shark dispersant into the water and hovered near the surface, allowing the chopper's downwash to scare the shark away. Two rescue swimmers jumped into the water, one carrying a bang stick in-case Noah returned. The other swimmer placed a harness around the boys and lifted them into the chopper. When everyone was safely aboard, the helicopter flew to the Naval Hospital, where Seth received eight sutures to close the gash across his nose.

Jake said, "Ugh, that's gonna leave a scar."

"I'd rather be Frankenstein than a brown-eyed-mullet."

Later that evening, the chopper video of the rescue replayed on the local news.

The coverage made Jake and Seth instant celebrities at school but not so popular with the locals. The natives believed Jake and Seth acted recklessly and disrespected the whales. Jake and Seth apologized and made amends by volunteering to join beach cleaning crews and educate themselves on whales' migratory habits. While on a cleaning crew near Laniakea Beach, where they wrecked the catamaran, they found Jake's tattered ball cap that blew off when they hit the first wave.

Jake said, "Wow, look at that... almost like new!"

"I wouldn't wear it on a date... Speaking of dates, how's your girlfriend doing?"

"Uh, don't know... I haven't talked to her since the beach party. She ditches me all the time... She'll call when she gets bored."

The following week, Jake worked the bag at the dojo, turned to Master Fuji, and asked, "When am I supposed to test again?"

Master Fuji looked up from his book, "If you're confident you know all the required elements, we can skip the formalities. Are you ready?"

"Yes, sir."

Master Fuji marked the page and placed the book on the floor, "Okay, show me Bassai Dai."

Without hesitation, Jake moved to the dojo center, performed the kata, and waited for Master Fuji's response.

"Well done. Do the tonfa form."

Jake picked up a pair of tonfas and went through the form. As he waited for Master Fuji to respond, a fly buzzed Jake's face and meandered away.

Master Fuji said, "I know you know your self-defense techniques. Show me a jumping spin kick."

Just as he prepared to kick, the fly circled back. Jake's eyes locked onto the pest, tracking it as it zig-zagged toward him. He jumped, whipped around, and kicked the fly, knocking it across the room like a BB.

Master Fuji said, "That couldn't be scripted better. I promote you to 2nd kyu. You can now wear a brown belt."

Jake bowed, "Thank you, Master Fuji," then stood there with a blank expression.

Master Fuji said, "What's the matter?"

"I don't feel any different. Shouldn't I have a new superpower or something?"

Master Fuji grinned.

Two weeks passed since Jake spoke to Sheri. Whenever he called, she couldn't come to the phone. Feeling she was avoiding him, Jake cruised by her house one afternoon. As he approached her home, he saw her in the driveway talking to an older handsome teenager. They were so captivated by each other; they didn't even notice when Jake rolled up on his skateboard. He quietly reversed direction and left the same way he came. *Wow, I can't believe this. No wonder she doesn't call. I'm some kind of fool.*

Ryan bought a used car with the money he was making working at a local pizza parlor. It was a two-door maroon Pontiac LeMans he called Dr. Pepper. Every weekend, Ryan and his friends would get together and work on their cars, upgrading engine parts, exhaust systems, and stereos. A 400 cubic inch V8 motor with an aftermarket gas-guzzling quadrajet intake powered the Pontiac. Gas on the island was twice the mainland price, which kept Dr. Pepper parked most of the time. Once in a while, Ryan would take Jake to the Ala Moana strip, where teenagers would gather in parking lots for impromptu parties and show off their cars.

Ryan and Jake drove to a bowling alley where over two dozen hot rods gathered. All the drivers tuned their radios to the same station, and music blasted through the parking lot. Ryan wandered off to look at a friend's new wheels when another car pulled-up. Several guys jumped out of the car and bolted toward Dr. Pepper. The driver, a linebacker type like Ryan, approached Jake and pushed him into the car.

"You the little Hammer?" he said, laughing.

Jake caught himself as he fell against the fender. He glanced back just in time to see the green bomber jacket Ryan was wearing, flying like Batman's cape as Ryan's fist smashed into the jerk's mouth, knocking him to the ground.

Ryan shook his finger at the guy. "Don't touch my brother!"

Kneeling on the ground with his bloody lip stamped to his braces, he cried, "I was kidding, Ryan, I was only kidding..."

Ryan gestured toward Jake. "Get in the car; we're leaving."

Smoking tires, spitting gravel, they sped away.

Jake said, "What was that about?"

"That's Diggy—I hate that guy!"

Jake laid on his back, tossing a baseball at the ceiling. In his mind, the right-hook replayed over and over. It reminded him how Ryan always stuck up for him more than anyone else, even giving Jake money when he was short on cash. Their father, a decorated war veteran, was never the same after Vietnam— distant and sometimes belligerent. Their mother usually took a second job to help pay the bills, leaving the kids alone to fend for themselves. Jake thought of his parents as disconnected from his life and rarely spoke to them.

The end of school was nearing, and like everyone else, Jake

prepared for final exams. He needed high scores because he'd flunked several daily tests dropping his grades. Seth and Bobco were of no help. Their grades were as bad as Jake's. As he left his locker, he bumped into Sheri and tried to act normal. She said, "You've been a stranger lately. What's up?"

"Oh, um... been busy... you know, finals. I need to pass."

"Hmm? Maybe, I can help. Why don't you come over?"

Jake wondered, *is she still seeing Ken doll?*

The following Saturday afternoon, Jake gathered his text-books and went to Sheri's house. Sitting at the kitchen table, they reviewed his old tests and worked on his weaknesses. After an hour, Jake closed a book and said, "My brain is swollen. Does my head look bigger?"

"Oh, it's ginormous. Let's take a break," Sheri replied.

Sheri grabbed two sodas from the fridge and sat next to Jake at the breakfast bar.

"It's been like forever since we've done anything," she said. "What have you been up to?"

"Oh, just hangin' out. I'm learning to drive. Getting my license next month."

Sipping from his soda, he raised a brow and said, "And, what's new with you?"

Sheri said, "Not much." She slumped back in her seat, fiddling with a glassfish on the counter. She said, "I'm going to visit family in San Fran this summer. "

"Cool, who lives there?" Jake asked.

"My dad and my brother."

"Oh," Jake said. "I didn't know you had a brother?"

"Ya, he was studying in Taiwan last year."

She turns a photo frame around and shows it to Jake. "This is us in Kona two years ago."

He leaned forward to look at the picture and gave himself a mental head slap. *Oh man, that's Kenny.*

Jake said, "Wow! Y'all look just alike."

"Oh," Sheri replied. "You think I look like a boy?"

"Uh, no, no, you look like a girl—very girly... Um, so, when are you going to Cali?"

She said, "In two weeks. When school is out."

"Bummer," he moaned.

# 16

At the end-of-year party, seniors whooped-it-up on a secluded beach around a large bonfire. For most, it was a jubilant goodbye celebration because they were leaving to attend colleges on the mainland. Whenever anyone asked Ryan about college, he answered, "I haven't decided yet."

Later that evening, as the party began to thin out, Jake found Ryan sitting alone on the trunk of Dr. Pepper staring out to sea. Jake leaned against the car, "Whatcha gonna do now?"

Ryan paused before responding. "I talked to an Army recruiter. I'm leaving in July."

"What? No way! You can't leave me here alone. What am I gonna do?"

"Don't know... but I gotta go. I can't stay here. I got nothin'."

Jakes' head dropped. "I can't believe this."

"Mom is moving back to Texas."

"Are they splitting up?"

"Don't know," Ryan replied. "Dad might retire."

"Man, I can't go back to Texas. I ain't start'n over again," Jake said. "This always happens. As soon as things are going good, they jerk us around."

"Hope things work out for ya."

"It isn't fair."

"I hear ya, bro... It's not fair."

Several weeks earlier, Lyndsey moved in with her boyfriend, Dave, on the hill. On Jake's birthday, she picked him up in her tiny Chevy Chevette and drove to the driver's license testing center. The little car made it much easier to parallel park and Jake passed. On the way home, he asked, "What's this about Mom moving back to Houston?"

Lyndsay replied, "Mom and Dad have been threatening to split for years."

"Like every argument," Jake said. "I never thought they would."

"Mom wants to go home," Lyndsey said.

"I can't move again."

"I know," Lyndsey said. "But, Mom is sick of fighting."

When Sheri returned from California, Jake borrowed his mother's Camaro to take her to the movies and stopped by the pizza parlor to grab a bite. Jake introduced Ryan to Sheri, whom he'd never met.

Ryan said, "Jake gets his magnetic personality from me."

"Really?" Sheri replied, "that's the part I don't like."

"Good comeback!" Ryan gave Jake a thumbs up. "She's a keeper."

Jake and Sheri ordered a pizza, grabbed a soda and some items from the salad bar, and sat in a booth. Ten minutes later, Ryan served them a piping hot specialty pizza. Sheri took a bite of pizza and her face contorted in all directions.

Jake said, "You gotta bad tooth?"

Sheri's eyes bugged out as she struggled to swallow. "No, I don't have a bad tooth!" She sucked on her soda straw. "This pizza is gross! Do they use ketchup for pizza sauce, or something?"

"You don't like ketchup?"

"No, thanks. I'll eat the salad."

They left, thanking Ryan for comping the check, and arrived at the mall twenty minutes early. Passing the shaved ice treats, Jake said, "Can I get you a rainbow?"

"Sure," she replied.

They grabbed their treats and sat down. Jake wrapped his mouth around a large spoonful of rainbow-colored ice. "Mmm-mm, this is the bomb."

Sheri took a bite and, a few seconds later, mashed her palm against her forehead.

"Ow... I can't eat this." She tossed her cup into a nearby trash can, "Let's go to the theatre."

Jake huffed down whatever he had left and followed her. While standing in line, Sheri grabbed Jake's arm, burying her head in Jake's chest, saying, "No, no, not now, no, not now!"

"What's wrong?" Jake asked, "You got brain freeze?"

Sheri's legs collapsed, and Jake caught her. He laid her gently on the floor where she started shaking. Jake didn't understand what was happening and yelled out, "Help, somebody, help!"

Several adults crowded around to assist.

Jake said, "What's happening?"

"She's having a seizure," a woman replied.

Sheri gained consciousness just before an ambulance arrived and loaded her onto a gurney. Standing outside the theater, Jake watched, shocked and confused as they sped away.

The next morning, Jake tried to phone Sheri but kept getting the answering machine. Later that afternoon, Sheri called, "Can you come over so we can talk?"

"I'll be right over."

Jake jumped on his skateboard and shuffled to Sheri's house. He knocked, and Sheri opened the door, looking apologetic. She led him to the upstairs lanai, where they sat overlooking the backyard. A gentle breeze blew, and a few strands of hair stuck to her cheek in the wetness of tears.

Jake asked, "What's wrong?"

"This might surprise you," Sheri replied, "There's something I haven't told you."

"What's that?"

Her eyes sank, "... I have epilepsy."

Jake leaned back and threw an arm over his backrest. "Whew, I thought you were gonna break-up with me."

Sheri smiled. "Didn't know we were going out?"

"Ya, but don't tell anyone. My friends think I'm a stud."

"Ha. You're such a goof."

Jake asked, "Is that why you don't swim?"

"Yes, can you imagine if I had a seizure while swimming? Yesterday was a bad one. Sorry, you had to experience it. You must've been scared."

"Ah nah, ...well, maybe just a little," he replied. "Isn't there a medicine you can take?"

"I have a few, but they don't work well... And, they have unpleasant side effects—they make me tired."

"Can I help?"

"Well," she said, "that's a lot of baggage for you. I understand if you don't want to hang out anymore. I don't want you to feel like you have to take care of me."

"Are you kidding?" Jake said, "I took a CPR class. I know mouth-to-mouth resuscitation. Wanna practice?"

"Haha." Sheri stood up and walked over to Jake and kissed him on the cheek.

Jake perked up. "I guess we're officially going out now, huh?"

"Sure," she said, "but you can't tell anyone."

Ryan packed a small carry bag with a comb, toothbrush, and a few magazines to read on his long flight to Fort Benning to start basic training. All the Von Hammers gathered at the airport to see Ryan off. Sergeant Von Hammer stood there in his uniform beaming with pride as Jake's mother and sister cried. Ryan smirked at the spectacle of it all and said to Jake, "Can you believe this? It's embarrassing!"

Jake replied, "I'd cry too, but I don't want you to remember me that way."

Ryan laughed. "Ya, that wouldn't be good."

"Well, bye for now, brah, visit when you can."

"Sure thing." Ryan reached in his pocket and pulled out a key and stuck it in Jake's chest, "She's yours."

Jake's eyes lit up, "No way, are you serious?"

Ryan dropped the keys into Jakes's hand and said, "I can't take her with me. Don't pounce on her too much. She's a gas guzzler. If you're looking for a job, Pearl City Pizza needs help. I left you something in the tape deck. Aloha, bro!"

Then Ryan walked through the gate and boarded the plane. The family stood and watched as the plane taxied down the runway and took-off. A tear welled up in Jake's eye and he silently prayed Ryan would be alright.

When the Von Hammers returned home, Jake jumped in Dr. Pepper's driver's seat, one hand resting on the wheel, the other caressing the maroon velour. In the console accessory box, he found a note Ryan left outlining the maintenance schedule. He inserted the key and held his breath as the 400 cubic inch engine cranked. Click, click, varoom! The motor rumbled, sending a surge of adrenaline through Jake's veins. He sat a moment feeling grateful then reached over and pushed play on the tape deck. Ozzy blasted out of the nine-inch triaxial speakers screaming, "Crazy..."

Jake gripped the steering wheel and drove to Seth's house to show off his new ride.

Seth said, "Take me for a spin."

Cruising down the boulevard, Jake lowered the windows and

cranked up the stereo. They came to an intersection on the main highway, where overgrown bushes blocked Jake's view to the left. He turned on his blinker and waited for the traffic to pass. A car stopped, the driver looked Dr. Pepper's way, and Jake thought she was letting him out. He eased off the brake, and the vehicle rolled forward. As it cleared the bushes, Jake saw a VW barrelling right at him. He slammed on the brake, and the car screeched to a stop. The Beetle clipped Dr. Pepper's front bumper, ripping the running board off, and bounced into the other vehicle. Jake watched it all happen in slow motion. The running board tumbled back to earth and landed only a few feet from Dr. Pepper.

A man ran over and knocked on Jake's window, "Are you boys all right?"

Jake's jaw hung slack as he turned to the man and nodded. In less than an hour, he'd wrecked Dr. Pepper and caused a three-car collision. Luckily, there were no injuries, but the VW was totaled, and the other vehicle needed a new front end. Dr. Pepper suffered only minor damage.

After exchanging information, Jake received a ticket for failure to yield. He drove himself home, bracing for a severe butt chewing from his father. Jake stood tall, accepting the blame, and told his father what happened. Sergeant Von Hammer calmly handed Jake the telephone and had him call the insurance company. After twenty minutes on the phone, Jake slogged his way to his room and curled up in bed. The following day, he drove to the pizza parlor to apply for a job and began working three days a week.

The waters around Oahu are calm in the summer months, and Jake convinced Sheri to go snorkeling. They practiced in Sheri's pool and devised a touch-sign so Sheri could signal Jake if she were about to have a seizure.

When she felt comfortable, Jake took her to the shallow

waters at Hanauma Bay. She put on a life jacket, and they slowly paddled out. The water buzzed with colorful parrot fish, tangs, butterflies around a vibrant coral reef. Sheri's head swiveled side to side as she took in the incredible beauty of it all. Jake guided her to a coral head where a sea turtle busily munched on algae. Jake watched as Sheri stopped paddling and floated above, transfixed by the honu. Twenty minutes later, Jake led Sheri back to the shore.

Sheri said, "That was awesome! Let's go again!"

"Whoa!" Jake replied. "Slow down. Don't you need to rest?"

"I'm rested. Let's go!"

They swam back to the reef again, and again, and again. Sheri couldn't get enough, but Jake finally convinced her to pack it in, promising to take her another day. They stopped by a souvenir shop and bought a shell to commemorate her first snorkeling adventure.

Over the next few weeks, Sheri became more adventurous as she and Jake spent a lot of time together. Seth started dating a new girl and suggested Jake bring Sheri to the park for a picnic. They invited Bobco and Alex and arranged for everyone to meet at a park near Waimea Bay to use the barbeque pits.

Bobco brought his longtime girlfriend, Claire, and Alex brought Pam, both friends of Seth's new girlfriend, Marsha. Jake and the guys were tossing around a frisbee, and Sheri joined them while the other girls remained seated in a huddle of gossip. No one expected Sheri to be a frisbee expert, but she threw better than the guys. When Alex threw the disc, a gust of wind blew it toward a group of older teens, landing just a few feet from a girl seated on a blanket. Jake trotted over to pick up the frisbee and apologized for the errant throw.

The girl said, "It's all right. Be more careful."

As Jake walked away, one of the older guys popped up and said, "Go home, haole punk."

Thinking, *that's odd coming from someone with a redneck accent,* Jake replied, "We're all from somewhere," and flashed the shaka sign and continued walking.

That didn't sit well with the older guy. He threw his cup down, splashing foamy beer all over, and yelled, "What d'you say?"

Turning toward him, Jake repeated, "We're all from somewhere, brah," and kept walking.

The guy didn't understand what Jake meant because he didn't know the word Haole means; a white guy from somewhere else. *I'm sure he didn't pick up that back-road Alabama accent on Molokai.*

The enraged guy charged at Jake and tried to sucker punch him from behind. Jake ducked under the punch and stepped aside, never touching the guy. Embarrassed, the beer-buzzed redneck cursed Jake.

Seth said, "Here we go. This will be interesting."

"What do we do?" Alex asked.

Seth folded his arms, "Just watch."

The guy approached Jake again and loaded up for a Superman punch. Jake remembered a drill Master Fuji called the Drunken Puncher. Master Fuji would play drunk and try to hit Jake with a wild punch or grab him and wrestle him to the ground. Master Fuji said, "If he puts his weight on his front foot, he's going that direction. Slip the other way and let the bum blow-by."

Jake leaned back, stepping to the side, and the redneck guy flew right past him. He turned to grab Jake, but Jake slipped the other direction. Every time the beer-buzzed joker lunged forward, Jake would slip one way or the other, step back, and slip again. It was getting so comical Jake started laughing. Now in a full-blown rage, the belligerent drunk thrust his whole self at Jake to hit him and missed. Now, everyone was laughing.

He mounted one last wild flurry of chaotic swings and flailing body parts. Jake matched him step for step and dodged everything he threw without ever touching him. The exhausted attacker doubled over with his hands on his knees, gasping for air. Jake chuckled and walked back to his table and tossed the frisbee to the nerve-frazzled Alex.

"You look like you need a skivvie check!"

Seth and Bobco chuckled.

Bobco asked, "Local?"

"Na, probably Navy. He's gotta anchor tatt on his wrist," Jake replied.

"We better leave," Alex said.

"Not until I get my burger," Jake replied. "Besides, I don't want them to see what car I drive so they can jump me later. Small island, you know."

Seth replied, "JVH... Can't take the bloke anywhere."

Bobco said, "It's dang good Jake is a ninja."

"Ha, that guy is slower than a sloth," Jake replied. "My sister could whoop him."

Seth said, "He wasn't that slow, just slower than you."

Bobco said, "I wanna be a ninja. How long will it take?"

"A long time. Ninjas don't exist," Jake replied.

The guys fired up the pit, and the other group gathered their belongings and left, taking their bewildered drunk friend with them. Jake and his friends enjoyed their lunch and cleaned up well. Jake and Seth even cleaned up the other group's site. The time spent on the beach cleaning crews had a lasting effect and fostered real respect for 'Aina (the land).

A few weeks later, Jake and Sheri were picnicing on the base beach. The park was empty except for a few couples and some kids boogie boarding small hull waves created by passing ships.

Jake said, "You gonna eat them chips?"

Sheri pushed the bag toward Jake. "Take 'em."

"You haven't eaten much. You feeling all right?"

"I need a nap. Can we go now?"

As they walked to the parking lot, Sheri grabbed Jake's arm driving her nails into his skin, a sure sign she was experiencing a seizure. Jake carried her to a shaded area and laid her down. He placed a towel under her head as her body became stiff and glanced at his watch. When she began convulsing, he rolled her on her side to keep her from choking.

"Don't worry, girl, I got ya... It'll pass. You're a fighter. It's gonna pass."

Sheri seized for almost a minute before coming around. Frightened, she lay there trembling.

Cradling her in his arms, Jake said, "You're okay, I got you. It's okay."

Jake carried her to the car and raced her home, honking the horn as he arrived. Her parents came out, and Jake ran to the other side of the vehicle.

"Help me!"

Sheri's mother ran to the side of the car and helped Sheri out. She took her straight inside while Jake stood in the driveway, explaining what happened to Dr. Taub.

"Jake, you did the right thing," Dr. Taub said. "All you can do is wait it out and keep her from banging her head."

"I wish I could do something for her?"

"We all do. Sheri has the best doctors and best medication available, but it's not helping much."

The next day, Jake went to see her. Sitting next to the pool, Sheri said, "Thanks for being there, again. I thought the new medication would control it, but I guess not."

Jake replied, "You don't have to thank me. I'd trade places with you if I could. I hate seeing you that way."

"I peed my pants. I hate you seeing me that way too."

# 17

A new school year started and Jake realized he'd been adrift while adjusting to his new home. He'd gotten away from serious practice, meditation, and study. Determined to be a better student, Jake created a detailed plan, setting three primary goals; improve his Karate, get better grades, and graduate from Radford.

Jake made a copy of his karate goals and carried it to the dojo and gave it to Master Fuji.

"Will you help with this?"

"If you are serious," Master Fuji replied, "we can train in the old manner. It's difficult, but it's the best way to harden your body and mind."

Jake popped his chest out. "I'm ready!"

Master Fuji and Jake faced each other in horse stances and locked arms in a block position pushing against one another.

"This is an isometric exercise," Master Fuji said. "It will strengthen the muscles from the floor to the contact point."

Every kind of push-up was on the menu including one-armed and fingertip variations. To strengthen his core, Jake carried heavy sacks of sand up and down the street. Master Fuji fastened a large ship mooring line to the high ceiling of the dojo. Every day, Jake climbed the thick rope using only his arms. Master Fuji increased the weight and difficulty of each drill whenever an exercise became easy. The makiwara and a bucket of sand hardened their hands while bamboo canes desensitized limbs.

The training often caused bruises and bleeding, but the results were noticeable as Jake's muscle volume and tone increased every few weeks. He spent a lot of time in after school study halls, and his grades started improving. Jake studied with Sheri too, but that was less productive because he goofed off most of the time. Sheri helped Jake as much as possible, but she was an honors student swamped with her own homework.

Jake received a letter from Ryan,

I hope everything is going well. I'm in Infantry school and trying to get accepted to Airborne training. Can you ask Sergeant Fujioka to put in a recommendation for me? Are Mom and Dad getting along better? Are you still dating that blonde? She's a winner! Write back when you get a chance.

Happy to hear from Ryan, Jake wrote him a long letter babbling everything he could think of, except wrecking Dr. Pepper. Jake was oblivious to his parent's problems because he was always busy with school, work, and practice, but he knew his parents would eventually split. They'd been threatening it for years, and now that Jake was nearing graduation, there was nothing to stop them.

One evening, working in the pizza parlor, Jake overheard customers talking about a tournament that paid cash prizes. Jake approached their table and asked, "When is the tournament?"

One guy handed him a flyer and asked, "What style do you practice?"

"Um, Karate."

"Shotokan, Gojo Ryu, Shinto Ryu?"

Jake's brows wrinkled. "I don't know."

They laughed. "Are you in a McDojo?"

"McDojo?"

They laughed again.

"Thanks for the info," Jake said as he turned and walked away.

"Hope to see you there." They continued laughing.

The next evening, Jake was in the dojo and asked, "Master Fuji, what's McDojo?"

"It's a slang term used to describe a fake martial arts school. Why do you ask?"

Jake said, "Some guys were in the pizza shop and gave me this tournament flyer. They asked me what style I'm learning. I didn't know, so they said this is a McDojo."

Master Fuji bristled. "We practice Karate. Style isn't important. Dedication is."

"Can I participate in the tournament?"

"That's up to you. Why do you want to compete?"

"Because they give cash prizes, and Dr. Pepper needs a new bumper."

"Well then, you better win."

Although Master Fuji was usually calm and measured, he took a slight offense to the McDojo insult. Master Fuji's father was a proud Japanese national who felt immense shame for his country's actions during WWII. He moved to the United States to teach Karate after the collapse of the Japanese economy. When Master Fuji was in high school, some kids, led by an overweight bully, spread rumors about his father's dojo, saying it was a fake karate school. Master Fuji wanted to challenge the bully to avenge his father's reputation, but his father wouldn't allow it and sent him to Okinawa to study with the Grandmaster.

Jake figured he only had to place in one section to get his

entry fee back and make a few extra bucks to get Dr. Pepper's bumper fixed. Jake's determination reminded Master Fuji of when Jake was just starting and eager to learn. Now, Jake had grown strong and become a good karate-ka. Master Fuji wanted him to do well because he'd been having a rough time dealing with his parents' problems and needed some wins.

He had concerns Jake might do too well and exhibit the attributes associated with the Wado juice. His physical abilities were maturing, and although Jake wasn't aware of them, they came out whenever his reflex response initiated. It was only a matter of time before Jake's abilities would fully develop, and then no one could defeat him, not even Master Fuji.

Master Fuji told Jake he could wear a black belt to compete because the tournament paid higher cash prizes to black belt ranks. With six weeks to prepare, Master Fuji suggested he practice the Bassai Dai kata and use a sword form for the weapon section.

As Jake practiced, he thought about how Sam might perform the kata. Through application, Jake strived to understand the meaning of the form and express it through dynamic movement. The sword form was a different beast, and Jake asked Master Fuji to help create a fast and powerful sequence. Jake spent two weeks working out arrangements before settling on the final version.

Seth came by the pizzeria, bummed a few slices and a drink, and then hung around playing video games until things got slow.

Seth said, "You've been on the walkabout lately. What've you been up to?"

"I've been training for a tourney. I'm competing next weekend. Trying to win some cash."

"How much is the purse?" Seth asked. "Maybe, I'll get in… haha."

"You'd do well."

"Ha. Nah, where is it? I'll come to cheer you on. Is your girl-friend going?"

"I haven't told her," Jake said. "She already thinks I'm a dork. Don't need to make it worse."

On the morning of the tournament, Master Fuji gave Jake a black belt and told him, "Wear it like you earned it."

Putting on the belt, Jake felt weird because it was a symbol of something he'd revered for a long time but didn't feel worthy.

As usual, he arrived at the arena early. It's a military thing, hurry up and wait, or as his father would say, if you're not ten minutes early, you're five minutes late. He ducked into a corner and loosened up as spectators arrived and filled in the seats. Jake noticed Seth come in and motioned him over to his side.

Seth said, "G'day mate, you got a promotion, aye?"

"Shhh, just for today," Jake said. "Thanks for coming. Don't know how long it'll be, but I'll be in the center ring."

"Alrighty then. I hope you don't mind, but I invited Marsha and Bobco for moral support."

"Oh jeez," Jake said. "Thanks for piling on the pressure!"

"No worries, mate. Nothing a black belt can't handle."

A few minutes later, Bobco, Alex, Marsha, and Claire arrived and sat next to Seth.

Jake looked at Seth shaking his head, and mouthed, "What the?"

Seth threw his arms up and shrugged as if he didn't know Bobco was bringing more people. Then Master Fuji, wearing street clothes, sat down in the front row beside Jake's friends.

The kata competition started almost immediately, and Jake followed Sam's routine of not watching the other competitors and visualized himself executing his form. The competitors performed one by one until they called Jake's number. He walked smartly to the middle of the ring, introduced himself, and bowed to the judges. Jake snapped into the first Bassai Dai position and paused for a moment before exploding into the form. Bassai Dai means 'storm the fortress,' and Jake showed power, balance, and technique throughout the kata earning him high marks from the judges. The last competitor performed a more difficult kata and scored higher, leaving Jake in second place. Jake received a small trophy and a check for one-hundred-fifty dollars, twice as much as his entry fees.

His friends cheered from the stands and did their best to embarrass him—which they liked to do. At a short break before the weapons competition, Master Fuji said, "Congratulations! You did well for your first Black Belt competition." He handed Jake an apple, "This will replace your energy."

When Sheri came into the hall and sat down with his friends, Jake didn't notice. He took out the sword and wiped away all fingerprints and smudges. The tournament officials reset the ring, and the weapons competition began. They arranged the competitors according to their placement in the kata event, so Jake was second to last. Jake saw the first competitor start and slipped into a meditation trance until they called his name. Jake opened his eyes and stood up and raised his hand, asking permission to enter the ring. Jake attached the scabbard to his side and stepped into the ring, faced the front judge, and said, "I am Jake Von Hammer. My sensei is Master Fujioka. Request permission to begin!"

The judge waved him on. Jake removed the apple from inside his gi, placed it on the floor in front of him, and backed up two steps. Everyone stopped talking and watched with extreme interest. He knelt into the seiza sitting position and moved his hand slowly across his body, and rested it on the handle of the katana. He paused, then drew the sword with lightning speed, cutting across his body to a solid stop. Standing slowly, he quickly turned to rear raising the sword overhead. Whirling around, he moved across the floor, striking and slicing. The shiny blade surrounded Jake in a halo of tracers. Jake stopped and sheathed his weapon and turned to the front. He slowly put his hand on the handle and drew the katana again, jumping and spinning three-hundred-sixty-degrees and charged forward, striking and slicing. The weapon whistled as it cut through the air. Jake did a forward flip striking downward before immediately flipping backward, cutting across his body. He moved sideways, spinning across the floor in a frenzied blur before coming to an abrupt stop in a forward strike position. Jake whipped around and stabbed the apple, flipped it into the air, spun like a top, slicing the orb in half as it came down. Jake froze, facing the primary judge while the pieces landed on the floor in front of him. He sheathed his sword and bowed to the judges. The crowd erupted in applause.

Jake received the highest score. The judges gave him a giant trophy and a check for two-hundred-fifty dollars.

Master Fuji told Jake, "Outstanding! That was fun to watch."

"I'm gonna win the sparring competition."

"You don't have to prove anything," Master Fuji said.

"I know, but Pepper needs a bumper."

Jake walked over to his friends, who waited for him. As he approached, he saw Sheri and bowed his head.

"Hey, Sheri, what're you doing here?"

"Uh, Bobco invited me because YOU didn't."

"Aya... I thought you didn't like Karate. I look like a dork anyway, sooo..."

"Well, that was fun. Are you finished now?"

"No, I have an hour before the sparring competition."

"Then you better take me to lunch. You should be able to afford it now."

The whole group shuffled down the road to McDonald's for

lunch, but Jake did not eat. He ordered a sprite and ate a few of Seth's fries.

Seth said, "You look hungry."

Jake replied, "I'm starving, but I don't want to spar on a full stomach. I hate to barf."

Jake turned to Sheri, "You don't have to stay if you don't want to. I know you don't like fighting."

"No way, I'm staying. I wanna see you barf. Besides, you might need someone to treat your wounds."

Back at the arena, Jake grabbed his equipment bag and got ready to spar while his friends found their seats. He saw the guy who made the McDojo remark and picked up his empty McDonald's cup, and shook the ice making sure the guy noticed. When he looked, Jake sucked a huge gurgling slurp through the straw.

Competitors lined up around the competition ring, and Jake went to join them. Along the way, Master Fuji approached and asked, "How are you feeling?"

Jake said, "I'm hungry."

Master Fuji smiled. "You should've eaten the apple."

The judges explained the rules to the competitors, and the matches began. Jake got the first match against a large opponent that tried to intimidate him by pounding his gloves together. They took their marks. Jake inserted his mouth guard, and they bowed. The lubber tried to rush, and Jake stepped aside, kicking him in the ribs as he passed by. The guy tried to counter with a roundhouse kick, but Jake backed out of reach. Jake faked a side-kick and hit him in the face with a backlist, then a roundhouse and a hard punch to the solar plexus. The big guy dropped to his knees and was TKO'd when he couldn't continue. Jake's fanbase cheered.

Jake watched a few matches before his next bout. This time his opponent was a small jittery guy. He kept faking a charge then dropping back to counter punch. *This guy drank too much java.* The more Jake watched him, the slower he seemed to move. Jake timed his movement and tagged him in the face with a jab. That excited Java Guy even more. He jumped around in a jerky unorthodox manner. Jake stayed calm and waited for Java Man to attack. When he did, Jake side-stepped, punching him twice in the head before kicking him in the chest with a round-house. Stunned, Java Dude staggered, and the judge called, "Time."

He grabbed his gloves to see if he was all right and reset the fighters. Java Guy jumped, and Jake stopped him cold with a front kick to the stomach. With time running out, Jake let him run around the ring and won the fight on points. His friends chanted, "JVH, JVH, JVH..."

Two matches took place before Jake's next fight against a Chuck looking second-degree black belt. He was a good fighter and caught Jake with a hook-punch to the kidney. *Owch!* Smarting from the blow, Jake backed away. His demeanor changed as his survival reflex engaged. When Chucky came after him again, Jake stepped in, jamming his attack, then delivered a sharp blow to his lower ribs. His opponent countered with a spinning back-fist, but Jake blocked it and crescent-kicked him in the back of the head. Chucky wobbled, and Jake closed in to finish him off. Chucky raised his hand and gave up the fight. The growing fan club chanted, "JVH, JVH, JVH..."

Five minutes passed before the judges called the fighters for the championship match. Jake entered the ring and stepped to the line. His opponent was a giant linebacker type kid. *Jeez, it's the Hulk.* Jake bit down on his mouthpiece, and the Hulk came out swinging. Jake backpedaled, ducking punches, and escaped. The giant chased him, swinging wildly. *So, this is what makes you green.*

Jake caught Hulk in the chin with a right-cross and kicked

him in the stomach. Hulk swung and missed. Jake jumped and hit him in the head with a spin-kick, knocking out his mouth-piece. Hulkster dropped to the mat with a thud, wallowing around for his mouthguard. He put it halfway into his mouth and tried to stand up, but the judge waved Jake off, ending the fight. His fan club and the arena cheered.

The judge lifted Jake's arm, declaring him the Jr Black Belt Champion, and gave him a five-foot shiny gold and blue trophy and a check for four-hundred dollars. Jake walked over to Master Fuji and gave him the award as camera flashes lit up the room. His friends piled on, knocking Jake to the ground.

A few days later, Jake carried his gym bag into the dojo and approached Master Fuji. He pulled the black belt from the pocket and folded it.

"Are you sure you don't want to keep it?" Master Fuji asked.

"No, sir, I'm not ready for it yet. I'll be ready when I earn it."

Master Fuji reached out, and Jake placed the belt in his hands. Jake smiled, and Master Fuji smiled back, never more proud of Jake-san.

## 18

Winter brought big waves back to the island. Jake strapped his board to the top of his car and met Seth on the North Shore for a day of surfing. After waxing the boards, they paddled out and waited for their set.

Seth said, "So, are you and Sheri still going out?"

"I guess... She still calls once in a while."

"Sounds like the perfect girlfriend."

Jake spotted his wave, "Ya, maybe," and started paddling.

The board lifted and started racing down the wave. Jake popped into a crouched position and turned into the wave, climbing higher until it began to break. He cut-back and became airborne. Floating weightless, cloaked in silence, time slowed to a standstill. Only he and the wave existed. *Woe, this is the Kwan!*

The board dropped onto the shoulder, and Jake regained his line. Wrapped in an envelope of blue crystal, Jake leaned back, dragging his fingertips through the glassy surface. The tube collapsed, and Jake bailed screaming, "Cheeee hoo!"

They surfed most of the afternoon and made a plan to do it again the following weekend. Jake headed back to Hickam to see

Sheri. He noticed Sheri looked tired. He sat beside her on the couch, "How are you feeling?"

"Not well," she responded. "The new medicine makes my head spin."

"Oh man, that sucks. Can I get you anything?"

She ran her hand across her head, "No, think I'll go to bed."

"Get some rest. I'll see you tomorrow."

"Thanks, Jake."

Jake drove home worried about Sheri, but he heard his parents yelling at each other when he turned off the car. Banging his head against the headrest, he thought, *Jeez, not again.*

He quietly backed out of the drive and drove to the dojo. Jake took his frustration out on the heavy bag. The harder and faster he punched, the more the bag buckled and swayed. The sound echoing off the metal hangar drowned out the screaming inside his head. Unaware, a seam on the leather bag was tearing, Jake continued thirty minutes until stuffing dumped onto the floor. He then turned his frustration toward the makiwara. It broke on the third strike. Fed up, Jake laid on a mat lamenting his lot in life and fell asleep.

The following morning, he wrapped duct tape around the bag and filled Ratcom's seed trays. He left a note for Master Fuji:

Sorry about the bag and makiwara. I'll replace them.

— Jake

When he arrived home, he found a postcard on the counter:

They accepted me to Airborne school. I graduate next month. Please give my thanks to Sergeant Fujioka. Anything new with you?

—Ryan

Jake cooked half a carton of eggs and drowsed them with A.I. sauce, a' la Bebout. While eating, he sat at his desk and wrote a short note:

I won some trophies at a tournament. Lyndsey is still living with the Navy guy. I got a raise at the pizza shop. Mom and dad fight all the time.

—Jake

A few days later, Jake arrived at the dojo and warmed up. He'd worked up a good sweat by the time Master Fuji came, so the test started right away. After completing all the required katas, he performed his weapon forms and finally demonstrated all the one-step-sparring techniques. Then Master Fuji put him through a barrage of physical exercises; running in place, push-ups, jumping jacks, carrying sandbags, climbing ropes, and dragging a large tire around the parking lot. Realizing Jake would not exhaust himself and even seemed to get stronger, Master Fuji taped a stripe around his belt and said, "Congratulations, Jake-san! You have earned the rank of 1st kyu. You may test for Shodan in one year."

Jake bowed, "Thank you, Master Fuji. I promise to work hard and be ready when that time comes."

The next day, Jake dropped by to see Sheri on his way home from work. Sitting by the pool, Jake said, "I got a promotion. 1st kyu now."

"I guess I don't need to defend you anymore, huh?"

Sheri started hitting Jake with play punches. "Hey, teach me some karate."

"Okay... This is how to punch."

Jake shows her a straight punch from a front stance. Sheri tried to copy him. He adjusted her stance and straightened her wrist. "You hit with these knuckles, so you want your wrist to be square."

Sheri had trouble making a fist. Jake giggled and said, "What are you doing?"

"I'm trying to make a fist." She kept trying. "I can't make a fist... Nobody ever taught me to fight."

"Uh, well... You wouldn't want to hit like that. You'd probably hurt yourself."

"What?... No," she turns her wrist, "Is this right?"

Jake says, "Hit me."

"Really?"

"Ya... Just hit me in the chest so you can see what it feels like. You won't hurt me."

Sheri took careful aim, thrust a punch into Jake's chest, and quickly pulled her hand back, "Ouch... that hurts!"

Jake laughs, "You need to strengthen your hands. Doing push-ups on your fists will help."

Her brow furls. "Push-ups? Can't I just do the no-push-up kind of karate?"

Jake and Sheri agreed to exchange Christmas gifts early because she would be in California for the holiday. The evening before she left, Jake cleaned Dr. Pepper and put on his best pair of shorts. He drove her to a restaurant in Haleiwa, where they ate a candlelight dinner sitting in the outdoor garden area. Jake pulled out a little box wrapped in snowflake paper and handed it to Sheri. She carefully unwrapped the small jewelry box and joked, "You're not proposing, are you?"

In the box, she found a silver necklace with a sea turtle pendant.

Jake said, "I hope it always reminds you of the day we went snorkeling with the honu."

Sheri got teary-eyed and handed Jake a small box wrapped in dark green paper with gold pinstripes. Jake opened the box and gazed at the jade ring for a moment before saying, "I do."

Sheri laughed. "That's not a wedding ring! Look close; you'll see a dragon etched into the ring with your initials, JVH. Dragons are the symbol of power and strength. Thank you for always being there to protect me."

"Always, Thank you," Jake replied.

Jake and Sheri walked to the beach and took a barefoot stroll in the sand along the water's edge. A quarter moon hung over the horizon, casting a soft glow over the winter surf crashing just offshore. Sheri stopped. Jake turned toward her and looked into her eyes as water lapped at their feet. He slowly leaned forward and kissed her, but Sheri didn't respond. She smiled and put her hands on his shoulders. A tingle shot up her spine, and her expression turned pale.

"Take me back to the car," she said.

Jake obliged, wondering why Sheri suddenly turned cold. Driving back to Hickam, he asked, "Are you okay?"

"Yes," Sheri replied.

"Are we okay?"

"Of course. I just need to get ready to fly to San Fran tomorrow."

"All right, I just thought something was wrong, that's all."

She reached across the console and lightly grabbed Jake's arm.

"No, tonight has been perfect. I don't want to mess it up."

The following day, Jake is at work bussing tables when he sees the guy who gave him the tournament flyer and suggested he might be in a McDojo.

He said, "Hey, I saw you at the tournament. Congratulations on your victories. Your instructor must be a great master. What school do you go to?"

"It's not a school. I'm his only student."

He handed Jake a business card. "Well, if you ever want to teach, we could always use a junior instructor like yourself."

Jake couldn't accept the offer because he wasn't really a black belt, but he thought, *if all else fails, I could teach karate someday.*

On Christmas Eve, Jake drove to the dojo and left a small gift for Master Fuji and some special treats for Ratcom. When he got home, no-one was there. He flopped onto the couch, looking up at the old artificial tree in the corner. It'd been in the family since anyone could remember. The branches were flat and entangled with old tinsel no one bothered to remove. A third of the lights were burned out, which is why they didn't plug it in anymore. His thoughts drifted back to past Christmases when they were younger, and the tree seemed so much taller. *The Christmas spent in a hotel room, the blizzard in Alaska, the car accident in Mississippi.*

Through all the diversity, the family stuck together. Those were happy times.

Now, the tree was just a sad remnant of a dysfunctional family and his parent's failing marriage. His parents were at that stage where they couldn't stand each other anymore. The stain on their breath left no doubt where they spent their time. When Jake's father was drunk, he'd often become belligerent and thought he was the Master Chief of the Air Force, barking out orders at everyone.

Jake looked at the ring that Sheri gave him and wondered how she was. He wasn't even sure how well that was going because Sheri often sent him mixed signals. He thought of Fritz. *I wonder if she ever thinks about me. Carla and Tammy, how are they? Benji? Bebout? Master Kim and Master Lahn? Master Yamada, Sam—*

A car door slammed shut. A moment later, the door flew open, and a dark, heavily burdened shadow stood in the doorway. *Oh man, I can't deal with this right now.*

Just as he was preparing his exit, he heard, "Get your butt up, Goobs!"

A buzz-cut soldier barged in and threw a duffle bag down.

Jake sat up, "Holy cow! What are you doing here?"

Fist on hips, Ryan looked around the room. "Does anyone live here? Look at that tree. That's pathetic!"

"Haha, no kidding!" Jake said. "Man, I'm glad to see you! How'd you get here!"

"I'm Airborne; we go everywhere! Seriously, I'm on leave before I head to Germany."

Jake said, "Well, Mele Kalikimaka!"

"Merry Christmas to you, too," Ryan replied. "Let's get outta here!"

Jake reached into his pocket and tossed the keys to Ryan, who exclaimed, "Be a Pepper!"

They jumped in and sped up the hill to Lyndsey's. She'd been cooking all day, preparing a turkey with all the fixings for her hungry brothers. Ryan looked Army fit, but Lyndsey and Ryan were both surprised at how big Jake had gotten in just a few months. Lyndsey said, "My goodness, I can't call him baby brother anymore."

After dinner, Lyndsey told the boys, "Mom and Dad are separating. I know you guys blame Mom, but it's not all her fault. They've been doing this to each other for a long time."

Jake said, "I hate it. I'm stuck in the middle."

Lyndsey said, "I know. Just keep doing the best you can."

They spent the rest of the night playing games and cracking jokes—that's how brats cope with stress.

The day after Christmas, a light breeze cleared the clouds away. Ryan took Jake to an airfield where they boarded a plane. The Twin Otter circled the island, climbing higher with each pass. From 18,000 feet, Jake could see most of the island of Oahu, nearby Molokai, and Maui covered in haze. Ryan put goggles on Jake, snapped his harness to his chest, and then gave a thumbs-up to the flight crew. The side door opened, and Ryan pushed Jake toward the door, hurling them into free-fall over the southern tip of Diamondhead Crater. Jake was sure they would hit the water, but he didn't care. For seventy seconds, they were in free-fall, and the wind whipping by washed every worry from Jake's mind. Ryan pulled the ripcord, and a bright yellow chute popped open overhead. Ryan steered them to a soft landing inside the crater. Jake popped up, bouncing foot to foot, talking non-stop.

Ryan laughed, "Things look a lot different through jump goggles, don't they?"

"Man, oh ya! That was crazy. I love it, love it, love it!"

A taxi drove them to the Shorebird Restaurant in Waikiki. While waiting for his Shoreburger, Jake asked, "What's the Army like?"

"Oh, man, how things have changed," Ryan said. "You just have to set a goal and work for it. In Infantry School, I qualified Expert with the rifle. That got me into sniper training. With Master Fuji's recommendation, I got into Airborne. I knew I was in the right place after my first jump. I loved it. I'm planning to go to school on the GI Bill when I get out."

Later that day, Jake jogged to the dojo to feed Ratcom and put in a short work-out. He found a box with a red bow sitting on the floor with a card that read,

Merry Christmas, Jake! Thank you so much for the teacups. I love them. See you in the new year. Enjoy! Master Fuji

Jake opened the box and found a new leather speed bag—the kind that attaches to the ceiling and floor with a bungee cord. The harder and faster he hit the bag, the faster and more it moved. Jake punched and kicked the bag non-stop for forty minutes. The next day, he replaced the top rope with a thick bungee to make it faster.

A few days later, Ryan packed his duffle bag to report to his new duty station in Wiesbaden, Germany. They were saying goodbye when Jake remembered he still had Ryan's jump goggles.

Ryan said, "You keep them. When things get you down, put on those goggles, and jump!"

# 19

The doctors gave Sheri a new medication that made her nauseous. On his way to work, Jake swung by to cheer her up. She lay on the couch, bundled in thick blankets. He pulled an airline barf bag from his pocket and unfolded it.

"I've been saving this for times like these."

Sheri half-smiled. "You win the terrible bedside manner award. "

"How ya feeling?" he asked.

"It's supposed to get better."

"I'll help any way I can." He perks up. "I can even do your homework."

"Um, no thanks."

Bobco, the best hurdler on the Radford track team, had never beaten Lars, a tall, long-legged Norwegian who attended their rival school. It was a kind of rub for Bobco, whose parents were both high school track stars who specialized in hurdles. They went to every track meet to watch Bobco finish just milliseconds behind Lars. One day, Bobco approached Jake and said, "Yo mon, how do ninjas get fast? Can you make my legs faster?"

"You should talk to Master Fuji. He's the expert."

The following evening, Bobco went to the dojo and told Master Fuji about his dilemma. Master Fuji said, "I've never trained a track athlete, but I suggest you increase fast-twitch muscle fibers and overall leg strength."

"Could ya show me?"

"Can you bring a hurdle to the dojo?"

"Yes, sir. I'll try."

The track coach lent Bobco a hurdle, and he practiced at the dojo twice a week. He and Jake would warm-up, and Bobco worked with Master Fuji for the rest of the evening. Master Fuji had Bobco raise the hurdle six inches higher than usual and jump it until he became sweaty. Then he'd sprint flights of stairs carrying sandbags until he almost collapsed. Jake helped him cool down, joining him on a light jog around the block. Then they'd hang from the rack letting gravity stretch their tendons and muscles. One evening, while hanging upside down, Jake said, "How did you get red hair anyway?"

"Ah ya, my family is creole. I gotta lotta red-headed cousins."

"And, the amber colored eyes? You should be in movies."

Almost every other weekend, Jake met Seth in Waimea Beach to surf. They paddled out and waited for a set.

Jake said, "Where you been hangin'?"

"My mother's boyfriend lets me stay in the lower guest room when he's away. It's a walkout to the beach."

"What more could a surfer want?"

"Twenty-foot barrels and a pair of sizzling hot Sheilas."

Jake smiled and started paddling to catch a wave. Just as he gained speed and popped-up, a newbie surfer cut him off, forcing Jake to bail-out to avoid hitting him. Seth saw this and berated the kook, who was unapologetic. After carving up a few sets, Jake and Seth packed it in and headed to the parking lot.

Along the way, Jake stopped to rinse sand off while Seth continued. The kook and his friend jumped Seth, pushing him against the car. Seth swung his board, hitting the skinny guy, and knocked him to the ground. The larger kook walloped Seth with a haymaker punch. Seth dropped to the ground, where he hit his head. Hearing the commotion, Jake ran to help. As he approached, the large guy attacked him. Jake backed him up with a stiff side-kick to the chest. He tried to help Seth to his feet, but the guy attacked from behind, taking another giant swing that grazed Jake's head as he ducked. Rising, Jake hit him with a solid uppercut to the jaw. He collapsed to the ground— knocked out cold. The skinny guy got to his feet and tried to tackle Jake from behind. Jake stomped his foot and elbowed his head. He let go and ran. Jake threw the boards into the car and raced Seth to a clinic. They gave Seth a few stitches and an ice pack to curb the swelling.

Seth said, "Thanks for the backup, mate."

"Ha, they shaved the side of your head. New Aussie fashion?"

"Aye, call me Koko Head."

One evening, Jake arrived at the dojo early and started working the speed bag. He became so enthralled, he didn't notice when Master Fuji entered the room. Tagging the target with straight punches, kicks, elbows, and spinning back fist, the bag became faster and more erratic with every blow. Jake matched every movement of the bag, no matter how abstract it became. Moving faster than an eye could process, Master Fuji knew it was time to tell Jake what was happening to him.

After practice, he said, "Jake-san, do you have any plans for this weekend."

"Nah, why?"

"I want to do some field training. Are you game?"

"Sounds fun."

They met early the following Saturday and drove across the island. The jungle floor was slippery from morning dew as they hiked into the Makua Keaau Forest. After hours on the trail, they came to a clearing surrounded by steep mountains.

Jake asked. "Where are we going?"

Master Fuji pointed to a steep face rising in front of them. When they reached the base, Master Fuji put a climbing harness on himself and helped Jake into his. He snapped a safety hook onto Jake's D-ring and said, "Pay attention and use the same handholds I do."

Carefully scaling the jagged face, they reached the halfway mark and stopped to rest. Master Fuji took a drink of water from a canteen, and Jake sniffed the air.

Jake said, "Froot Loops."

"Froot Loops?"

"I smell Froot Loops cereal." Jake gazed upward. "It's coming from up there."

They continued the climb, making it to the top around lunchtime. Following his nose, Jake tracked the scent leading him to a spot.

He pointed. "That's where the smell is coming from."

"That's what we came for," Master Fuji said.

Jake snarled. "That ugly plant."

Master Fuji replied, "That ugly plant is a Wado bush."

"Looks like a weed to me."

"Maybe, but it has medicinal properties. It enhances senses, strength, reflexes, and other things."

"Looks like you found the Fountain of Youth! I always thought you were quite spry for someone your age."

"It's not for me, Jake."

"Um, then who?"

"You."

"Huh? Why do I need it? I'm already young."

"That's not what I mean."

"Is that the plant you used when I got bit by the cobra? Benji told me."

"I had to give it to you," Master Fuji said. "You would've died without it."

"Okay, but there ain't no cobras in Hawaii, so why do I need it?"

"You might feel unusually tired for no reason. If that happens, drink a cup of the sanpincha tea I keep in the dojo. I mix Wado leaves with it to help you rejuvenate."

"So, those are the 'special herbs.'"

"Yes. It's toxic except to survivors. They are called, Hābu-Té."

"Ha boo tae?"

"It means born again. Sometimes, the Wado is given to a sick child when there are no other options. If they survive, they may develop sustained effects. You are one of only a few who have survived."

"What does that mean?"

"It means you are stronger and faster than you should be. You might even develop other things depending on how the Wado affects you."

"Do I get to wear a cape?"

"I'm serious, Jake. You must not tell anyone about this."

Jake sat and unpacked his lunch as Master Fuji pulled a half-frozen fish from his lunch kit and laid it on a rock. As it thawed, it stank worse than Limburger cheese. Master Fuji grabbed a large knife and scored the fish. Jake watched out the corner of his eye and held his breath, waiting for Master Fuji to eat the smelly mackerel. Jake swallowed a bite of his sandwich and said. "You making kimchi?"

Master Fuji replied, "I'm not going to eat the fish, Jake. I'm feeding the plant."

"Oh, I thought it was one of those Asian delicacies."

"Nutrients are scarce up here. Without the fish, the plant would starve."

Master Fuji dug a hole under a plant and placed the fish there, covering it with soil.

"Why don't you just grow it at home?"

"That's the first place they'd look."

"Who?"

"Some people."

They finished their lunch and climbed down the mountain the same way they came. Jake was silent the entire time.

When they arrived at the dojo, Master Fuji said, "You will meet Grandmaster Matsumura soon, and things will become clear."

"Is Grandmaster, some people?"

"Grandmaster is good people. Keep a low profile."

"Yes, Sir."

Sheri didn't have a lot of friends. She was a social introvert and tried to hide her illness from everyone. Many people misinterpreted her behavior, earning her the reputation of spoiled snob among other kids. Her birthday just happened to be on St Patrick's Day. Jake thought, *What's more Irish than golf?*

He arranged for the gang to meet for a game of putt-putt golf. Everyone arrived at the game center and grabbed putters. Sheri shot first because it was her birthday. She aimed carefully and struck the ball hard, pinging it off the barrier. As it careened off a wall, everyone ducked, and it bounced into another area.

Sheri covered her mouth. "Oops."

Seth leaned over and whispered in Jake's ear, "Letting her win could take a while."

"Aya," Jake replied. "She might need unlimited mulligans."

When the game was over, everyone gathered in a small corner in the game center where Jake had arranged a white-frosted cake decorated with four-leaf clovers. They lit sixteen candles and sang Happy Birthday. Sheri blushed and silently wished, as she did every year, to be healthy and blew out the candles.

Jake gave Sheri a square box wrapped in rainbow-colored paper with a green bow. She carefully removed the wrapping to find a Pearl Harbor Pizza box.

Her nose wrinkled-up. "Oh gee, Jake. You know how I love Pearl pizza."

Jake laughed. "Open the box."

Sheri lifted the top and taped to the lid, where she found the latest album from her favorite band and two tickets to the upcoming show.

"Oh my god, Oh my god, Oh my god... you didn't... I can't believe, Oh my god..." Sheri jumped up and hugged Jake. "Thank you, thank you... and thank you, Seth, and Marsha, and Bobco, and Claire, and Pam, and Alex. This is the best birthday ever."

Jake and Sheri said bye to everyone and left the game center, and drove across the island to Haleiwa for dinner. They dined on fresh seafood amongst the fragrant flowers at an outside table in the restaurant's garden area. When they finished their meal, they drove the shoreline road as Sheri sang along with every song on the radio. The setting sun cast a blanket of orange across the sky as they passed Kaiaka Bay Beach Park.

Sheri slapped the dash. "Pull over, pull over."

They grabbed the beach towels Jake always kept in the trunk and trotted to the beach, kicked off their shoes, and waded knee-deep into the water.

"I love sunsets," Sheri said.

Jake gestured toward the horizon, "Just for you. Ta' La' ga'... "

"What does that mean?"

"Don't know. It's from a whiskey commercial in the Philippines."

"Haha, I swear you live the life of Riley."

"Who's Riley?"

"Don't you ever read?" She scoops a handful of water at Jake, "It means a privileged life."

Jake shakes off the spray, "I doubt Riley works at Pearl Harbor Pizza."

"Haha, you're such a goofball."

Sheri high stepped it to the beach and sat on a towel, hugging her knees. Jake spread his towel beside her and sat down. Palms gently swayed in soft tropical breezes as the setting Sun bathed the bay in orange, red, and violet.

Sheri said, "I'm scared."

Jake replied, "I'm scared too."

"I mean, it's not fair," Sheri said. "Why me? I wanna be a doctor, but I can't even help myself."

"You don't deserve it—nobody does. Don't give up. You'll be the one who finds the cure."

She rested her head on her knees, "I need a miracle."

Jake wrapped an arm around her. "I'm right here."

After a slight delay, Sheri started laughing. "Gosh, I hate you sometimes."

The following weekend, a chill sea wind blew in, dusting the bleachers with a dewy glaze. Using a beach towel, Jake dried the bench, and he and Sheri took a seat. Jake huddled close to Sheri, trying to stay warm.

Sheri said, "I thought you lived in Alaska."

Shivering, Jake replied, "That was eons ago, and we had parkas and snow pants. Besides, aren't you from San Fran? You've got goosebumps. Didn't Jack London say, 'The coldest winter I ever spent was summer in San Francisco?'"

"Actually, I think that was Mark Twain. "

"Oh, see, I don't read."

Bobco's parents came and sat just a few rows away. Seth, Marsha, and Claire came a few minutes later. Sheri pointed toward the track, "Hey, isn't that Master Fuji down there?"

Jake replied, "Ya, I didn't know he was coming."

"Why don't you invite him to sit with us?"

"He knows where we are."

"How do you know, maybe he didn't see us?"

"He's Master Fuji. He sees everything. I'll bet if you kiss me, he'll say something about it next time I see him. Go ahead, try it."

"I'm not falling for your stupid tricks, Jake!"

As they lined up for the relay, Jake and Seth got Bobco's, and everyone else's attention, by cheering for Lars, who wasn't even in the race. Bobco smiled and made an impolite hand gesture. The gun sounded, and the runners took off. The first runner handed the baton to Bobco, who switched on the afterburners and gave his team a comfortable lead. They held the lead until the last runner fumbled the baton transfer. Radford settled for second place behind the Spartans.

With an hour to burn before the hurdle heats began, Jake and Sheri went to the concession stand to grab a couple of ice cream cones. They walked behind the bleachers and leaned against a fence to enjoy their snack. While Jake lapped at his cone, Sheri asked, "So, how many girls have you kissed?"

Jake swallowed. "Oh, bunches."

Sheri's eyes grew large. "Oh, ya. Name them."

"I can't remember them all."

Jake continued sheepishly licking his cone as Sheri picked at her napkin. Sheri squared up to Jake and said, "Kiss me."

"Wha... Really?"

"Ya, go ahead."

He licked his lips. "Hold my cone."

"What do you need your hands for?"

He gave her the cone and placed his hands on her waist. Looking into her sparkling blue eyes, he gently leaned in, following the warmth of her breath until his lips touched hers. Softly, he pressed against her and heard the cones splat on the ground.

Jake pulled away. "Are you all right?"

Sheri exhaled and opened her eyes. "Do it again."

The track teams set the hurdles for the final heat. The air crackled with tension rising from Bobco's fan group as Jake and Sheri took their seats. Master Fuji sat in the front row, projecting an atmosphere of calm, as always. The gun sounded, and the racers left their blocks. Bobco led Lars by a full stride as usual, but Lars usually finished strong. After the second hurdle, Lars gained on Bobco and almost closed the gap as they approached the third hurdle. At the jump, Lars clipped the hurdle and lost a step. Bobco increased his lead. When they came to the final hurdle, Bobco had a quarter step lead and cleared the hurdle just before Lars. As they sprinted to the finish line, Bobco surged forward, beating Lars by a half-second. The Radford crowd cheered wildly. Bobco pointed toward his family and friends holding his hand over his heart.

A few days later, Bobco stopped by the dojo to pick up the hurdle. Master Fuji sat at his desk, reading papers.

Bobco approached Master Fuji and said, "Thanks for the help. I couldn't do it without you."

Master Fuji replied, "You always had it in you, Bobco. Training made you stronger and more determined. Keep working hard. You'll succeed more than you ever dreamed."

The day Jake's mother left, he came home from school to find a note on his desk that read:

The reason I can't stay has nothing to do with you. Your father isn't the person he used to be, and I can't live like this anymore. I understand why you feel your friends are more family than the one you've come to know. I'm sorry about that. I hope one day you can forgive us. Love you, Mom

Jake fought back tears as he prepared for work. He looked out a window and saw the neighbor's young kids trading cards in the driveway. Jake grabbed a box from the top of his closet and placed it on the bed. He took out a few cards and remembered a time when they meant something more to him. When a neighbor gave Jake the box of baseball cards a decade earlier, it took him weeks to organize all seven hundred cards, including complete sets of hard to find vintage collectibles. He closed the box and walked outside.

"Hey guys, Y'all want more cards?"

The kids looked up and nodded and Jake sat down and showed them how the cards were arranged by team and year. After seeing the excitement on their faces, Jake drove to work feeling much better.

When he came home, the house was full of smoke. He ran to the kitchen and removed a burning pot of beans from the stovetop and opened the windows to vent the fumes, Jake threw a blanket over his father, who lay passed out drunk in a papasan chair, and went to bed.

## 20

R umors claimed she put her head on the desk and started shaking, unresponsive for several minutes, and the paramedics took her away. Jake left school and sped to the hospital, but they'd already discharged her. No-one answered at her house, so he scratched out a note and stuck it to the door.

The rest of the day and night, Jake waited to hear something, but no-one returned his calls. The following day, he skipped school and stayed near the phone—still, nothing. As he prepared for work, Jake slipped on the jade ring Sheri gave him and stared at the etching. *Where are you?*

Every time the phone rang at the pizza parlor, he answered, hoping to hear Sheri's voice, but they were just pizza orders. When his shift ended, he raced home and played phone messages. Among others was one from Sheri.

"I guess you heard what happened? My mother took me to Lahaina to recoup. Be back in a few days. Bye."

Jake exhaled and shuffled to the kitchen to get a drink. That's when he saw the note his father tacked to the refrigerator:

Jake, I'm retiring. I'm going to Houston to patch things up with your mother. You can come with me or stay here, but you'll have to find a place to live.

Lyndsey and her boyfriend, Dave, lived in a small house a few miles up the mountain. They kept a travel trailer in the backyard and occasionally let friends use it when they visited.

She told Jake, "I talked to Dave. He said you could stay there if you help mow the lawn and feed the dog."

The trailer was small, but it had a microwave, bunk, and shower. Jake boxed up his room and watched the movers load them for the trip back to Texas. He packed clothes, some personal items, and a few comic books into his car along with his surfboard. He propped the board against the trailer, hung the jump goggles next to the door, and made himself at home.

The dog, Sambo, a black and tan collie Lyndsey rescued from an abusive owner, would lie under the trailer and wait for Jake to return home. Sambo had non-stop energy and liked to play frisbee. He instinctively knew how to jump and catch the flying disc. Sometimes, he'd even spin in mid-air just to show off. Jake brought Sambo to the beach one day, and everyone stopped to watch the acrobatic hound. Before long, Sambo had his fan club taking pictures with the dog. Jake and Seth joked, "Sambo has more girlfriends than we do."

The school year ended just in time for Jake. With all his family problems, his grades slipped, and he barely escaped with passing grades. The doctors changed Sheri's medication. She felt better and regained her strength.

"We don't have to go," Jake said. "I can sell the tickets."

"No way Von Hammer. I'm going to the concert if I have to go alone."

Two hours before the concert, Jake picked up Sheri and met Seth and the gang at the pizza shop. They formed a caravan and headed toward the Honolulu Convention Center, where air buzzed with excitement. As Jake and his friends zig-zagged through the parking lot, the local radio station pumped Journey songs into their speakers. Everyone on Oahu was there, including half the kids from neighboring islands. Inside the convention hall, the loud noise and jammed hallways made it hard to move. Jake grabbed Sheri's hand and weaved through the crowd to get to their seats. They sat down just as the sound-check finished.

Sheri squeezed Jake's hand. "I'm so excited. Thanks for bringing me."

"For a minute there, I thought you were gonna bailout."

"Fat chance, Von Hammer."

It wasn't twenty minutes before the lights dimmed and the band appeared on the stage playing, Just the Same Way. Sheri jumped to her feet and joined the crowd singing every word along with Steve Perry. Beaming lasers, colorful lights, flashing strobes, Sheri sang and danced song after song. When her favorite song, Any Way You Want It, played, Sheri sat down. Jake sat beside her, "Are you all right?"

"I'm okay. Just resting."

A few minutes later, Sheri asked Jake to take her to the restroom. Jake led her up the stairs to the concourse where the line for the ladies' room was short. Jake waited in the hallway, peeking into the show now and then.

He saw girls walk in and out of the restroom, but Sheri remained inside. Jake wondered, *what is taking so long.*

He stopped a girl and gave her a description of Sheri. "Can you check on her, please?

The girl entered the restroom and came back a minute later, "I didn't see her. Maybe she's in a stall and not answering."

"Okay, thanks."

Jake hesitated to enter the ladies' room, but despite the odd looks, he ran inside anyway. He looked under the doors and recognized her shoes in the last stall. Without thinking, he sprung to the top of the booth and straddled the walls scaring other girls who left the bathroom screaming. Sheri lay slumped against the wall. Jake climbed down and tried to wake her, but she remained unconscious. He unlocked the stall door and yelled, "HELP!" and carried her to the middle of the floor. A police officer entered the bathroom.

Jake said, "She's having an epileptic seizure."

The officer called for paramedics, who placed Sheri on a gurney and rolled her to a waiting ambulance. Jake ran to Dr. Pepper and raced to the hospital, begging anyone to tell him how Sheri was doing.

Dr. Taub stepped out and motioned for Jake, "Sheri had a grand mal seizure and suffered a heart attack."

"Can I see her?"

Dr. Taub put his arm around Jake and led him to her room. Sheri was lying in a pitiful state with tubes in her arms and a ventilator strapped to her face. Jake stood beside the bed, looking at her.

*How could something so perfect be so damaged?*

Dr. Taub came into the room, "Jake, we need to let her rest. I put you on the visitor list. You can come back in the morning."

As soon as the sun came up, Jake jumped in his car and darted to the hospital. Sheri sat up when Jake entered the room, carrying a colorful bouquet.

"I'm sorry," She said. "I ruined it for you."

"Ah, ah, no worries. It was almost over anyway." Jake held up a concert shirt, "Got this for you!"

Sheri's eyes lit up, "Oh, my gosh! Thank you!"

Jake draped the shirt over Sheri's hospital gown. She hugged the shirt, "You're the best."

Jake stayed and talked non-stop until the nurses threw him out.

Two weeks later, Sheri was resting on her patio when Jake arrived with some fish tacos. He held up the bag and said, "Fish oil is good for your heart."

Sheri tried to smile. "I'm homeschooling next year. I can't risk having another seizure at school." She looked away to hide her tears. "I don't know what to do anymore. My parents can't help. Doctors can't help. Nothing helps."

Jake placed the bag on the table and sat down. "I don't know what to say. It totally sucks. I wish I could do something."

"I know. I'm just too messed up. I need a miracle."

Jake reached into the bag. "Let's eat. You need your strength. What do you wanna drink?"

"Oh, tea, I guess."

When Jake heard that, he paused, then bit his lip and carried on. "I'll get that for ya."

Afterward, Jake grabbed his board and headed to the beach. Calm wind and flat surf made the bay smooth as glass. He paddled out and spotted a sea turtle gliding below. Legend holds that the sea turtles known as Honu led the first Polynesians to the islands and are navigators of the sea. They travel vast swaths of ocean and somehow return each year to the beaches where they were born. Jake remembered how excited Sheri was the first time she saw one when they were snorkeling. *How ironic is it that the Honu, Sheri's favorite creature, is the symbol of health and longevity, of which she has neither?*

The next day, Jake went for a jog to relieve the tension bubbling-up inside. No matter how fast he ran, he couldn't outrun the questions rifling through his head. *What do I do? What if she gets sick? What if she dies? Will Master Fuji help?*

He found himself running down Sheri's street and knocked

on the door. She answered and looked him up and down, "Ew, you're sweaty."

He stepped into the foyer and whipped around, "We gotta talk."

"You're acting weird. Are you sick?"

"I know, I mean, no, I know. I mean, there's a way I can help, you, I mean."

"What?"

"Sorry. I mean, I can fix your epilepsy, maybe."

"How's that? You barely passed fundamental biology."

He paced around, clutching his head with both hands. "I know It sounds crazy, but there's a magic plant."

"Oh Jake, you're lightheaded." Sheri sighed. "Did you eat too many Lucky Charms."

He turned to her. "No, no, no, listen. It saved my life. Maybe it can work for you?"

"Hmm? It didn't save your brain."

Jake covered his mouth and mumbled, "Oh gosh, how can I convince you." He snapped his fingers. "Your heart just skipped a beat."

"What? How do you know that?"

"My spidey sense detected it."

She laughed. "You must've fallen asleep reading a comic."

"No listen. For a second, you believed me. That's all I'm asking. Just try to believe."

Sheri rolled her head. "I want to believe you. Heck, I'd try anything, even if it kills me."

"That's good—because it might."

"Oh jeez, go home and take a shower. You stink."

When Jake got home, he immediately picked up the phone and dialed Sheri's number. The phone rang half a dozen times before she answered.

Jake said, "So, when do you want to try the magic potion?"

"Oh my gosh, you're losing it."

"Yeah, nah, yeah, maybe. I dunno. I'm nervous."

"Ho-hum, my parents are going to San Diego the week after next. Maybe then."

"Okay, but what if it makes you sick?"

"What?" Sheri asked. "This is your idea. Are you getting scaared?"

"Kinda. I don't know what's gonna happen."

"Are you afraid I'll be able to kick your butt?"

"Um, that'll never happen. I just don't want you to get sick."

"Well, I could have a seizure and die tomorrow."

The day before her parents' trip, Jake crept into the jungle and made his way to the mountain. Free climbing, he paused near the same spot he and Master Fuji rested. A double rainbow looping over the valley caught his attention. *There's a sign. Rainbows are a symbol of transformation, and Sheri, you're about to be transformed.*

Jake reached the top and pulled a plastic bag containing a wet rag from his pocket. He spread the cloth on the ground next to the Wado plant. Jake carefully dug up the plant using a pocket knife, folded the napkin around it, and placed it in a plastic bag. He returned to his car and smashed his forehead against the steering wheel. *What am I doing? Master Fuji is going to kill me. I could put it back... but what about Sheri? I could play dumb, 'huh? I don't know what happened' He'd never believe it? Ah man, I'm so screwed.*

Sheri told her mother, "I'll be fine. Marsha is coming over to stay the weekend. I have all the emergency numbers written down, just in case."

Her mom replied, "When's she going to be here?"

"Soon. Go ahead. I'm okay."

"Are you sure?"

"Ya, go ahead. I'm fine. You don't want to miss your plane."

"All right, but keep the phone close by."

Sheri held up the phone. "Got it. Have a good trip."

When her parents drove away, she called Jake. "Hey Merlin, bring on your magic potion."

Jake arrived a half-hour later and pulled the plastic bag from his pocket. He removed the Wado plant and placed it on the kitchen counter. Sheri came over, and they hovered over it.

Sheri said, "Doesn't look magical to me."

"Kinda ugly, huh?"

"Looks like rotten spinach."

Sheri followed Jake into the living room, where he asked her to recline in a chair. His hands trembled as he used his pocket knife to cut away the root's thick covering. Jake squeezed the yellowish squash like pulp until a drop of nectar formed. Sheri tilted her head back and squeezed her eyes shut. Jake dripped juice into her nostrils, then put his mouth over her nose and blew. The syrup shot down her throat. She coughed, gagging on the bitter goop, and sat up. "Ugh... That's so gross!"

Jake replied, "That bad?"

"It's awful. This better work, or I'm gonna kill you."

"Um, you and Master Fuji."

"Get me some water."

Jake handed her a glass and said, "Soon, you'll be dodging bullets and leaping tall buildings in a single bound."

Sheri rolled her eyes and laid back in the chair. Jake wiped down the counters, checked his watch, swept the floors, checked his watch, emptied the dishwasher, bagged the trash, and stared at the clock.

Sheri said, "Will you stop it? You're driving me crazy!"

He asked, "Anything yet?"

"No!. Just a gawd awful taste in my mouth and burn in my throat."

She hopped up. "I'm going to brush my teeth."

Sheri returned and reclined in the chair, staring at the ceiling with such intensity Jake thought she'd burn a hole through it.

Ten minutes passed before she sat up and burped. She stood and walked a few steps, holding her stomach, then doubled over with cramps. Jake helped her to the couch, where she started to puke. Jake grabbed the closest container, a bowl of chips, and held it under her to catch the vomit. He set the bowl down and offered her some water.

"Ugh," she pushed it away. "Get that outta my face."

She palmed her forehead and laid down. "I feel dizzy."

Jake covered her with a blanket. *Gosh, I hope I didn't give her too much.*

He tried to lighten the mood by reading articles from a glamour magazine he found on the table. As he talked, Sheri drifted off. Exhausted himself, he laid his head next to her and fell asleep, dreaming they were walking on the beach with turtles hatching all around. Sheri named each one as they scuttled toward the sea.

At sunrise, the dogs barked and woke Jake up. He turned to Sheri, but she was still asleep, so he got up and fed the hounds. He gathered items from the bathroom and returned with a warm washrag, and wiped away her sweat. Using lip balm, he painted her dry lips and brushed her hair back. Every time he checked Sheri's pulse, it seemed weaker and slower than before. Her breathing slowed to nothing, and Jake gently shook her, trying to wake her.

"Sheri, wake up, please... c'mon, Sheri! Please wake up. Come on, girl, wake up!"

She laid there unresponsive while Jake paced the floor holding his head in his hands.

"God, don't take her. Please. Don't let her die. Take me."

By afternoon, Sheri hadn't moved, her skin turned pale, and her hands were cold. Jake collapsed to the floor, shaking.

"I'm sorry, so sorry... I didn't know. I swear I didn't know. I'm so sorry..."

After some time, he picked himself off the floor and stumbled into the kitchen.

Shaking, he leaned against the counter. *I gotta call someone.*

## 21

Jake wiped his face dry and picked up the phone. When Master Fuji answered, he told him what they'd done. Master Fuji came right away, and Jake showed him where Sheri was lying. Master Fuji sat on the edge of the couch and touched her cheek, squeezed her arm, and listened to her heart. He shook his head and pulled the cover over her shoulders. He sat for a long minute, looking at Sheri.

"She's not dead."

Jake perked up, "She's not dead!"

"She's in a coma."

"Is she gonna be okay?"

"I didn't say that. I don't know. The coma should last a day or two."

"Should we take her to the hospital?"

"They can't help her. She has to process the poison if she can."

"What can I do to help?"

"Talk to her."

"She can hear?"

"I believe so. In any case, it won't hurt."

Master Fuji picked up her hand and rubbed it, "Keep her warm. Move her arms and feet, so she knows she's here. Girls mature faster than boys. Hopefully, her hormones will pull her through. What you did was stupid. Take care of her and pray a lot." He gave Jake some tea. "When she wakes up, give her this to drink."

Jake thanked Master Fuji and walked him out. He locked the door and sat next to Sheri and massaged her feet, told her corny jokes, and sang her silly songs. "Sheri, you're gonna be a doctor... if you don't sleep too long. If you don't wake-up, you'll miss college. I'm gonna eat all the cheesecake..."

Sheri slept the rest of the day and woke early Sunday morning. She placed her arm across her forehead, "Oh my head... How long have I been sleeping?"

Jake perked up, "Almost two days. Thank God you're awake. How ya feelin'?"

"Like roadkill."

"I one it, you two it..."

"What're you talking about?"

"Nevermind. Have some Fuji tea. It'll make you feel better."

He poured her a cup and prepared a light breakfast. A rosy glow returned to her cheeks as Jake sat down and watched Sheri devour her eggs.

She said, "Are you going to eat that?" and reached across the table, stabbing Jake's bacon and stuffed it in her mouth, and commenced to finish off his plate."

Jake looked at her and said, "I'm gonna call you, chipmunk."

"Shut up. I'm so hungry."

Jake smiled. "Want some chips?"

When the food was gone, Sheri left to take a shower. Jake placed the rest of the Wado plant in a small pink accessory box he found in a junk drawer. Then, as brats do, he spit-shined the entire house leaving nothing that might give them away.

Sheri and Jake were sitting by the pool when her parents got home. It surprised her mother to see Jake, and she asked, "What have you two been up to?"

Sheri said, "Marsha had to leave early, and I wasn't feeling well, so Jake brought some tea."

Her mother replied, "We have tea."

"This is better. It's a special Okinawan blend."

"Hmm... Maybe I should have a cup?"

When Jake saw Sheri doing better, he left, taking the tea and the rest of the Wado plant. He cruised home and slept for the rest of the day.

The next evening, Jake dropped in to check on Sheri before heading to work. With a sheepish grin, he said, "You look much better!"

Sheri smiled. "You've seen me at my worst, and you're still not scared away. What do I have to do to get rid of you, JVH?"

"It's not easy. Small island, you know."

A few days later, Jake went to the dojo and swept the floor, trying to think of a way to apologize. Jake heard Master Fuji's truck arrive, and the door slammed shut. Swallowing the lump in his throat, Jake waited for his punishment. Master Fuji walked into the dojo and motioned Jake over. He leaned the broom against the wall and walked over to Master Fuji, avoiding eye contact.

Jake said, "I messed up... I'm really sorry... I'll do whatever I can to repay you. I left what was left of the plant in the refrigerator."

Master Fuji replied, "How is Sheri?"

"She's doing better today."

"Jake, I know how you feel about Sheri. I know you were trying to help her. I might have done the same thing if I was you."

Jake looked up, "So, you're not mad?"

"I'm disappointed, but I'm happy Sheri is okay."

"I'll do whatever you need. I want to repay you."

"We need to take a trip to Okinawa soon. Make sure Sheri tells no one about the Wado. Do you understand?"

"Yes, Master Fuji, I understand."

## 22

Over the next few weeks, Sheri got stronger and joined Jake on an easy hike to majestic Manoa Waterfall. They rested on rocks near the falls, and Jake pulled two water bottles from his backpack. He handed one to Sheri and said, "How ya feeling?"

She removed the cap from the bottle, "Great," took a drink and swallowed, "Enjoying the hike."

"Maybe the Wado is working?"

"I had a small seizure last week... it didn't last long."

"Dang, I hoped it would work."

"I know, but, thanks for trying." She recapped her drink, "By the way, I got my transcripts. I'll be graduating in December."

"Wow! That's great. I have to take a quick trip with Master Fuji, but I'll be back before school starts."

"Safe travels."

A few days before his senior year started, Jake and Master Fuji prepared to board a C-5 Galaxy transport aircraft for a ten-hour flight to Okinawa. It excited Jake because he'd never been to Okinawa or been in a Galaxy aircraft. As they climbed the ramp, Jake rolled his head around to scan the cavernous airplane and remarked, "It's bigger than the Astrodome."

While Master Fuji placed Ratcom in a special animal transport carrier, a crewman handed Jake a pair of earplugs and a blanket. "You'll need these."

The crew loaded the last of the cargo pallets and closed the massive rear door. Jake and Master Fuji took their backward facing seats. As the four enormous turbo-fan engines powered up, an ear-piercing whine filled the cabin, and the C-5 crept forward. Jake scrambled to insert the earplugs and jokingly flashed hand signs at Master Fuji. Master Fuji signed back.

Jake yelled, "I don't really know sign language."

Master Fuji signed, 'I know,' by touching his fingertips to his forehead."

*Jeesh, is there any language Fuji doesn't know?*

A thunderous clamor shook the aircraft as it gained speed and lifted off the flight line. With no windows to look out, Jake pulled a magazine from his bag and started reading. Halfway through the flight Jake wrapped the blanket around his freezing legs. A crewman handed him a MRE (meals ready to eat) complete with canned water. Jake squeezed chicken paste onto a cracker and took a bite. As the full essence of the paste expanded through his mouth, Jake's face twisted and contorted.

Master Fuji laughed, "You gotta be pretty hungry to eat that one."

After the most uncomfortable flight Jake could remember, the plane landed at Kadena Air Base in Okinawa at 3:00 am local time. Master Fuji and Jake grabbed an early morning bite at the mess hall before driving to the city of Naha, where Master Fuji kept a small home. Jake put Ratcom in cages and trudged off to bed.

Suffering extreme jet lag, he slept until afternoon. Jake fed Ratcom a snack and rode with Master Fuji to one of his favorite restaurants. Unable to read the menu, Jake pointed to a picture, "I'll have one of those."

"Would you like the snail raw or boiled?"

"Um, nevermind. Just order me something American, please."

"How about a burger?"

"Cha-Ching!"

Needing groceries, they walked to the public market where food vendors and clothing boutiques clogged the street. Steam and cooking aromas wafted into the walking areas inviting visitors to sample a smorgasbord of edible delights. Jake stopped to gaze at a pig's head hanging over a display when a vendor reached out and offered him a taste.

He responded, "Thanks," and popped it into his mouth. "Wow, this is good. What is it?"

The shopkeeper smiled. "Mimiga."

Jake had a puzzled look on his face, so Master Fuji translated, "Pig ears."

Jake's jaw dropped. *Oh my gosh, I ate a dog treat.* He grabbed his throat and with a grovely voice he said, "Soda, soda?"

Later that evening, Master Fuji told Jake, "We can take advantage of jet lag and do some Wado maintenance tonight."

"I'm game."

They drove to the southern coast and hiked several miles along the cliffs. When they reached the mountain, Master Fuji said, "Focus on what's in front of you."

Jake followed Master Fuji up the cliff face and stopped on the ledge. Master Fuji peered out to sea, "I stop here every time. I like the view."

"Ya, it's pretty... dark."

They climbed higher until they reached an outcropping. Master Fuji pointed, "This is where we have to jump up to the next ledge." Master Fuji jumped, caught the ledge, and pulled himself up. As Jake worked into position and prepared to jump, he looked down and said, "So, this is how it ends?"

"It's not as hard as it looks," Master Fuji replied. "Have faith."

Jake focused on the small ridge and sprung, snagging the rim one-handed, and dangled there looking out to the sea. He swung side to side and threw his leg over the top, and climbed onto the ridge.

Master Fuji said, "That was different."

Jake shrugged. "What?"

Master Fuji led Jake through the tunnel and stopped. He stood motionless for several seconds before collapsing to his knees.

Jake leaned over and said, "What's wrong?"

Master Fuji didn't respond. Jake knelt beside him, "Are you having a heart attack? I know CPR."

Motionless, Master Fuji sat with his mouth agape.

"Okay, breathe slowly," Jake said reassuringly.

"The Wado," Master Fuji said. "It's gone!"

"What? Where did it go?"

"I don't know. It's gone."

"No biggie, we'll find another?"

"Oh, Jake, you don't understand."

Jake stood and walked toward the empty plot. "Maybe, we can find a seed or something?"

"You don't get it, Jake."

Master Fuji took a few minutes to gather himself before he led Jake back across the cliff face. He didn't speak a word the entire way home. Jake slogged off to bed and lay there, tossing and turning till morning. By the time Master Fuji came out of his room, Jake had eaten half a box of cereal.

Master Fuji said, "How are you this morning?"

"Meh, couldn't sleep."

"It didn't affect your appetite."

"Ho no, I'm feeling lucky." Jake lifted his spoon, "Look, green clovers."

Master Fuji smiled. "Let's hope so."

After breakfast, they walked a few blocks to a narrow alley leading to a blue door. Master Fuji knocked two, then three times, and waited. A minute later, a deadbolt slide broke the silence, and slowly, the door opened.

Master Fuji said, "Remove your shoes."

They stepped inside, and Jake saw an old man with thick white brows and a Fu Manchu-style mustache. Deep long wrinkles, rutting his face, gave him a serious scowl that unnerved Jake.

Master Fuji said, "Jake, this is Grandmaster Matsumura."

Jake stared for a second, "Nice to meet you, sir," and bowed.

Grandmaster said, "Hello, Jake-san. Nice to meet you too. Master Fujioka taught you well."

Jake grinned. "Yes sir. Thank you, Grandmaster."

Master Fuji turned to Jake and said, "Grandmaster and I have some matters to discuss. Make yourself at home. Try not to break anything."

They entered the office and closed the door while Jake snooped around. No bags, training dummies, or weights, just a makiwara and a bo leaning against the far wall. Jake grabbed the sturdy old bo and spun it around. He liked the weight, and the octagon shape allowed for a tighter grip.

Meanwhile, in the other room, Master Fuji speaking in Okinawan, "Grandmaster, I have terrible news. The Wado is missing."

Grandmaster replied, "How?"

"Someone dug it up."

"Find them."

"Yes, Grandmaster."

Master Fuji returned to the dojo where Jake was moving in a

full-blown blaze. Jake saw Master Fuji and halted. Master Fuji said, "I must leave for a few hours. Can you wait here?"

Jake's face twisted up.

Master Fuji said, "If you ask kindly, Grandmaster might teach you how to use that."

Jake grinned. "Okay, bring me back some tacos," and continued swinging the staff.

Twenty minutes later, Grandmaster walked into the dojo where Jake was hanging from the stretching bar. When he saw Grandmaster, he tried to untangle himself and fell awkwardly to the floor. Jake popped up and bowed. His face turned cherry red.

Grandmaster smiled and motioned. "Jake-san, come sit with me."

Kneeling in the traditional seiza position, Grandmaster peered at Jake with penetrating eyes. Jake turned away, glancing down at Grandmaster's hands. Swollen knuckles covered with thick leathery callouses gave his hands a permanent cup.

"How are you, Jake?"

"I'm fine, Grandmaster."

"You are quiet. What are you thinking about?"

Jake raised his eyes. "Worried I guess."

Grandmaster smiled, "You needn't worry. Come, I'll show you."

Jake followed Grandmaster into an office filled with bookshelves and pictures. Pointing to a photo, Grandmaster said, "This is Master Fujioka after winning the All Asian Kumite. One of my best students."

The phone rang, and Grandmaster said, "Excuse me, I have to answer that."

Jake wandered around the office, looking at pictures. When Grandmaster finished his phone conversation, he found Jake looking at an old sword mounted to the wall. Grandmaster removed the blade and handed it to Jake, "My sensei gave me this many years ago."

Jake held the sword. "Wow, it's heavy."

Pulling the blade from the scabbard, he noticed the cutting edge. *That's weird.*

"Do you know how to use it?" Grandmaster asked.

"I'm learning."

"Show me."

Jake walked to the center of the dojo floor and attached the scabbard to his belt. He bowed and performed his tournament kata the way Master Fuji taught it to him.

"Well done, Jake-san."

"Thank you, Grandmaster."

"Do you have questions?"

Jake replied, "Yes..."

Grandmaster lifted a brow prompting Jake to finish his thought.

Jake said, "Am I the only Hābu-Té?"

"There have been others."

"Who?"

"I can't say."

"Where did the Wado come from?"

"A sailor named Annan brought it here. He lived in a cave near the sea."

"Did he teach karate?"

"No, he was an expert in Chinese Boxing. However, he did teach a kata called Chintō. I will teach it to you the way I was taught."

With surprising power and speed, Grandmaster performed the kata in the original Annan manner. Afterward, Jake said, "I've seen Master Fujioka do that one, but he called it Gakuku or something."

Grandmaster replied, "Ah, yes. Gankaku, that's what the Shotokan practitioners call it."

Jake spent the rest of the morning practicing the kata the way Grandmaster taught him.

Meanwhile, Master Fuji traveled to the town of Tomigusuku and met with his trusted friend Hiro.

Hiro said, "Your old buddy, Neiko, is floating around Naha, living quite miserably."

"Thank you," Master Fuji replied, "Next time we'll visit longer."

Neiko's unkempt lawn and boarded-up windows told Master Fuji he wasn't there. Master Fuji wanted to avoid Neiko's sister, but he had no choice because he was desperate for information. He knocked on the door and waited for Mieko to answer, kind of hoping she wouldn't. The last time he saw her, she cried, but he had a plane to catch, and she wouldn't go with him.

The doorknob clicked, and the door opened. A slender figure with silky black hair wearing a flowery blouse stared back at him. The sight of her made Master Fuji stuck for words. She smiled, breaking the awkward standoff. "Well, Teruo, what a surprise! It's been too long."

"Yes, it has."

She stepped aside. "Would you like to come in?"

"Oh, yes, thank you. I would like that."

Leading him to a nicely furnished room, she said, "It's such a surprise to see you. Please, make yourself at home. I'll get some tea."

Master Fuji sat on the edge of the couch with his hands clasped in front. Meiko entered carrying a tea tray and set it on the table. She offered a cup to Master Fuji and placed the tray on the coffee table.

Meiko picked up her cup and stirred. "What brings you to Naha?"

"I was hoping to speak to Neiko. Do you know where I might find him?"

"I can't say. He's binging again. I haven't seen him for several months."

"That's disappointing to hear..." Master Fuji took a sip of tea. "Are you alright? Still teaching?"

"Yes, thanks for asking. I'm teaching at the college and have many talented students."

"They're in good hands."

"Awe, thanks, and you? Are you still saving the World?"

"Doing our best. "Master Fuji takes another sip and swallows. "Thank you for the tea. I wish I could stay."

"Still using that line?"

Master Fuji dropped his head and cracked a half-smile. "You know how to contact me if you need anything."

"And, you know where to find me."

Master Fuji placed the cup on the tray. "Thanks again." He walked toward the door, turned, and said, "Good to see you again."

Meiko replied, "You too," and closed the door behind him.

After speaking to Meiko, Master Fuji had a good idea of where to find Neiko. He made his way to the port area where bars operated illegal gambling rooms. A bartender told him Neiko frequented the pub at the end of the dock. As he entered the club, Master Fuji went blind in the dim light. As his eyes adjusted, he scanned the faces of the patrons and locked eyes on Neiko.

Neiko pointed. "Look what the tide washed in."

Master Fuji replied, "I knew you'd be lurking around here somewhere."

Neiko stood and motioned toward Master Fuji. "Hey everyone, this is the great Master Fujioka. The best fighter in all of Naha. Five-thousand yen says he can take all of you!"

Master Fuji understood what Neiko was doing, but several men stood up before he could say anything, and the largest stepped forward aggressively. Master Fuji raised his hand and said, "I'm just here to talk to Neiko."

The large male slammed his fist into a table and moved toward Master Fuji, lifting his arm over his head to strike. Master Fuji deflected the hammer fist and hit him with a straight punch in the solar plexus knocking his breath out. Just then, another man attacked, grabbing Master Fuji by the shirt and punching. Master Fuji locked up the man's arms and flipped him onto an empty table. Two other men came at Master Fuji. He kicked one into the other, knocking both to the floor. Neiko tried to run during the scuffle, but Master Fuji found him hiding behind a curtain in the pub's corner. He dragged Neiko into the parking lot and held him against a wall, twisting his arm behind him, "I'll break your arm if you keep fighting. What did you do with the Wado Neiko?"

"What... what d'you mean?"

"Don't lie to me, Neiko!" Master Fuji bent his arm farther.

"Kay, Okay... I didn't mean it. I didn't want to."

"What did you do, Neiko?"

"I had to pay my debts."

"To who?"

"To whoever. What does it matter?"

"Do you realize what you've done!"

"I'm sorry, Teruo, so sorry..."

"Tell it to Grandmaster."

When Master Fuji returned to the dojo, Jake was still practicing the Channan kata. Master Fuji and Grandmaster walked into the office and shut the door.

Grandmaster Matsumura said, "Teruo, what did you find?"

Master Fuji replied, "It was Neiko."

"That's unfortunate. Take Jake-san to the castle. I'll deal with Neiko."

Master Fuji took Jake to the Shureimon Castle. As they walked through the gate, Master Fuji explained, "The original castle was built in the 16th century and destroyed in the Battle for Okinawa during World War Two. In 1950, they rebuilt the gate and the castle." Inside the museum, Jake saw pictures of the castle before its destruction and detailed reconstruction photos.

Meanwhile, nervous Neiko prepared a departure. He packed a small bag of essential items and headed to the airport to catch a plane destined for Buenos Aires, where all wayward spies hide. While waiting to board his flight, a man sat beside him and dropped a small black stone in his lap. Neiko looked down at the rock, and his aspirations of life on the lam fluttered away. When you join the OTé, you give the Grandmaster a stone. When the Grandmaster returns your stone, you're presumed dead.

The associate took Nieko to the dojo, where Grandmaster greeted him, "Neiko, you've been busy."

"It's not like that. I can explain."

"Yes, Neiko, tell me everything."

"I got into trouble. I ran up a huge debt, and they threatened to harm my family."

"Who?"

"The Hong Kong syndicate."

"Name?"

Neiko clutched his chest. "I don't know."

"You've done irreparable harm."

Clasping his hands together, Neiko said, "I'm sorry. I'll make it up to you. I promise. Please!"

"You don't belong here."

"Please, Grandmaster, please!"

"Run, Neiko, run."

The following day, Master Fuji let Jake sleep late and traveled to the dojo to speak to Grandmaster. He found Grandmaster sitting alone, sat beside him, and asked, "Grandmaster, what did Neiko say?"

"Do not speak his name again."

"I'll find it."

"It's gone, Teruo."

"I can retrace the steps?"

"Two hundred-year-old footprints?."

"Let me try."

"If you must, take Jake-san."

"He's only seventeen."

"He's Hābu-Té. Tell him the truth."

"What about you?"

"I'm old, Teruo, My Sun sets—Jake's star rises."

Master Fuji drove home and found Jake sitting Indian style on the garage floor with Griffiss and Travis.

Jake said, "Watch, Travis thinks he's Willie Mays."

He threw a piece, and Travis caught it on the run. Jake pointed, "Did you see that?"

Master Fuji said, "Yes, that's impressive. Where's Elm?"

"Dunno. She doesn't play ball."

Master Fuji turned a metal chair around and straddled it, resting his elbows on the back.

"We need to talk."

Jake threw Griffiss a piece. "I'm listening."

"I'm going to China to find another Wado plant."

"Cool, sounds like fun." Jake tosses Travis another kernel. "But, why can't you just get one from your friends?"

"Because I had the only plant... Don't think it's gettin' bigger."

Jake sinks. "Oh, ya... Sorry."

"I'm sending you home. I'll be back in a week or two."

"Why go through all the trouble? Do ya really need it?"

"No, you do."

Jake's head pops back. "What do I need it for?" And, pushes another handful of popcorn into his mouth.

"So you don't go into a coma."

Jake's eyes grow big, and his head swivels toward Master Fuji. "Huh?" As pieces of popcorn eject from his mouth. "What? I'm going into coma?"

"No, not if I can find another Wado."

"Oh god... I'm gonna die!"

"When's the last time you drank the tea?"

"I dunno, a month ago, why?"

"How do you feel?"

"Okay, I guess."

"You should be okay for awhile. As you get older, you'll need it more often. Grandmaster drinks a cup almost every day."

"Grandmaster is Hābu-Té?"

"Yes."

"Oh, no!" Jake brings his hand to his face. "Am I gonna look like Grandmaster? ...Oh gosh, I'm gonna be sick!"

Master Fuji left to allow Jake time to absorb the situation.

*This can't be happening. No way, Moms gonna trip. it's gotta be a mistake. I can't believe it. Gee wiz, what have I been working for? ...Oh my god, what's gonna happen to Sheri? What's she gonna do? This is the worst. Unbelievable!*

Griffiss climbed into Jake's lap and rolled onto his back. While scratching his chest, Jake's shock gave way to numbness. "You know Griff; it's all been a lie. That dang cobra is gonna win after all. Just kill me—I'm dead." Griffiss wriggled deeper into the crook of Jake's lap. "Sometimes I think you're the only one who understands, but what can I do? What would you do? Man... wish I could talk to Ryan. What d'ya think he'd say? ...oh, I see him now, chin up, chest out, 'SUCK IT UP GOOBS! Whatta you gonna do, QUIT? Is that what The Fuge taught ya? Don't be a LOSER—KEEP SWINGIN'—YA MIGHT HIT SOMETHIN'"

Jake wiped the corner of his eye. "He's right, ya know... he's always right."

Griffiss snored. Jake lifted a brow and looked down at him. "Griff, you're a genius!"

Jake picked up Griffiss's four-pound mass and placed him in his cage, where he rolled into a ball and continued sleeping. Entering the kitchen, Jake found Master Fuji at the table leaning over a map. He stopped at the door and said firmly, "Sir, I'm going with you."

Master Fuji removed his glasses and looked at Jake. "I understand how you feel, but it's dangerous. We might not make it back."

"Well, then it won't matter, anyway—I'll be toast just the same." Jake snorted. "Besides, how are you gonna find it if you can't smell it?"

"Elm and I can manage."

Jake bristled. "It's my life. I don't wanna die here doin' nothin'."

Master Fuji rubbed the back of his neck and said, "Grandmaster said you should go."

"I'm excited!" Jake replied.

"You could miss a few days of school."

"I'm really excited!"

# 23

————

Master Fuji took Jake to a warehouse where they met with a counterfeiter. They posed for headshots, and the man created fake travel documents for them. Jake looked at his passport and said, "Who is Binh?"

"That's your name. Remember it."

"Binh?"

"C'mon," Master Fuji said. "We need to go shopping."

"Ah, Binh loves to shop."

They drove a few blocks and stopped at a resale store.

Walking in, Jake asked, "What are we doing here?"

"Looking for clothes. You can't wear Levis in China."

Jake's eyebrows lifted. "We're really going undercover, huh?" He posed. "Can Binh wear a kung fu uniform?"

"Sure, if Binh wants to wear a prison uniform."

"Oh, nevermind. Binh waits for your recommendation."

Master Fuji pulled some clothes from a rack and handed them to Jake.

"Here, try these on."

Jake walked out of the dressing room wearing a loose-fitting grey Tang suit with knot buttons and a mandarin collar. "Now, I feel like a real-life spy."

After dinner, Jake packed seeds and fruit into his bag for the two-day trip to China. They herded Ratcom into a shoulder satchel and gave them cardboard to pacify them during the taxi ride to the docks. A light rain fell as they climbed the gangway of a cargo ship, making final preparations to depart. They followed a crew member through a tight passageway to a berthing compartment where he showed them their bunks. Jake looked at his tiny bed and remarked, "Do you have this in California king?"

The crewman leered at Jake and pointed at the deck. Jake thought, *Lucky me, two joyful days with Grumpzilla.* Master Fuji unfolded a portable cage and directed Ratcom inside while Jake prepped the seed dish.

An hour later, the rain subsided, and the ship slipped its mooring lines. As a tugboat guided the vessel to open water, Jake climbed the ladder leading to the main deck and leaned against the gunnel. A brisk breeze blew as the ship's giant propellers started churning and the tug cast off. The shore lights faded away, and the Moon ducked behind swift-moving clouds. Something caught Jake's eye, and he turned to see a beam of eerie green light bending from the clouds to the sea. Seconds later, the lunar rainbow disappeared. *Woe, why does that feel like an omen?*

Rain chased the freighter all the way to China and poured steadily when the ship entered the Quanzhou Approaches along the southern coast. Master Fuji and Jake gathered Ratcom and their belongings and prepared to disembark. A crewman lowered the gangway, and a small sampan boat came alongside. Master Fuji and Jake scampered down the ladder and boarded the craft seeking shelter in the cabin. The sampan joined a flotilla of other fishing boats headed into Quanzhou Bay.

After several hours, the little boat headed up the Jinjiang River and docked in a small marina. Within minutes a pair of Chinese police officers boarded the boat and demanded documents from the crew. Master Fuji peeked out the window and waved off Jake, signaling him to stay put.

Master Fuji went topside as Jake ducked into a corner and threw a blanket over his head. The inspectors poked around the upper deck and grew suspicious, questioning Master Fuji. Unable to understand what was being said, Jake became scared when one officer raised his voice. Master Fuji remained calm and gave the inspectors the documents they wanted. One officer entered the cabin and looked around, jabbing the blanket with his baton. He hit something squishy and became suspicious. He reached down and ripped away the blanket and found a bag of rice. The officers left, and Jake crawled out of the engine compartment. "Whew, that was close!"

They took a taxi to a hotel, just a block from the Shaolin Temple. After a sleepless night, Jake woke early and peeked out the window. A group of people gathered in a square across from the hotel were doing temple exercises.

Jake said, "Look, Master Fuji, just like Master Lanh."

"Close the curtain. Eyes are everywhere. We don't want to arouse suspicion."

Jake and Master Fuji gathered their Ratcom and walked to the temple.

Entering the main chamber, Master Fuji said, "Do as I do."

"Aye, aye, mon Capitan."

They remained in the rear of the prayer room where Master Fuji pulled the ultrasonic whistle from his shirt pocket and blew it. Elm climbed out of the pouch onto Master Fuji's shoulder. He gave her a sunflower seed, placed her on the floor, and blew a short sequence of commands, and she hurried away.

"Where's she going?" Jake asked.

"Searching for Wado. If she finds it, she'll bring back a piece. Do you smell your cereal?"

"All I can smell is incense. Do you think they have food here?"

"Nothing you'd like."

"Oh um, ...can I get some sunflower seeds?"

When the monks returned from their morning walk, Master Fuji approached and offered a gift. The monks graciously accepted the tea, and Master Fuji, speaking in Mandarin, said, "May I speak to the abbot?"

They took master Fuji and Jake to a small room where he and Jake waited to talk to the leader. Twenty minutes passed before three monks entered the room and exchanged greetings.

Master Fuji said, "We're searching for information on a man named Channan who visited this temple two hundred years ago. Do you know of him?"

"I'm afraid not," the Abbot replied. "You might find the information you seek in the old logs. You're welcome to look through them if you wish."

Master Fuji and Jake followed the monks to the room where two hundred-year-old texts were stored. Unable to read Chinese, Jake played with Griffiss and nibbled on sunflower seeds. After an hour of skimming pages, Master Fuji ran across a reference to an herbalist from Wuyishan, an expert in Chuan fa. Master Fuji and Jake left the library and returned to the main prayer room. Master Fuji blew his whistle three times and waited. Elm returned without Wado and crawled back into the bag. Jake said, "What now?"

"Looks like we're going to Wuyishan."

"Where's that?"

"Three hundred miles northeast."

"Sheesh, can we grab some grub?"

"Yes, but first, we need a cover for your hair."

They walked a block and ducked into a store where Master Fuji spotted a conical rice hat. "Try this one."

Jake's eyes sparkled. "A hat for Binh."

"It's called a dǒulì."

Jake placed it on his head and posed. "Me like."

Passing a slurry of street vendors, Jake said, "I want General Tso's Chicken."

Master Fuji replied, "Bù hǎo."

Jake's brow furled. "Poo how?"

"It means not good, in Chinese."

"Doesn't sound good in English either."

"General Tso's chicken is American, not Chinese."

"Oh. How 'bout Orange Chicken?"

"How 'bout dumplings and veggie rolls?"

"Oh, poo."

Master Fuji paid for the food and steered Jake back to the hotel to eat while Ratcom stretched their legs. When they finished, Jake packed their bags while Master Fuji checked out of the hotel. Avoiding the main roads, they walked to the rail station and bought tickets for the five-hour train ride to Wuyishan. Jake settled into his window seat and gazed out the window.

He turned to Master Fuji, "What's war sickness?"

"It's a term for people suffering from stress anxiety. When someone goes through a traumatic event, they can experience flashbacks and nightmares."

"Does it ever go away?"

"With therapy, you can learn to cope. Why do you ask?"

"Ryan said my dad has it."

"He had a rough go in Vietnam."

"What happened?"

"It's classified. Let's just say he probably sleeps with his eyes wide open."

The Unreal Adventures of Jake Von Hammer

Jake rubbed his cheek. "I believe that."

The train chugged seven hours, winding through mountains, over rivers, and through tunnels, reaching Wuyishan City in the early evening. Master Fuji and Jake left the station and walked through town to find a Chinese medicine store. Master Fuji described the Wado plant to the apothecary.

The owner replied, "I'm not familiar with any plants like that, but an herbalist named Ling who lives in the valley might." He grabbed a map from the shelf and marked the location. "She lives here."

Master Fuji thanked the man and bought the map. He and Jake left Ratcom in a hotel room and spent the rest of the evening collecting supplies for the long trip ahead. The next morning, they ate breakfast and headed out. Following the map given to them by the medicine man, they traveled by taxi through the Wuyi Mountains. Tucked into a bend along the Jiuqu River, they found a wood and stone dwelling with meticulously manicured grounds.

"This looks like the place," Master Fuji said.

He opened the gate and rang the bell. A tiny woman speaking Mandarin greeted them. "Can I help you?"

"We're looking for Ms. Ling."

"I am she. How can I help?"

Master Fuji pulled a paper from his pocket and showed her a drawing. "We're looking for an herb like this. Have you seen it?"

Ms. Ling squinted at the picture. "I need my glasses. Come inside."

She put on her glasses and studied the picture. "I've not seen a plant like this, but sometimes I receive ground and partial plants in trade. Look in here."

They followed her to a room containing a table full of jars filled with seeds, leaves, and powders. She removed the lids of several jars until the aroma of Froot Loops caught Jake's attention. He piped up, "That one."

Ms. Ling handed the jar to Master Fuji, who dumped a small hardened piece into his palm.

He rolled it around. "Root." He looked at Ms. Ling, "Where did you get this?"

Ms. Ling replied, "A man picked it on Forbidden Mountain many, many years ago."

He unfolded a map. "Can you show me where?"

She touched her forehead.

"Been a long time." She pointed to a spot upriver. "I think here... You should not go there—bad spirits."

Master Fuji bought the Wado along with a few other herbs and tucked them into his hiking bag.

"Thank you, Ms. Ling. We will be on our way now."

The taxi took them through mountain roads until the car could no longer pass. Master Fuji paid the driver and sent him on his way.

Jake said, "I never thought China would look like this. It's unreal, like a fictional world."

"This area is one of the most biodiverse regions on Earth. There are plants and animals here not found anywhere else. It's not surprising the Wado comes from here."

Master Fuji pointed to Jake's feet. "Watch your step. Lots of venomous snakes here."

"Oh, now you say."

Walking along the bank of Jiuqu Xi river, they found an abandoned canoe. Master Fuji pushed it into the water and rocked it. "Looks seaworthy. This will save us a lot of time. Climb in."

They paddled upstream against the lazy river current.

Jake said, "All this work is making me hungry."

He dug through the backpacks and found a bag of beef jerky.

He bit down on a piece and ripped off a chunk, and started chewing.

He turned facing Master Fuji and said, "How high can Grandmaster jump?"

Master Fuji continued paddling. "Don't know. Why?"

"Isn't he like me?"

"Yes, and no. They gave Grandmaster Wado when he became sick with cholera. The Wado tends to counter whatever ails you. Cholera is a bacterial infection, and Grandmaster developed a powerful immune system—he never gets sick. He's a skilled martial artist because he's lived a long time and practices a lot."

"What about me?"

"Cobra venom is different. It's a neurotoxin that affects the central nervous system. The nervous system controls every aspect of movement, senses, and awareness. That's why you have quick reflexes, strong senses, and who knows? Your perception may be unlimited."

At dusk, they searched for a campsite and pulled the canoe onto the bank. While Master Fuji prepared a simple meal of herbs and noodles, Jake gathered wood and started a campfire. While the noodles warmed, Master Fuji opened a bag of rice cakes and gave one to Jake. Jake chewed slowly and tried to feed a piece to Griffiss.

Master Fuji said, "I thought you were hungry?"

"Ya well, Rice cakes aren't my favorite. Look, even Griff won't eat it."

"Do you know how to fish?"

Jake stood. "Aye, Binh loves to fish."

Using a technique he learned in Texas, Jake spooled a line around a soup can and baited the hook with a bit of rice cake. *I don't know if this is gonna work.* He slung the hook into the water, letting the line slip off the end of the can. A few minutes later, he felt a nibble and hooked a small panfish.

He held it up. "Sunfish eat rice cake."

In a short time, he caught several more until Master Fuji said, "That's enough," and pulled out a knife and started cleaning. "We'll cook them all and save the rest for breakfast."

A while later, Jake laid back and covered his face with his dǒulì hat. His mind drifted through a portal of time where he dreamt he was a fisherman. As he cast a net into the river, he saw a woman washing clothes beside the bank. An eagle swept down and snatched a fish from the surface and soared into the Sun.

Master Fuji shook him. Jake woke up and looked around. Realizing it was morning, Master Fuji handed him a can of cold noodles with fish. Jake looked into the can and moaned, "Poo how."

In the late-afternoon, Master Fuji saw a mountain and checked the map. It wasn't there.

"That's it," he said.

They pulled the canoe ashore and hid it under a thicket of dense foliage. Walking beside a bluff, Jake and Master Fuji found a small rivulet of water streaming down the hill. Master Fuji leaned in and filled his canteen, took a large drink, and filled it again. He looked at Jake. "Do you smell anything?"

"The body odor is strong with Binh.

## 24

Master Fuji removed the duffle from his shoulder and let Elm, Griffiss, and Travis climb the mountain. Jake and Master Fuji discovered a footpath leading into the forest. Steep terrain and loose rock slowed their progress, and after an hour, they'd made only a mile of headway.

"Let's find another route," Master Fuji said.

Jake stopped to wipe the sweat from his brow and said, "Dang, I left my hat in the canoe. Are you sure this is the right hill? "He pointed, "That one looks a lot easier to climb."

"Let's take a break and hydrate."

Leaning against a large boulder, Jake sipped from his canteen, then wrinkled up his nose, "Whew, something stinks."

Master Fuji sniffed, "I smell nothing."

Jake spun around. Behind him lay a pile of bones and animal carcasses, "Oh yuck! You gotta see this."

Master Fuji recapped his canteen and walked over to where Jake was standing, and said, "Looks like a large carnivore lives nearby."

Jake pointed. "Isn't that skull human?"

"We need to be careful."

Jake capped his canteen. "I'm beginning to believe in bad spirits."

"We should go."

They packed their canteens and walked back toward the river along the trail they came in on. "Wish I had a camera, "Jake said. "No one's gonna believe this."

Master Fuji replied, "Remember, we were never here."

As they entered the forest, men painted black and white, like skeletons, surrounded them.

Jake said, "Whoa! This gets more Halloweeny by the minute."

They stripped Jake and Master Fuji of their backpacks and nudged them down another trail at spear point. "Do as they say, Jake."

"I ain't arguing. Maybe if we give 'em some candy, they'll let us go?"

The trail led to a large cavern where they stood before a stone altar. Standing above them, a towering man dressed in bronze armor, with a spiked helmet, shoulder pads, and shin plates extending over his feet. He thumped his chest, "Pa', Pa', Pa'."

"We get it, your name is Pa', "Jake said, cranking his neck to see Pa's face. "Geez, he's gotta be eight-foot-tall. "Jake lifted a cupped hand and said, "Trick or treat."

"Quiet, Jake," Master Fiji scolded.

In a language, even Master Fuji could barely understand, Pa' shouted and banged his fist.

Master Fuji said, "They call themselves the Fāngshi."

"Hope that doesn't mean cannibals."

Pa' motioned to his men. Two warriors stepped forward and struck Jake and Master Fuji behind the legs forcing them to their knees.

Master Fuji said, "We need to get out of here."

"Uh, just say when," Jake replied.

Master Fuji jumped to his feet, elbowed a guard, and took his spear, smacking another in the head. Jake back-fisted the closest man and kicked him into several others. He snapped-off the end of a spear and made a staff. Whorling around, he smashed heads, cracked knees, clearing a path to the door. Jake turned and called Master Fuji to follow. Master Fuji lunged forward, but a guard whacked him in the head and knocked him to the ground. A warrior shoved a spear deep into Master Fuji's shoulder, pinning him there, and another stepped on his chest, threatening to kill him with a spear to the throat. Jake dropped his weapon and pleaded, "No! Stop! Please stop! Don't kill him!"

The guards forced Jake to the ground, tied his hands and feet, and then did the same to Master Fuji. Pa' waved his arm. "Sow po, sow po!"

Several sentries left and returned carrying clay pots.

"What the...?" Jake said.

The guards removed the lids, and with metal tongs, extracted two angry brown snakes. Jake's eyes popped out. "What're you doing?"

The guards held a serpent next to Jake's neck. He turned his face away as adrenaline surged through his veins.

The warriors chanted, "Caw, caw, caw..."

The serpent's fangs clamped down on Jake's neck. "Aghhh... You animals. I'm gonna kill you. All of you. Everyone! You savages!"

The sentries carried Jake and Master Fuji outside to a bottomless pit and dropped them into the darkness. Jake landed hard and laid there a minute, smarting from the pain. He rolled to his side and laid there until his eyes adjusted. The sound of labored breathing led his eyes to Master Fuji, who was lying face down. He wriggled over and pushed Master Fuji onto his back and spotted the fang marks. "You got bit on the neck too. And, your shoulder is bleeding."

Breathing hard, Master Fuji said, "I'm sorry, Jake. I never imagined this would happen."

"How long we got?"

"Not long. Save yourself if you can."

As a thick fog descended the mountain, The Fāngshi sentries walked away, leaving them to die. Jake took the hypersonic whistle from Master Fuji's pocket and blew it several times.

"Hang on Master Fuji—help is on the way. " Master Fuji didn't respond. Jake bumped him, "Wake up. "Still, no response. Soon, Jake heard the patter of little feet and tapped the whistle against the ground, calling attention to his hands. Elm gnawed the bindings until Jake could free his hands. He untied his feet and tried to wake Master Fuji. Jake licked the back of his hand and held it under Master Fuji's nose, detecting barely a whiff of air.

He untied Master Fuji and propped him up. "Elm, the venom is getting to him."

*Think, Jake, think, think. What do I do? What do I do?...Wait! Why ain't I sick?*

Jake rubbed his neck. *Why isn't the poison getting me like Fuji? ...the Wado... That's it, the Wado.*

"Hold on, Master Fuji. I'll be back." He pointed at Elm, "Don't let him die!"

Jake sprung out of the pit and hid behind a clump of trees. Voices of Fāngshi warriors carried up the hillside and pushed him higher until he found another cavern leading into the mountain. The passage led to the main chamber, where Pa' sat with his guards. Scanning the room, he spotted weapons stacked in a nearby corner and the backpacks in the center of the room.

As Jake prepared to dart into the room to snatch Master Fuji's backpack, Travis climbed onto a table, and a sentry drew his weapon. Travis sat-up on his hind legs like a puppy begging for attention. The guard smiled and sheathed his sword. He reached out to pet the little creature. For a moment, Travis appeared to enjoy the attention, then viciously bit his finger and ran away. The sentry and several others chased Travis, who escaped into another room.

*Whoa! Travis, you rock!. This is my best chance.*

Jake jumped into the room and dashed for the weapons. He grabbed a bow and notched an arrow, drew back the string, and released it before Pa' even turned to look at him. Jake watched the arrow fly straight toward the back of Pa's head. Just as the arrow arrived, Pa' turned to look at Jake and flicked the arrow away like an annoying fly. Seeing this, Jake realized Pa' was like himself—Hābu-Té.

Jake fired six more arrows, snuffing out the lamps, and plunging the room into complete darkness. After a half-a-dozen seconds, Jake's vision adjusted, and he could see Pa's silhouette against the background, but the warriors fumbled around blind. Pa' smirked at Jake and dipped his head as if to recognize his prowess. His quiver empty, Jake grabbed a sword and crept down the steps leading to the main floor.

Pa' removed his heavy golden shoulder armor and drew his sword. Jake stepped down onto the main floor facing Pa' and holding his sword in the front guard position. Pa' attacked Jake with such fury, Jake couldn't stay with him. Knocked to his knees, Jake's knelt there as his weapon lay on the floor. Pa' stood on his blade, rendering Jake defenseless. Pa' hovered over him, lifted his sword overhead to unleash a fatal blow. Out of nowhere, Griffiss pounced onto Pa's face, biting and clawing his eyes. Pa shook his head, stepped backward, grabbed Griffiss by the neck skin, and pulled him away. Griffiss fought to shake free, but Pa lifted him high and leered at him before skewering him with his sword.

"Noooo!" Jake screamed and picked up his sword, thrusting it deep into Pa's thigh and left it there. Pa stared at the blade protruding from his leg, dropped his sword, and fell against the altar as Griffiss lay on the floor bleeding. Jake scurried over to Griffiss and scooped him up. He grabbed Pa's sword, darted to the backpacks, and rifled through them, searching for the Wado. He grabbed the jar, tucked Griffis under his shirt, and ran to the upper chamber carrying Pa's sword, and escaped just as the guards relit the lamps. The guards found Pa' lying across the altar steps with a sword stuck in his leg. Furious, Pa' grasped the handle and pulled the sword out himself.

Jake ran to the pit to rescue Master Fuji, but twenty-some-odd warriors carried Master Fuji's body away when he arrived. Jake fled up the mountainside and found a hollow to hide. He rolled inside, holding Griffiss tight against his pounding chest. He thought he heard something and leaned out, eyes flicking side to side, "They're coming. Griff, what do I do? Stay, run? ... No, wait. No, they're leaving?" Several minutes passed, and Jake's heart rate slowed to a mild panic level. "Where are they? Why aren't they chasing us?"

Griffiss stopped moving, and Jake laid him on the ground. He removed the Wado from the jar and discovered it was dry and brittle, "No juice... Hold on. I've got an idea."

He used a stone to grind it into a powder and sprinkled it into Griffiss's nostrils. Jake wrapped his lips around Griffiss's nose and blew. "Breathe, c'mon, do it."

Griffiss's jaw fell open, and his tongue lay limp to the side. "Don't go, Griff, don't go, don't leave me. Please, don't leave me—don't leave me alone."

Griffiss's eyes sunk into his head, and his light faded. Tears fell like rain as Jake picked up his oldest friend and held him close. Rocking back and forth, he mumbled, "Sorry, Griff ... so sorry... It's my fault. All my fault.... I'm so sorry..."

Jake cleared a spot and padded it with leaves, resting Griffiss on top. He covered his body with stones, saving the last one for himself, and put it in his pocket. Jake sat a long while staring at Griffiss's grave, remembering how Griffiss comforted him whenever he felt blue.

An hour passed, and Jake succumbed to the realization of his situation. He placed his hands over the grave as if to touch Griffiss's spirit. "I'll never forget you. Take care, my friend."

## 25

J ake grabbed the sword and climbed the mountain, searching for a better shelter. Walking along an outcropping, he spotted a cave below. *That looks like a good hiding place.*

He leaned over the edge. *Hmm? That pile of brush might make a soft landing.*

He squared-up and aimed for the middle.

"Oomph!" *Bad idea,* he thought, while struggling to sit up. *Oh, what stinks?*

He looked around.

*What the halo... bones, fuzz, teeth? Sheeze, this is the animal den. I gotta get outta here.*

He shimmied up the ridge in a hurry and ran to a ledge overlooking the hillside.

*Whew, that was close. I need to be more careful. Good thing Chewy wasn't home.*

Jake searched the hillside for landmarks to orient himself and saw a crescent moon hanging over the horizon.

*There you are. Will you send a message for me? Tell Master Fuji, I'm sorry. Tell Ryan, I miss him. Tell Sheri, I love her.*

He lifted an ear toward the mountain as a distant dribble caught his attention and followed the sound. As he drew near, his path became blocked by dense shrubbery. Jake used the sword to cut a hole through the thicket and crawled on his hands and knees, emerging next to a stream trickling into a small pond. Remembering the Jungle Survival Class, Master Fuji instructed them, "Never drink from still water."

Jake leaned forward and placed his face near the flow, and stuck out his tongue, letting the water drench lips. Jake pulled his head back, licking his upper lip. *Yum, this is good, real good, like popsicles, cotton candy... Like, Wado!*


As Jake lapped at the fountain, a strange sensation overcame him. *Somebody's watching me!*

He backed out of the brush and hiked up the hill, stopping on a ledge overlooking his path. *If someone is following me, they'll cross below.* A moment later, Jake's eyes popped. *Holy macaroni, look at that, a real-life tiger. Wow, if he only knew how hungry I am, he wouldn't come closer. Hmm, I wonder what tiger tastes like? I'm startin' to understand Chinese cuisine—when you're hungry—you'll eat anything.*

Following the stream, Jake came to a small clearing. There, propped against rocks in the sitting position, he found human skeletons dressed in armor. An impulse to flee tried to pull Jake away, but curiosity held him there. Hand and feet bones were thick and long. Gashes appeared on extremities, and dents blistered the armor, telltale signs of a great battle. He crept closer, tipping the helmet off one skull, and gasped. A gaping hole showed he'd suffered a violent death. Jake lifted Pa's sword and matched the edge to the contour of the fracture.

*Oh wow! Perfect match. This sword killed this guy.*

When he checked the blade against other skeletons, some gashes matched, and some didn't.

"... Why?"

The small stream led Jake to a spring bubbling out of the hillside. Beside it, a long-rooted weed stretched out, sapping moisture from the rill. He plucked a leaf and popped it into his mouth. *Oh my gosh, that's good.* Reveling a moment in Wado bliss, Jake experienced a surge of energy throughout his body. He cupped the plant in his hand. *Dang, this booger is barely bigger than Fuji's.*

Jake used the sword tip to pry the earth away from the plant. He squatted and set the sword on the ground. While reaching down to pluck the plant, he heard a twig snap. Jake moved his hand over the blade and peered out of the corner of his eye. In a flash, he whipped around, slicing through the air. He froze, glaring into the darkness. A shadowy figure took shape—*Pa'*.

Jake slid to his left and raised the sword to the front guard position. Pa' held a sword and a short spear. Pa' threw the spear causing Jake to duck. Quickly, he jumped to his feet as Pa' lunged forward with his sword. Jake blocked his blow and backed away. Dang, he's fast, Jake thought. Pa' attacked with a downward strike and skinned Jake's arm. Jake countered with a horizontal strike, but Pa' blocked him. Pa' spun around with an angular strike and knocked Jake's weapon out of his hand. Defenseless, Jake retreated and stumbled over a rock. Trapped between a steep wall and the Fāngshi leader, Jake prepared to jump. Pa' closed in—Jake pushed off and face-planted at Pa's feet. Not wanting to get hit in the face, Jake didn't look up. He thought about his family and tried to imagine Sheri.

A low tonal rumble stopped Jake's heart, and Pa' froze. Both of them turned and locked their eyes on a large tiger lurking nearby. As the tiger crept forward growling, Pa' eased away, holding his sword in the front guard. The cat roared, and Pa' turned and ran, leaving Jake helpless. Jake lay there unable to move, staring into the tiger's eyes, smothered by the cat's heavy breath. He thought, *Could tonight get any worse?*

The tiger crouched, snarling, ready to pounce. The cat hissed and leaped upward and ran away.

"What the heck?"

Jake sat up and focused on the dark shape in front of him. There stood a rat with a mouthful of orange fur.

"Oh my gosh," Jake said. "Travis, come here, you little tart."

Jake scooped up Travis and dashed to the Wado plant, and stopped, *It's gone!*

He reached down and felt the ground. *Pa' took it.*

He dropped to his knees, *What am I gonna do now?*

Jake dug into the soil with his fingers and pulled out a thumb-sized chunk, "Pa' ripped the plant out so fast he left a root. What can I do with that?"

Travis crawled into his pocket. Jake dropped the root into the other and picked up the sword. He climbed the mountain, far away from the tiger and the Fāngshi. Way up in a tree, Jake nestled into a crook for the night.

## 26

The following morning, Travis stirred and woke Jake. "Oh," patting his pockets, "I've still got Master Fuji's whistle." He wiped it off and blew it three times. "Maybe she's still with us?" Jake's stomach growled, and he worried the noise would attract the tiger. Falling back on his jungle training, he foraged for edible plants, picking up tidbits here and there. As the hunger pangs increased, Jake started digging for protein in the form of worms. He found a few and swallowed them whole so that they wouldn't squish in his mouth. Travis wasn't as squeamish chewed them up like taffy.

A clacking sound reverberated throughout the hillside. Jake became curious and descended the mountain in search of the source. Perched above a clearing, he spotted Fāngshi warriors beating sticks to scare away the tiger prowling nearby.

"Wow, that cat gets around."

The sentries tied a small deer to a pole and left the area. Moments later, Jake watched as the tiger returned and attacked the poor animal. He wondered if the reason the Fāngshi didn't come up the mountain was because of the tiger. The tiger suffocated the deer and dragged it away.

With the tiger preoccupied, Jake ran to the stream and guzzled as much water as he could. As he sat wiping his chin, Travis squealed, and Jake jumped to his feet, gripping the sword. Moments later, an intruder came into view.

"Elm!"

Jake held out his hand, and Elm jumped onto his shoulder.

"Where have you been?"

Jake's reached over and scratched her back. Her whiskers tickled his neck, "Ha, I'm glad to see you too."

Jake held her up, looking for injuries. She spit out a whole sunflower seed that hit Jake's arm and fell to the ground. He put her down and picked up the seed, rolling it between his fingers, staring at the grain.

"Elm, is Master Fuji alive?"

The sound of water trickling in the background jogged Jake's memory. On the way up, he and Master Fuji stopped to fill canteens. *Master Fuji drank Wado water. It's weak, but he drank a lot.* Jake gasped, "HE'S ALIVE!" He pulled the piece of root from his pocket, "Take this to Master Fuji." Elm stuffed it into her cheek pouch and scurried off.

Walking along a patch of bamboo, a memory flashed into Jake's mind—Benji teaching him how to strip bark from bamboo. *Bingo!.*

He chopped down large stalks and stripped the bark to make strapping material. Benji taught him how Filippino farmers strapped bamboo canes together to make structures. Jake used the same technique to make a large cage. He latched onto the pen and dragged it onto a trail. *Umph, who knew bamboo could be so heavy?*

*Man, this better work,* he thought as he covered it with foliage.

Jake huffed it down the mountain and traipsed around the tiger den. Alerted by the heavy scent, he felt the tiger's glare cut him up like a juicy steak. Playing cat and mouse, he led the tiger through the forest, keeping a safe distance. When they arrived at the cage, the tiger crouched, watching. Jake squatted to make himself small and easier to ambush. He aimed his ear toward the tiger and tuned into its breathing. When it slowed, Jake knew he was about to pounce. *Patience, patience, if I move too soon, I'll blow the whole thing.*

The tiger sprang, bearing teeth and claws. At the instant the tiger's paws were to clutch Jake in his grasp, Jake shot upward. The big cat missed and flew into the cage. Jake slammed the door shut and jammed a thick stick through the bars, locking it in place. The angry cat flung around in a frenzy, trying to escape.

"Sorry Chewy, can't let you eat us."

Jake grabbed Travis and the sword and went searching for an escape route. He found a narrow pass through the rocks leading to a cliff above the Jiuqu Xi River on the far side of the mountain. Leaning over the cliff, he spit and watched it fall for several seconds.

"Jeesh, that's a long way down."

As night fell, Jake wrestled with his thoughts. *I need a plan. Think, think, think, how can I beat Pa'? He's bigger, faster, stronger, experienced, older... Older, that's it.*

*Pa' wasn't there looking for me; he was there to get the Wado. He's getting tired and needed a bump.*

The Fāngshi warriors gathered around the tiger pole performing some ritual, and Jake sprinted to the creepy burial site of Pa' people. He examined the skeletons and their armor, noting where the dents and wounds were. In his mind, he recreated each of their battles and compared them to Pa's style. *That's it—that's Pa's weakness.*

Jake removed the armor from a skeleton and put it on. *Gee wiz, all these guys have big heads.* He tried another. *This one's a little better.*

He continued to fit himself with armor, making adjustments until he had a full set. He looked at Travis and said, "Keep your whiskers crossed."

The Fāngshi tied Master Fuji to the stake and engaged in some chant.

"Now we know," Jake whispered, "they capture people and feed them to Chewy."

A skeleton decorated warrior approached Master Fuji carrying a large knife and held it against his ribcage. *It's now or never. Do your best Marilyn Monroe.*

Jake walked out of the shadows, standing tall as he could, projecting an air of omnipotence. The chanting stopped, and the Fāngshi leered at Jake as he walked toward Master Fuji. The warrior holding the blade turned to Jake, pointing the knife, and dropped to his knees, and the others followed suit. *These guys take their Halloween seriously.* With a whiff of the blade, Jake cut the ties holding Master Fuji to the stake.

Jake said, "You look better?"

"Feeling better."

"Vámonos."

As Jake and Master Fuji tread nervously across the clearing, Jake said, "I smell Wado."

Just then, Pa' and ten of his elite guards emerged and blocked their path.

Master Fuji said, "Jake, give me the sword and make a run for it."

"Nah, I've got the armor. Besides, Pa' is Hābu-Té. He's faster than the Flash. He'll cut us both down before we get halfway across the field. When they're distracted, run up the mountain. They won't follow you. I'll meet you there."

Jake stepped forward with the sword dangling by his side. Dressed in full armor, Pa' walked to the middle of the clearing.

Travis jumped out of Jake's pocket and hurried over to Master Fuji.

Jake met Pa' in the center of the arena and inhaled.

"Eh, you got your bump," Jake said. "I smell it on your breath. You can't hide that from me. I'm the son of an alcoholic. En garde, sucker!"

Pa' lifted his weapon, and Jake assumed the guard position. Jake nodded as if to invite Pa' to attack, and he did, charging forward like a freight train. Jake darted to the side and avoided the attack. No sooner did he reset, and Pa' charged again, this time hitting Jake on the chest plate and knocking him down. "Wow, you ARE amped up."

Jake jumped to his feet, and Pa' rained down strike after strike, beating Jake to the ground like a nail. Jake, bleeding from his forearm, retreated and set his feet as Pa' whirled in like a buzz saw, cutting across Jake's thigh.

"Yo, braddah, that hurt!" *Rope a dope time.*

Jake leaned his back against the wooden pole for support. Pa' prepared to finish him off. With a big swing, Pa' lunged in, Jake ducked and Pa's sword hit the pole and stuck there. Rolling out ninja-style, Jake whacked the back of Pa's ankle and cut his Achilles tendon. Stunned, Pa' stood holding the sword handle for support. Jake jump-kicked him in the side, and a long-stemmed leaf fell from Pa's chest armor.

"Ahh," Jake pointed, "hiding something?"

Jake kicked Pa' in the chest with a spinning back-kick. Pa' crashed to the ground.

The impact ejected the Wado plant from Pa's chest plate. Pa' waffled around searching for the plant and snatched it up. Jake stood over him and put the point of his weapon on his stomach. Peering into Pa's cold grey eyes, Jake remembered what he did to Griffiss, but all he could see was desperation and fear as Pa' lay there clutching the Wado plant close to his chest. Jake dropped the sword next to Pa' and walked away, stopping at the long-stemmed leaf. He picked-up and let it dangle from his lips like a cigarette and told Master Fuji, "Let's go."

Jake stripped off the armor and left it there. When they exited the clearing, the Fāngshi started following, slowly at first, then quicker. Jake looked at Master Fuji and said, "Run for it!"

Master Fuji stayed close behind as Jake tore a path up the mountain with the Fāngshi in hot pursuit.

Master Fuji said, "I thought you said they wouldn't go up?"

"I guess they're evolving," Jake said. "I've got a plan. Follow me this way."

Jake led Master Fuji to the tiger cage, removed the leaf covering, and poked the beast with a stick. Agitated, the tiger thrashed about, snarling. The Fāngshi stopped at the foot of the trail.

Jake pointed. "See, they're afraid of Chewy."

Master Fuji replied, "They're not afraid of the tiger, Jake—they worship it."

Jake's brows lifted. "Oh!"

Jake turned to the Fāngshi warriors creeping ever closer. He grabbed the stick locking the door, and yelled, "Run!" while pulling it out.

The tiger burst from the cage and barreled down the hill toward the Fāngshi who turned and ran. Master Fuji and Jake went the other way to the high cliff above the Jiuqu Xi River.

Jake said, "Jump out as far as you can. It's a long way down."

Master Fuji tucked Travis into his shirt and said, "Be sure to cross your legs, so you don't rack yourself."

"Best tip I've heard all day."

Jae vaulted into the darkness. "Geronimo!"

Followed by Master Fuji.

As Jake fell, he looked at the stars glowing brightly above and thought, *It'd be so cool to be an astronaut.* Seconds later, splashdown. Jake plunged into the river and splayed out his arms; his butt touched the bottom. He shot to the surface and called out, "Master Fuji... Fuji, Fuji, are you here?"

Master Fuji bobbed to the surface, and Jake swam over to him, "Are you all right?"

"Ya, but I lost Travis."

Jake swam around in circles, searching, "Travis, Travis."

He felt something climb onto his back, "There you are... I got him."

"Great," Master Fuji replied. "Let's find the canoe."

They swam the river, holding close to the bank so the Fangshi couldn't see them from above. After what seemed like an hour, they reached the landing and dragged the canoe to the river's edge. Jake reached into the dugout. "Look, Binh found his hat."

Jake put on the hat and pulled the whistle from his pocket. Shaking out the water, he said, "Gotta give Elm a chance." Jake put it to his lips and gave it three sharp shots.

Master Fuji asked, "Where's Griffiss?"

Jake dropped his head. "Pa' killed him."

"Oh, I'm sorry, Jake. I know how much he meant to you."

"He gets the Medal of Valor." A tear ran down Jake's cheek. "He saved my life."

"I bet he did. Griffiss was an exceptional commando."

A few minutes later, Jake and Master Fuji prepared to launch when they heard something in the brush. Jake and Master Fuji grabbed oars and readied to defend themselves. Elm popped out of the dark and scampered toward them. Jake picked her up. "Thank goodness you're okay."

Master Fuji pushed off, and Jake paddled until they were well clear of the mountain. When he paused to look at the stars, Elm climbed onto his lap and spat something out.

"What's this?" Jake picked it up and rolled it between his fingers.

Realizing it was the Wado root, he turned to Master Fuji and said, "I thought Elm gave this to you."

"They held me under guard the whole time. The last time I remember seeing Elm was when we released them to climb the hill."

"Then, how did you recover from the snakebite?"

"I don't know." Master Fuji replied. He leaned forward and asked, "How is your leg?"

"It stopped bleeding," Jake said. "Good thing I'm up on my vaccinations, huh?"

Master Fuji grabbed his shoulder. "That makes two of us."

The Jiuqu Xi River meandered around mountains, twisting and turning through the valley. Jake grew tired and allowed the canoe to drift with the river current until the boat ran aground on a shoal. Master Fuji and Jake laid back and fell asleep. Jake started dreaming. Pa' chased him across a field wielding a knife. Running as fast as he could, but Pa' kept getting closer and Jake accidentally ran off a cliff. As he fell, he looked up, but Pa' was gone. Just before he hit the ground, he woke-up startled by his dream. His heart racing, he sat up to catch his breath and saw Master Fuji sound asleep. He wiped the sweat from his brow and laid back looking up at the heavens. He lay there thinking how things that frighten him often show up in dreams and thought, *Wow, Dad's nightmares must scare the bejeebers out of him.*

The morning sunlight illuminated the mountain tops, and Master Fuji and Jake ungrounded the canoe and paddled onward. Late in the afternoon, the canoe rounded a bend, and Jake saw a small house with nicely kept grounds. Jake steered toward the bank and pulled the boat onto the shore. Ms. Ling came out and saw Jake standing there. Jake pointed to Master Fuji, and she ushered them into the house where she cleaned their wounds with a tincture of antiseptic herbs. She gave them some of her late husband's clothes, fed them, and put them up in a spare room. Master Fuji and Jake stayed with Ms. Ling for several days, while Master Fuji regained his strength. To repay Ms. Ling for her hospitality, Jake did some heavy lifting and odd chores around the house.

## 27

J ake and Master Fuji took a train back to Fuzhou and boarded another freighter. After three days at sea, they returned to Okinawa with Elm and Travis. Jake took them to the garage, filled their water bottles, and gave them cardboard to chew. Standing in front of Griff's cage, he remembered his loyal friend who always comforted him when he was down. As tears rolled off his cheeks, Elm climbed onto his shoulder and rubbed her head on his chin.

Jake reached up to pet her. "We all miss him."

He placed Elm back in her cage and gave her a peanut. Feeling exhausted, he wandered into the living room and fell asleep on the couch.

Master Fuji left to run errands and consult with Grandmaster Matsumura. When he arrived at the Grandmaster's dojo, no-one answered, and the door was locked. He used his key to open the door and stepped inside. Having spent many years of his youth here, he knew the building well. By the dust build-up, he knew no-one had been there for weeks. In the office, he noticed a photo of himself and Grandmaster hanging slightly crooked. He removed the picture and found a key taped to the back. From the stamp on the key bow, he knew it belonged to a safe deposit box at a local bank.

Master Fuji locked-up the dojo and walked to the bank a few blocks away. As he entered the bank, an employee approached. "Sir, what can we do for you today?"

"I'd like to see a safe deposit box, please."

"No problem, Sir, I just need a photo I.D."

He handed him a driver's license and waited. The banker looked-up his name in a ledger and handed a pen to Master Fuji. "Could you verify your name and sign the book?"

Master Fuji signed the book, and the banker smiled, "We're all set."

He stood and motioned to Master Fuji, "Let me show you to the vault room."

Master Fuji followed him to the vault, where the banker pointed to a box and said, "This one is yours. I'll leave you alone. When you're finished, push the green button by the door."

"Thank you."

Master Fuji inserted the key, removed the box from the wall, placing it on the table. He pulled a chair over and sat down, squaring the container in front of him. Carefully, he lifted the lid and found a note. He picked-up the note and underneath that, laid a familiar box.

The note, written in Okinawan, said:

You made me proud, Teruo. Take the box and the sword and give them to Jake-san. Till we meet again.

Master Fuji picked up the box and opened it. Inside, he found the Wado leaves he'd given to Grandmaster before they left for China, and then some. He choked back tears as he slid the box and letter into his pocket and pushed the button.

He left the bank and walked the neighborhood remembering Grandmaster. As a young teen, Master Fuji had gotten into several fights at school after his mother died of cancer. His father thought he'd benefit from a change of location and sent him to Okinawa.

As he passed a convenience store, he recalled a time when Grandmaster locked him and Nieko out of the dojo after they got caught stealing gum. They tried to join another dojo, unaware that Grandmaster had asked the other masters to send them away. Grandmaster made young Master Fuji and Nieko clean the store for six weeks to atone for their poor judgment. Afterward, Grandmaster tried to teach Master Fuji and Neiko to refocus their destructive energy. Master Fuji became an ardent student spending much of his free time practicing. Neiko didn't work as hard and came to resent Master Fuji for being, "A suck up."

Master Fuji arrived home with a bag of groceries, including Jake's favorite cereal. Jake ate half the box of Lucky Charms before guzzling down two glasses of orange juice.

"Well Jake, looks like your appetite has returned."

"It never left. I think I lost ten pounds."

"Hold down the fort," Master Fuji said. "I'm going to take a shower."

A few minutes later, the phone rang. Jake answered, "Hello, Sergeant Fujioka's residence. This is Jake speaking."

"Hello Jake, this is Atto. May I speak to Sergeant Fujioka?"

"Hold on, let me see if he's out of the shower yet."

Walking into the master bedroom, Jake heard the shower running and said, "He'll have to call you back. Do you want to leave a number?"

"He has it. Just tell him I called."

"Okay, bye."

Putting the phone down, Jake noticed the pink box on Master Fuji's dresser, "What the heck?" He unfolded the note but couldn't read Okinawan.

When Master Fuji finished his shower, he found Jake in the

backyard sitting in a chair with the letter dangling from his fingertips.

Master Fuji sat next to him. "Are you all right?"

Jake staring into space replied, "He's gone, isn't he?"

"I'm afraid so."

Jake's eyes dropped. "I'm gonna die just like him, ain't I?" Master Fuji didn't answer and Jake turned and looked at him. "Why did this happen?"

"I don't know," Master Fuji replied. "I believe things happen for a reason. Grandmaster believed that too." Master Fuji lifted Grandmaster's sword and said, "He left this and the box of leaves for you."

Jake took the sword, pulled it halfway out of the scabbard, and studied the edge. "This is Pa's sister sword. This has a right bevel, Pa's is left." Jake slid the sword back into the scabbard. "I don't want it. You keep it," and held it out for Master Fuji.

Master Fuji took the sword. "I'm sure Grandmaster didn't know, ...but he left enough leaves to last a while. There's a good chance the root Elm saved is viable. We can use it to grow a new plant. By the time the leaves run out, it could be large enough to sustain you."

Jake didn't respond.

Master Fuji said, "Why didn't you take the Wado plant from Pa' when you had the chance?"

"I couldn't. When I looked into his eyes, I saw myself."

"You're not like him."

"I'm just like him."

Master Fuji leaned forward, "You took the higher path."

Jake shrugged. "Maybe."

Master Fuji stood. "I have to stay here for a while, but I'm sending you back to Hickam. Can you take care of Elm and Travis?"

"Of course. They're all I have left."

The following day, Jake packed the Wado and put Ratcom into a pet carrier. Master Fuji drove Jake to the flight line and helped him board a military DC-8 bound for Anderson Air Force Base, Guam. The plane touched down two hours later and taxied to a refueling station where Jake got out to stretch his legs. A massive B-52 Bomber roared down and adjacent runway and took off. Jake watched it climb until it was dot and wondered, *how's Ryan's doing? Does he still like the Army?*

The crew signaled passengers to re-board the plane for the trip to Hickam. The airliner landed at Hickam around midnight Honolulu time. A courtesy driver drove Jake to the warehouse, where he transferred Travis and Elm to their cages. After he filled their water bottles and seed dishes. he pulled the stone from Griffiss's grave from his pocket and placed it on his cage. He put the Wado leaves in the refrigerator and retrieved Dr. Pepper's keys from the drawer.

He looked at the calendar hanging above the table and counted the days he'd been away—three weeks. The battery had gotten weak while sitting, and Dr. Pepper was slow to turn over. *Can things get any worse?*

After several attempts, the engine sprung to life. Jake backed the car into the alley and locked-up the dojo. Physically drained, Jake stopped by McDonald's on his way home to grab a breakfast-biscuit and wolfed it down. He staggered up the trailer steps sipping his soda, flung the door open, and flopped down on stale couch cushions. "Sambo, where's Sambo... Nevermind, I'm too whipped to care."

He set the cup on the table and lay there looking out the door, trying to digest the past few weeks. His eyes drifted upwards and caught sight of the jump goggles hanging beside the door. He leaned forward and grabbed the goggles and pulled them over his head.

He slumped back in the seat, fell asleep, and started dreaming. Trapped in a cave, he heard Sheri calling out to him, "Jake... Jake, answer."

Drifting through dark passages, he searched but couldn't find her. Sheri called out again, "Jake, where are you? Jake..."

Jake woke-up staring at a blurry image. He lifted the foggy goggles and saw Sheri banging on his trailer door. "Jake... open the dang door before I tear it off the hinges!"

Jake shot upright, dropping the goggles under the table and opened the door. "Oh Sheri, glad you're here. Come in, come in."

Sheri climbed the steps and hugged Jake, "Wow, you smell! ...Where have you been?"

Jake pointed to the east. "Thatta way."

"Are you okay? Where is Master Fuji?"

"I'm fine. Master Fuji is okay. How are you?"

"I'm great. Just got worried when you didn't come back."

Sheri sat down on the opposite side of the tiny table.

Jake said, "Oops, I dropped the goggles."

He reached under the table, but they were just out of reach. He stretched out and slipped, his other hand accidentally knocked the soda off the table.

Jake sat up. "Oh, crud."

Leaning to look over the side of the table, he expected to find a mess, but instead, he saw the cup balanced upright on Sheri's foot. Jake stared at the cup, then slowly turned to Sheri.

"Nice reflexes."

Sheri smiled, "Got tea?"

## NAMASTE

This isn't the end for Jake and Sheri. Their saga continues in Book 2, American Ninja, due to be released in the fall of 2022.

I hope you enjoyed this book. Thanks for reading.

RN Shelly

RNShelly616@gmail.com

www.RNShelly.com